He examined the door, still blinking furiously.
Felt like he had bleach in his eyes, dammit.

It turned into a moot point, because under the sound of his breath and the persistent thudding of his heart, another music intruded.

Footsteps.

He hopped onto the shelf-bed, the lance's light growing steadier. The lives he took vanished into its hungry core, and battle only made them both stronger. Something had drained the lance, but he might get a chance to add strength in the next few moments.

Creaking. Dusty clockwork cogs shrieking as they turned, grudging each inch of motion. Whoever it was hadn't taken any chances; they wanted him to stay. Even cold iron might not cut through such a door.

Unwinter has me. I'm not dead.

Of the two sentences, he couldn't say which was more disturbing.

The groaning and shuddering increased. Finally, with a rusting scream, the door hauled itself open an inch, another. Ruddy torchlight sliced through and Jeremiah folded into a crouch, the lance keening softly as it clove air in small precise circles and found no resistance. It would show him a map of the battle inside his head.

If only there was a battle to be fought.

A low, chill laugh echoed in the hall. Jeremiah's breath turned to puffs of white cloud, the cold rasping against his armor as if it wished to work through and cat-lick living skin.

"Gallow." The single word was a frigid caress.

PRAISE FOR THE WORKS OF
LILITH SAINTCROW:

Dante Valentine

"She's a brave, charismatic protagonist with a smart mouth and a suicidal streak. What's not to love? Fans of Laurell K. Hamilton should warm to Saintcrow's dark evocative debut."

—*Publishers Weekly*

"Saintcrow's amazing protagonist is gutsy, stubborn to a fault and vaguely suicidal, meaning there's never a dull moment.... This is the ultimate in urban fantasy!"

—*RT Book Reviews* (Top Pick!)

"Dark, gritty urban fantasy at its best."　　　—blogcritics.org

Jill Kismet

"Nonstop rough-and-tumble action combined with compelling characterization and a plot that twists and turns all over the place. Saintcrow...never fails to deliver excitement."

—RT Book Reviews

"Loaded with action and starring a kick-butt heroine who from the opening scene until the final climax is donkey-kicking seemingly every character in sight."

—Harriet Klausner

"Lilith has again created a vibrant, strong female heroine who keeps you running behind her in a breathless charge against forces you just know you would never be able to walk away from completely unscathed."

—myfavouritebooks.blogspot.com

"This mind-blowing series remains a must-read for all urban fantasy lovers."　　　—Bitten by Books

Bannon & Clare

"Saintcrow scores a hit with this terrific steampunk series that rockets through a Britain-that-wasn't with magic and industrial mayhem with a firm nod to Holmes. Genius and a rocking good time."
                                                        —Patricia Briggs

"Saintcrow melds a complex magic system with a subtle but effective steampunk society, adds fully fleshed and complicated characters, and delivers a clever and highly engaging mystery that kept me turning pages, fascinated to the very end."
                                                        —Laura Anne Gilman

"Innovative world-building, powerful steampunk, master storyteller at her best. Don't miss this one. . . . She's fabulous."
                                                        —Christine Feehan

"Lilith Saintcrow spins a world of deadly magic, grand adventure, and fast-paced intrigue through the clattering streets of a maze-like mechanized Londonium. *The Iron Wyrm Affair* is a fantastic mix of action, steam, and mystery dredged in dark magic with a hint of romance. Loved it! Do not miss this wonderful addition to the steampunk genre."   —Devon Monk

"Lilith Saintcrow's foray into steampunk plunges the reader into a Victorian England rife with magic and menace, where clockwork horses pace the cobbled streets, dragons rule the ironworks, and it will take a sorceress's discipline and a logician's powers of deduction to unravel a bloody conspiracy."
                                                        —Jacqueline Carey

BY LILITH SAINTCROW
Blood Call

GALLOW AND RAGGED
Trailer Park Fae
Roadside Magic
Wasteland King

BANNON & CLARE
The Iron Wyrm Affair
The Red Plague Affair
The Ripper Affair

DANTE VALENTINE NOVELS
Working for the Devil
Dead Man Rising
The Devil's Right Hand
Saint City Sinners
To Hell and Back
Dante Valentine (omnibus)

JILL KISMET NOVELS
Night Shift
Hunter's Prayer
Redemption Alley
Flesh Circus
Heaven's Spite
Angel Town
Jill Kismet (omnibus)

A ROMANCE OF ARQUITAINE NOVELS
The Hedgewitch Queen
The Bandit King

AS LILI ST. CROW

THE STRANGE ANGELS SERIES
Strange Angels
Betrayals
Jealousy
Defiance
Reckoning

WASTELAND KING

Gallow and Ragged:
BOOK THREE

LILITH SAINTCROW

orbit

www.orbitbooks.net

Copyright © 2016 by Lilith Saintcrow
Excerpt from *Lilith Saintcrow #1* copyright © 2016 by Lilith Saintcrow
Excerpt from *Wake of Vultures* copyright © 2015 by D. S. Dawson

Cover design by Lauren Panepinto
Cover illustration by David Seidman
Cover copyright © 2016 by Hachette Book Group, Inc.

Orbit
Hachette Book Group
1290 Avenue of the Americas
New York, NY 10104
orbitbooks.net

First Edition: June 2016

Orbit is an imprint of Hachette Book Group.
The Orbit name and logo are trademarks of Little, Brown Book Group Limited.

The publisher is not responsible for websites (or their content) that are not owned by the publisher.

The Hachette Speakers Bureau provides a wide range of authors for speaking events. To find out more, go to www.hachettespeakersbureau.com or call (866) 376-6591.

Library of Congress Cataloging-in-Publication Data

Names: Saintcrow, Lilith, author.
Title: Wasteland king / Lilith Saintcrow.
Description: First edition. | New York, NY : Orbit, 2016. | Series: Gallow and Ragged ; book 3
Identifiers: LCCN 2016015118| ISBN 9780316277914 (softcover) | ISBN 9781478964384 (audio book downloadable) | ISBN 9780316277907 (ebook)
Subjects: LCSH: Fairies—Fiction. | Kings and rulers—Fiction. | BISAC: FICTION / Fantasy / Urban Life. | FICTION / Romance / Fantasy. | FICTION / Fantasy / Paranormal. | FICTION / Fantasy / Contemporary. | GSAFD: Fantasy fiction.
Classification: LCC PS3619.A3984 W37 2016 | DDC 813/.6—dc23 LC record available at https://lccn.loc.gov/2016015118

ISBNs: 978-0-316-27791-4 (trade paperback), 978-0-316-27790-7 (ebook)

Printed in the United States of America

RRD-C

10 9 8 7 6 5 4 3 2 1

Once more, to L.I.
Peace, the charm's wound up.

TRUTH

Love all comes down to revenge, sweetheart.
—NICHOLAS DEANGELO

MOVE AND THINK

The assassin and the redhaired girl burst onto the shuttered, dark fairway, and Crenn almost thought they had a shot at escaping unseen—until the shadows at the far end, under the Ferris wheel's spidery bulk, birthed a cold gleam and clawed silvershod hoofbeats rang on packed dirt. The rider, a black paper cutout, smoked with wrongness, and Robin's despairing, mewling little cry ignited something in Crenn's bones.

"That way!" he said, and pushed her. The dog took over, hauling her up a rickety ramp, bursting through a chain into a dark passageway beyond. A gigantic clown was painted above, its gaping mouth the entryway, its rubber-red lips leering in the low lamplight. FUNHOUSE FUNHOUSE FUNHOUSE, *the painted boards cried, and below,* IT'S A SCREAM!

No doubt Gallow would do something stupid, like charging the rider with his lance out. Crenn's hands moved, the curve of wood strapped to his back yanked free, and a word of chantment snapped the bow out, its arms gracefully bending into tension as his fingers felt along fletchings and found the one he wanted.

He nocked and drew back to his ear, a subtle breath-humming becoming an invisible string, the silver whistle-blast of Unwinter's hunters becoming a high keening of prey found, prey found! *The dogs would be along any moment now.*

Still, he took his time, the world becoming a still, small point as if he balanced on a bough in the Marrowdowne, waiting to send a flint-needle arrow through a sparrow's eye. This bolt was fletched heavily, and its head was cold iron; the hoop in Crenn's ear burned as chantment woke, humming.

He loosed.

The nightmare mount's steady jog turned to an uncertain, pawing walk as the rider stiffened, a grotesque choking audible down the fairway. The rider slumped, the arrow a flagpole poking from the jousting helm's eye-bar. Crenn didn't wait to see him hit the ground, just spun and plunged after Robin and the dog.

Complete darkness. Choked cries, shattering glass. A whining bark, and he blundered into a hallway lined with mirrors, faint light from the end reflected over and over. Robin, trying to scream, reeled drunkenly from side to side, her reflections distorted-dancing; he ran into her with an oof! *that might have been amusing if he hadn't heard more urgent silver whistles filtering in from outside.*

"Don't look!" he snapped, and grabbed at her, earning himself a flurry of blows as she kicked. Maddened with fear, she even bit him as he hauled her through the hallway, and the flooring underneath shifted treacherously, groaning under Pepperbuckle's weight. They pressed forward in a tangle, and he realized he was cursing, swallowed half an anatomical term a woman should never hear, and got his hand over her eyes. "Don't look, damn you! Keep moving!"

Turns in quick succession, and all of a sudden a doorway loomed, the dog leapt and carried it down in a shatter of splinters. Back on the fairway, Robin's eyes tightly closed as she ran, clinging to his hand.

Don't just move, *Jeremiah Gallow had always said.* Move and think, *that's the ticket.*

As if that bastard had any other setting than just charging in with that goddamn pigsticker of his.

Crenn skidded to a stop at the end of the fairway. His ears tingled, perking. They were loud, and the hounds were belling now. The dog pressed close, whining; he calculated its size, and hers.

"Listen." He dropped his bow, caught her face. Her eyes flew open and she stared, witless with terror, perhaps, or just numb. "Listen to me, pretty girl. The dog will take you, I'll hold them. You run, you stay alive, and I will find you. I promise."

Her mouth worked for a moment. Her skin was so soft. What was she doing tangled up in this?

"I hate you," she whispered under the ultrasonic thrills. Close now, the net tightening, but there was a hole in it and he was about to send her through it. The dog was fast, and one sidhe with a bow and a habit of hunting could make merry hob of a pursuit.

With a little luck, that is.

"I hate you," she repeated, and sense flooded her dark-blue eyes. "I remember what you did!" Her voice was a husk of itself, broken into pieces.

He shook his hair back, stared down at her. "You can't," he told her, "hate me any more than I hate myself, Robin Ragged." He beckoned the hound, who pressed close, shivering and sweating: Crenn lifted her by the waist, so close he could smell the sunlight in her hair. She grabbed at fur, righted herself, and he'd be damned if the beast didn't bulk up a little, its legs thickening to carry her weight. "Now run. I'll find you later."

"I'll kill you," she informed him, with the utter calm of despair. "I will rip your heart out, Alastair Crenn."

Looking forward to it, pretty girl. He stepped aside, and the dog jetted forward, a coppergold blur.

Crenn scooped his bow up, closed his eyes, and listened.

Hoofbeats. Whistling. The pads of Unwinter's hounds, a frantic baying. The receding soft thump-thump *of Pepperbuckle's feet. And, to top it all off, a clamor of mortal voices. The carnival folk were beginning to wake to strangeness in their midst.*

"Time to hunt," he murmured, and drew another arrow from the quiver by touch. He held it loosely nocked, and ran toward the noise.

PART ONE

SOME FAINT COMFORT

1

Gray highway ribboned over tawny hills touched with dusty green smears of sagebrush clinging to any scrap of moisture it could find, heat-haze shimmering above sandy slope and concrete alike. The morning sun was a brazen coin, hanging above a bleached horizon as if it intended to stay in that spot forever, a bright nail to hang an endless weary day upon. The chill of a desert night whisked itself away, an escaping guest.

Cars shimmered in the middle distance, announced their presence with a faint drone, and passed with a glare and blare of engine and tire-friction. Most didn't stop, even though two signs, each leaning somewhere between ten and twenty-three degrees away from true, proclaimed LAST GAS FOR 80 MI.

An ancient pair of gas pumps squatted under a rusting roof; they and the convenience store keeping watch over them had last been refurbished around twenty years ago. Tinny country music blatted from old loudspeakers on listing poles, the tired breeze dragged shackles made of paper cups, glittering dust, and a dry skunky whiff of weedsmoke through umber shade and gold-treacle sunshine.

A burst of static cut through the music just as the thin slice of shade on the north side of the building rippled. A single point of brilliance, lost in the glare of day, dilated, and there was a flutter of russet, of indigo, of cream and black velvet.

One moment empty, the next, full; a large dog winked into being a split second before a slim female shape appeared, clinging to the canine's back as the Veil between real and more-than-real flexed. The dog staggered, its proud head hanging low, and slumped against the building. The girl slid from its broad back— the thing was *huge*—and her hair was a coppergold gleam, firing even in the shade. Tattered black velvet clung to her, swirling as it struggled to keep up with the transition, the hood not quite covering her bright, chopped-close curls. She heaved, dryly, a cricketwhisper cough under the tinpan cowboy beat.

Robin Ragged's stomach cramped, unhappy with the seawater she'd swallowed *and* the butter she'd filched. The fuel from milkfat had already worn off, and her throat was on fire again. Her hands spread against dusty grit, there was a simmering reek from around the corner of the building that shouted *Dumpster*, and the music was a tinkling ballad about mothers not letting their children grow up to be cowboys.

Good advice, maybe. But you had to grow up to be something, even if you were a Half, mortal and sidhe in equal measure. It was her mortal part that had trouble blinking through the Veil like this. It was much better to use a proper entrance, or some place where the lands of the free sidhe overlapped, rubbing through what mortals called "real" like a needle dragged along paper. Creasing, not quite breaking, almost-visible.

Pepperbuckle made a low, unhappy noise. The dog had carried her away from the nighttime carnival, hauling her through folds and pockets, light and shade pressing against Robin's closed eyes in strobe flashes. He'd be weary. They'd run past dawn, the silver huntwhistles further and further behind them.

Like any close escape, it made for nausea.

Concentrate. Four in, four out. The discipline of breath returned. A lifetime's worth of habit helped—if you couldn't breathe, you couldn't sing, and the song was her only defense.

She might have broken her voice, though, by screaming with shusweed juice still coating her throat. The prospect was enough to bring a cold sweat out all over her, even though it was a scorching midmorning outside the small shade where she and Pepperbuckle cowered.

Where are we?

She sniffed, gulping down mortal air full of exhaust and the dry nasal rasp of baking metal and sand. A whiff of something green and leather-tough—sagebrush? No hint of anything sidhe except her and the dog, his sides heaving under glossy, red-tipped golden fur. His fine tail drooped a bit, and he eyed her sidelong, his irises now a brighter blue and the pupils uneven ovoids. It gave his gaze an uncanny quality.

He hadn't left her behind. In for a penny, in for a pound, and all the old clichés. There was the large unsound of wind, and a drone that could have been traffic in the very far distance.

The cowboy ballad wound down, and another song started. Someone was standing by her man. A wheezing noise was an ancient air-conditioning unit on the roof.

Robin shuddered. She pushed herself upright, making her knees unbend because there was no other choice. Pepperbuckle was depending on her, and while the mortal sun was up, they were safe enough from Unwinter's hunt.

It was some faint comfort that Summer would think Robin still trapped or dead, and wouldn't be looking for her.

Don't think about that. Her lips cracked as she parted them. She wanted to say Pepperbuckle's name, stopped herself. She had to shepherd her voice carefully. No more raving at that treacherous bastard Crenn when she had the breath to permit it, while the wind and the Veil snatched the curses from her lips as soon as she uttered them.

You can't hate me any more than I hate myself, he'd informed her, calmly enough, before stepping back so Pepperbuckle could bear her away. Why had he bothered to save her, after he'd delivered her to Summer's not-so-tender mercies?

Had he also betrayed Gallow? It was entirely likely. Not that it mattered, Unwinter's poison had most likely finished off her dead sister's husband.

Daisy. Shining surfaces holding broken reflections danced inside her head. Her sister's teeth broken stumps, safety glass caught in corpsetangled hair...

Don't think about that either. Her head throbbed.

She uncurled, one arm a bar across her midriff to hold her aching belly in. The night was a whirl of impressions, everything inside her skull fracturing like broken—

Mirrors?

She shook her head, violently. *Glass,* like broken *glass.* That word wasn't as troubling as the other, the *m*-word, the terrifying idea of a reflection lurching for her while it wheezed, and choked, and cracked a leather belt in its bloody, too-big hands.

Robin's shoulder struck something solid, jolting her back into herself. She glanced around wildly, her shorn hair whipping—it stood out around her head now, a halo of coppery cowlicks. The gold hoops in her ears swung, tapping her cheeks, and she forced herself to straighten again.

She'd fetch up against the prefabricated concrete wall, either painted a dingy yellow or simply sandblasted to that color. The angle of the shade and the taste of the air said *morning,* and it was going to be a hot day. Pepperbuckle sat down, his sides heaving as he panted and his teeth gleamed bright-white. The scrubland here was full of small, empty hills, and if she peered around the corner she could see ancient cracked pavement and the two gas pumps.

A little *ding* sounded, and her breath stopped as a lean dark-haired mortal boy with a certain sullen handsomeness to his sharp face stepped out into the sun. He hunched his shoulders, lit a cigarette, and ambled for the pumps. A red polyester vest proclaimed him as an employee of HAPPY HARRY'S STOP 'N' SIP. Harry was apparently a cartoon beaver, even though such an animal had very likely never been sighted in this part of the country, let alone one wearing a yellow hat and a wide, unsettling bucktooth grin.

Robin exhaled softly. Pumps meant a convenience store. They would have a refrigerator. Very likely, there was milk. The burning in her throat increased a notch as she contemplated this.

She glanced at Pepperbuckle, who hauled himself up wearily and followed as she edged for the back of the building.

She didn't think using the front door would be wise.

PIXIES
2

Matt Grogan liked leaning against the gas pumps and having a smoke, even if the bossman would give him hell about safety. It wasn't like anyone ever used the damn things, despite the fact that they were live. You had to walk inside to pay for your go-juice, and nobody wanted to do that. They wanted the pumps with the credit card readers, not ancient ones probably full of water and air bubbles, so they drove straight on to Barton to the shiny stop-and-robs there.

When he came back in, he thought he was dreaming.

Nobody had driven up, but there was a redheaded punk girl in a long black velvet coat in front of the ancient cooler-case, the glass door open and letting out a sourish frigid breeze as she drank from a quart of milk, probably right at its sell-by date. Christ knew the tourists never bought anything here but cigarettes and Doritos, pity-buys really so they could use the small, filthy customers only bathroom around the side.

Her throat worked in long swallows, her weed-whacker-cut coppergold hair glowing under the fluorescents, and she was a stone *fox* even if she was drinking straight out of the carton.

Skinny in all the right ways, but with nice tatas, and wearing a pair of black heels, too.

The only problem was, she was drinking without paying, and right next to her was a huge reddish hound who stared at Matt with the sky-blue, intelligent eyes of a husky. A dog shouldn't look that damn *thoughtful*, as if it was weighing you up.

"Hey!" Matt's voice broke, too. Cracked right in the middle. Bobby Grogan, the football savior of Barton High and Matt's older brother, had a nice low baritone, but Matt's had just fractured its way all through school, even though he would have given anything to sound tough just once. Just that once, when it counted.

Instead it was *crybaby Matt*, and the only thing worse was the pity on Bobby's face in the parking lot. *Lay off him, he's my brother.*

She didn't stop drinking, her eyes closed and her slim throat moving just like an actress's. She finished off the whole damn quart, dropped it and gasped, then reached for another.

"Hey!" Matt repeated. "You gonna pay for that?"

Her eyes opened just a little. They were dark blue, and she gave him a single dismissive glance, tearing the top off the fresh carton in one movement. Milk splashed, and she bent like a ballerina to put the milk on the piss-yellow linoleum with little orange sparkles. The dog dipped his long snout in and began to drink as well.

Oh, man. "You can't just *do* that, man! You gotta pay for it!"

She reached into the case again, little curls of steam rising off her bare wrist as the cooler wheezed. Those two quarts were all the whole milk they had, so she grabbed the lone container of half-and-half—ordered weekly because the bossman said offering free coffee would make someone buy it—and bent back the cardboard wings to open it. The spout was formed with a neat little twist of her wrist, and she lifted it to her lips, all while the dog made a wet bubbling noise that was probably enjoyment.

Oh, hell no. "You can't *do* that!" He outright yelled. "Imma call the cops, lady! You're gonna get *arrested!*"

The instant he said it, he felt ridiculous.

She drank all the half-and-half and dropped that carton too, wiping at her mouth with the back of her left hand. Then she stared at Matt, like he was some sort of bug crawling around in her Cheerios.

Just like Cindy Parmentier, as a matter of fact, who let Matt feel her up behind the bleachers once but kept asking him to introduce her to Bobby. Then she spread that goddamn rumor about him being a fag, and even Bobby looked at him like he thought it might be true.

The woman's mouth opened slightly. She still said nothing. The dog kept sucking at the opened quart on the floor, but one wary eye was half open now.

"And you can't have dogs in here! Service animals only!" He sounded ridiculous even to himself.

She tipped her head back, and for a moment Matt thought she was going to scream. Instead, she laughed, deep rich chuckles spilling out and away, bright as the gold hoops in her ears. Matt flat-out stared, spellbound.

When she finished laughing, the dog was licking the floor clean, its nose bumping the empty cartons with snorfling sounds. She wiped away crystal teardrops on her beautiful cheeks, and walked right past Matt. She smelled like spice and fruit, something exotic, a warm draft that made him think of that day behind the bleachers, soft sloping breasts under his fumbling fingers and Cindy Parmentier's quick, light breathing scented with Juicy Fruit gum.

The dog passed, its tail whacking him a good one across the

shins, way harder and bonier than a dog's tail had any right to be. Matt staggered. The door opened, early-summer heat breathing into the store's cave, and Matt ran after her. "*You didn't pay!*" he yelled, but he slipped on something a little weird underfoot, like the floor itself was moving to throw him off.

He went down hard, almost cracking his skull on the racks of nudie mags they couldn't sell inside the Barton city limits. *That* was the real reason this place held on, and once he started working here the kids at school started laughing even more.

"Ow!" Matt rolled, thrashing to get back up. Something jabbed at his cheek, and something else poked his finger. Tiny, vicious little stings all over him.

The bell over the door tinkled again. "Stop that," the voice said, low and sweet as warm caramel, with a hidden fierceness. Just those two words made the sweat spring out all over him.

It was a good thing his eyes were closed, or he would have seen the tiny flying things, their faces set in scowling mutiny, their wings fluttering and a deep throbbing blue spreading through the glow surrounding each one of them, spheres of brilliance bleached by both day and fluorescent light but still bolder, richer than the colors of the tired mortal world. Some had gleaming, tiny sewing-needle blades, and their mouths opened to show sharp pearly teeth.

A low, thunderous growl. It was the dog, and Matt rolled around some more, suddenly terrified of opening his eyes. His bladder let go in a warm gush, and the stinging continued.

"I said, *Stop it.*" Everything inside the store rattled. The floor heaved a little again, and that was when he opened his eyes and saw... them. The little people, some naked and others in tiny rags of fluttering clothing, their delicate insect-veined wings, their sharp noses and the wicked merriment of their sweet, chiming pinprick voices as they chorused.

16

They darted at him, but the woman said, "No," again, firmly, even as they piped indignantly at her. "Leave him alone. He's just a kid."

They winked out. The door closed with a whoosh, and he lay there in his own urine, quivering. Her footsteps were light tiptaps on the tarmac outside before they were swallowed up by the hum of air-conditioning.

And a faint, low, deadly chiming. Little pinpricks of light bloomed around him again, and he began to scream.

Not long afterward Matt Grogan got up, tiny teethmarks pressed into his flesh on his face and hands, bloody pinpricks decking every inch of exposed skin. He bolted through the door without waiting for it to open, shattering glass into the parking lot.

He ran into the sagebrush wilderness, and nobody in Barton ever saw him again.

MISLAID

3

Summerhome rose upon its green hill, its pennants in wind-driven tatters. The walls should have been gloss-white and greenstone, the towers strong and fair like the slim necks of ghilliedhu girls, and around its pearly sword-shapes the green hills and shaded dells should have rippled rich and verdant. The Road should have dipped and swayed easily, describing crest and hollow with a lover's caress; there were many paths, but they all led Home.

The hills and valleys were green and fragrant, copse and meadow drowsing under a golden sun. They were not as rich and fair as they had been before, nor did they recline under their own vivid dreams as in Unwinter's half of the year. The ghilliedhu girls did not dance as they were wont to do from morning to dusk in their shady damp homes; the pixies did not flit from flower to flower gathering crystal dewdrops. The air shimmered, but not with enticement or promise. Strange patches spread over the landscape of the more-than-real, oddly bleached, a fraying paper screen losing its color.

The trees themselves drew back into the hollows, the shade under their branches full of strange whispers, passing rumor from bole to branch.

Rumor—and something else.

Occasionally, a tree would begin to shake. Its spirit, a dryad slim or stocky, hair tangling and fingers knotting, would go into convulsions, black boils bursting from almost-ageless flesh. First there were the spots and streaks of leprous green, then the blackboil, then the convulsions.

And then, a sidhe died, the tree withering into a rotting stump oozing brackish filth.

The dwarven doors were shut tight, admitting neither friend nor foe, and the free sidhe hid elsewhere, perhaps hoping the cold iron of the mortal world would provide an inoculation just as mortal blood did. Some whispered the plague was an invention of the mortals, jealous of the sidhe's frolicsome immortality, but it was always answered with the lament that no mortal believed in the Good Folk anymore, so that was impossible.

Summerhome's towers were bleached bone, and the greenstone upon them had paled to pastel instead of forest. A pall hung over the heart of Summer, the fount the Seelie held all Danu's folk flowed from. The vapor carried an unfamiliar reek of burning, perhaps left over from the disposal of quick-rotting bodies, both from Unwinter's recent raid and from the plague itself.

Sparse though the latter was, there was no real hope of it abating. Not now that Summer's borders had been breached, and the sickness brought in.

From the sugarwhite shores of the Dreaming Sea to the green stillness of Marrowdowne, from the high moors where the giants strode and those of the trollfolk allied to Summer crouched and ruminated in their slow bass grumbles to the grottos where naiads peered anxiously into still water to reassure themselves that their skin was unmarked, Summer quivered with fear and fever.

Inside the Home's high-vaulted halls, brughnies scurried

back and forth in the kitchens, but no dryads flocked to carry hair ribbons and little chantment spangles for their betters. The highborn fullbloods, most vulnerable to the plague, kept an unwonted distance from each other, and some had slipped away to other estates and winter homes, no doubt on urgent business.

On a low bench on a high dais, among the repaired columns of Summer's throne room, *she* sat, slim and straight and lovely still, her hands clasped tight in her lap. Her mantle was deep green, her shoulders peeking glow-nacreous through artful rends in rich fabric. The Jewel on Summer's forehead glowed, a low dull-emerald glare. It was not the hurtful radiance of her former glory, but her golden hair was still long and lustrous, and her smile was still as soft and wicked as she viewed the knights arrayed among the forest of fluted stone.

Broghan the Black, called Trollsbane, the glass badge of Armormaster upon his chest, stood on the third step of the dais. He did not glance at the knight who knelt on the second, a dark-haired lord in full armor chased with glowing sungold. Dwarven work, and very fine; Broghan's own unrelieved black was all the more restrained in comparison.

Or so he wished to think.

The golden knight with the *brun* mane, Summer's current favorite, stared at her slippered feet, waiting for a word. Once, he had worn small golden flowers in his hair, when his lady had been one of the Queen's handmaidens.

No more.

Summer did not let him wait long. "Braghn Moran." Soft, so dulcet-sweet, the most winning of her voices. The air filled with appleblossom scent, white petals showering from above as layers of chantment, applied at festival after festival, woke in response to her will. "A fair lord, and a fell one."

"Your Majesty does me much honor," he murmured in reply.

No ripple stirred among the serried ranks, though no doubt a few of them grudged him said honor. They had already forgotten a wheat-haired mortal boy's brief tenure as the apple of Summer's black, black eye, and Braghn Moran's sighs and hollow cheeks during it.

The wiser knew it was only a matter of time before any favor she bestowed upon him was lost in due course. *Fickle as Summer*, some said—though never very loudly. Braghn Moran's golden-haired lover had left Court not long ago, when Summer's gaze had snared the one who wore her flowers.

The sidhe did not share. But when Summer took, what could another elf-maid do? The Feathersalt was of an old and pure name, and her absence was perhaps not *quite* with Summer's leave... but that was a matter for later.

"Something troubles me, Braghn."

The knight could have observed that there were many troublesome things afoot among the sidhe lately, but he did not—perhaps a mark of wisdom in itself. He simply examined the toe of Summer's green velvet slipper, peeking out from under the heavy folds of her mantle. If he compared it to another lady's, none could tell.

Summer pressed onward. "I seek a certain troublesome sprite, and I would have you find him for me."

"Who could not come, when you call?" Broghan the Black commented.

Summer did not spare him so much as a glance. "I believe Puck Goodfellow is leading a certain former Armormaster down many a path."

A rustle now *did* pass through the ranks of Seelie knights.

Gallow. The Half who had committed the unforgivable, who had killed a peaceful envoy, then insulted Summer and all of Seelie to boot.

"You wish me to kill Gallow?" Braghn Moran did not sound as if he considered it much of a challenge.

Summer's faint smile widened a trifle. "No, my dear Braghn. Puck Goodfellow has mislaid his head; it belongs upon my mantelpiece where I may gaze upon it. I have had enough of his play at neutrality. If the free sidhe are not with us, they are with Unwinter." Cruel and cold, her beauty now, not the visage of the simple nymph it otherwise pleased her to wear. This was a different face, one haughty and motionless as marble. "And I will not tolerate Unwinter's insolence further."

Braghn Moran rose. He glittered as he stood before Summer, stray gleams of sunshine striking from dwarven-carved lines on breastplate, greaves, armplates. Fine strands of honey in his chestnut hair caught the light as well. "Yes, my Queen."

"Do this, and you shall be my lord." She smiled, softening, a kittenish moue on her glossy carmine lips. Petals showered through the air, shying away from each sidhe's breathing cloak of chantment.

Moran made no reply, merely turned on his heel. The ranks parted for him, and some may have noticed he did not swear to her before he left, nor did he glance back. His face was set and dark, and when the doors closed behind him, Summer's smile fled.

"The rest of you," she continued, "are required for other work."

Tension crackled between the floating petals, each exuding a crisp apple scent as it touched the floor. For Summer to expend her strength on this glamouring, for her to appear thus, was perhaps not quite wise in her recent state.

But who would tell *her* as much?

She finally gave them their task. "Jeremiah Gallow, once Armormaster, offends your queen." Her hands tightened against each other in her lap. "Kill him, and bring Unwinter's Horn to me."

NOT YET
4

Blackness. And cold. At least the great high-crested waves of agony, each with their glassy teeth tearing at his flesh, had stopped. They receded like chill water along a rock-strewn beach, and he was left in womblike dark, upon cold stone.

Jeremiah Gallow curled around his own heartbeat, the dumb persistent rhythm that had accompanied him from the beginning. His mortal mother, laboring in agony and dying as he first drew breath, could never tell him who his father was. Nor could the black-suited Fathers at the orphanage, preferring instead to ascribe all the boys under their care to the persistence of many-headed Sin itself.

Sin, like Charity and Obedience, was often upon the Fathers' lips, and meant something different each time they said it. In that, they were like the sidhe.

Jeremiah saw the orphanage again, the dingy halls ruthlessly scrubbed, the scratchy uniforms, the cold, narrow benches where boys sat in rows to learn by rote. The wooden paddles, polished with many beatings. Finding out how to whisper the locks and escape had filled him with a heady sense of invincibility, one that hadn't fully deserted him through all the subsequent years.

Until Daisy died. The mortal girl he'd left Summer for, swearing to himself that he was different, not a faithless fickle sidhe who would abandon a woman after a season.

No, instead there had been the car accident. Her mortal fragility, shattered. The machines keeping her alive, and the silence when they halted.

Which brought him, finally, to Robin.

I won't ever be my sister.

What did it make him, now that Daisy's face blurred and a sharper, finer one took its place, with the gloss of sidhe beauty? Coppergold hair, dark-blue eyes, a sweet mouth . . . but it wasn't there the real loveliness lay.

No, it was in other places. *A Half girl truer than cold iron itself, who makes you look the faithless hag you are.* He almost wished she'd been there, in Summerhome, to hear him say it.

Was she still alive? They'd taken her locket, it would be a simple matter to track her from true metal she'd worn at her throat for so long. She *needed* him.

Which brought him to full consciousness, alert in the dark, abed on cold stone, a gush of sweat breaking from his skin as he uncurled. His body responded with its usual alacrity, no dragging slowness, none of the agonizing spiked heat of poison along his side where Unwinter's knifeblade had stroked.

He was on a stone shelf, and he still wore his old armor—the first set of sidhe work he'd ever bargained for and won. It was of a cut not favored by Summer's knights, and for a pikeman who needed room to maneuver besides. Not for him an elf-horse and a broadsword or a sickle newmoon blade, though he could fight mounted, if he had to. And had, more than once.

His arms tingled. If there was any light, he'd be able to see the marks moving on his skin. Mortals would mistake them for tribal tattoos, maybe. Daisy had asked him if he was a sailor or a biker, one of her few questions.

Now he wondered why she never asked more.

He staggered the dimensions of the cell. Five strides by five, barking his shins on the bed. A wet bandage against his eyes, claustrophobia briefly closing his throat. Sidhe were creatures of air, if not light, and any mortal would be uncomfortable locked in a stone cube, too.

His arms ran with prickles, just treading the edge of actual pain. The medallion against his chest, a circle of burning frost, was a good reminder of why he was here.

Unwinter hadn't killed him. Instead, the lord of the Unseelie had taken the poison from the wound, and left him here to rot. A Half wouldn't starve to death, but he could grow attenuated indeed, and waste away of solitude itself.

No. Clarity returned. *Robin.*

If he was still alive, he needed to be fighting. But really, why hadn't Unwinter just fucking killed him? It didn't make *sense.*

Gallow exhaled, concentrating. It was hard, at first—that was new. The prickles turned to needles piercing skin and flesh underneath, and he couldn't ever remember the lance being so sluggish. Not since the first time he'd called it out of the dwarven-inked marks, and almost died.

A faint gleam around his fingers stung his dark-adapted eyes. He exhaled, harshly, and familiar solidity thocked into his palms. Shorter than usual, because of the confined space, the lance hummed, the tassels of its blunt end dripping a low punky moonfire. Gallow blinked rapidly. The faint light *hurt*, not along the marks but scouring his eyes. The dark was better, but he squinted, ignoring hot welling tears.

Cold gray stone, almost like slate, but with thin colorless

veins. There was only one place, in the real or more-than-real, where the cells were built of thanstone, meant to keep chantment and glamour from effecting a release of the poor assholes caught in them. There was a door, too, of sheer dark metal. It looked goddamn imposing, and the thin colorless veins in the thanstone had branched into its fabric, little clutching fingers deadening both chantment and light.

The lance's leaf-shaped blade lengthened slightly. It quivered, nowhere near its full substantial strength. Gallow concentrated, and the blade-edge flushed with rose-ruddy heat.

Iron, that most inimical of mortal metals. Only a Half could survive the marriage of the lance—too much mortal, and the weapon would kill you before it would yield, too much sidhe, and it would ironblight you from the marks inward. The dwarves had said it was *possible*—a weapon you could never lose, a weapon that would never break.

Jeremiah Gallow had brought the dwarves what was required, and said *Do it*. It was probably the last real decision he'd made. Everything after that had just been...well, a man did what he had to.

Even a Half. Pushed along by one bloodline, pulled by the other.

He examined the door, still blinking furiously. Felt like he had bleach in his eyes, dammit.

It turned into a moot point, because under the sound of his breath and the persistent thudding of his heart, another music intruded.

Footsteps.

He hopped onto the shelf-bed, the lance's light growing steadier. The lives he took vanished into its hungry core, and battle only made them both stronger. Something had drained the lance, but he might get a chance to add strength in the next few moments.

Creaking. Dusty clockwork cogs shrieking as they turned, grudging each inch of motion. Whoever it was hadn't taken any chances; they wanted him to stay. Even cold iron might not cut through such a door.

Unwinter has me. I'm not dead.

Of the two sentences, he couldn't say which was more disturbing.

The groaning and shuddering increased. Finally, with a rusting scream, the door hauled itself open an inch, another. Ruddy torchlight sliced through and Jeremiah folded into a crouch, the lance keening softly as it clove air in small precise circles and found no resistance. It would show him a map of the battle inside his head.

If only there was a battle to be fought.

A low, chill laugh echoed in the hall. Jeremiah's breath turned to puffs of white cloud, the cold rasping against his armor as if it wished to work through and cat-lick living skin.

"*Gallow.*" The single word was a frigid caress.

He set his jaw, wishing he could open his eyes. He was facing the lord of the Unseelie, the Lion of Danu, Summer's once-Consort. And Gallow's face was screwed up like a child waiting for a whipping, hot saltwater trickling down his cheeks.

He had to cough to clear his throat. His mouth tasted like he'd been working asphalt all day and drinking all night—a feat he'd performed once or twice before losing interest.

It was just too damn expensive to get enough mortal booze to make a Half even faintly tipsy. "As you see me, Unwinter."

Silence. Then another low grating sound struck the shivering air.

Laughter. Unwinter found him *amusing.*

"*This,*" the Unseelie said, "*is why I have not killed you yet.*"

"Because of my wit?" The lance hummed, eagerly, but there

29

was nothing for it to latch onto. The medallion at Jeremiah's chest was cold enough to burn, but it didn't. Unwinter had worn the thing for many a long year as both mortals and sidhe reckoned.

Had *he* ever felt it chill-scald like this?

"*What little you have? No.*" Another low grinding, but thinner than the last. "*You may be beaten, and you may be killed. But you do not submit.*"

Sheer idiot persistence, nothing more. Maybe he should tell Unwinter as much. "Never got the habit." The burning was going down, but he didn't dare open his eyes just yet.

"*Good.*" Unwinter sounded thoughtful. "*There is a task for thee.*"

I suspected as much, since you didn't let the poison take me. "Wonderful." His throat was so dry. What he wouldn't give for some Coors. Or better, milk. Even skim sounded good. Cream would be better.

"*You may always refuse.*" As if Unwinter didn't know he had Gallow by the balls.

So Jeremiah said the only thing he could. "Robin."

Unwinter did not laugh. "*You may even live to see her again.*"

It wasn't quite a promise, but it was all he was going to get. "Lead the way, then."

No, it wasn't submitting. He still couldn't see a damn thing, but he heard soft footsteps, each one crackling slightly as resisting air coated itself with ice, and followed in their wake. His shoulder hit the doorjamb, he blinked more hot water out of his eyes, and found he could squint at a long, cobweb-festooned hall. Retreating down its funhouse sway was a black-clad back and a head of thistledown hair, bound by a pale silvery fillet.

Gallow, half blind and unsteady, staggered after Unwinter.

ONE BEFORE DAWN
5

Smoke clung to Alastair Crenn's shoulders; the scream of the last Unseelie knight he'd killed still reverberated in his hands and throat and knees. His shoulder ground with pain, he was down to his last arrow, and the only thing that had saved him was mortal dawn's painting the sagebrushed hills with red.

A bloody dawn, indeed. Sailors take warning.

Crenn coughed, spat, and eyed the twisting, writhing almost-corpse splayed on the pavement.

The drow cursed at him, fragments of the Old Language fluttering blackwing-bird free of its mouth and struggling to flap into free air. They were too weak to do more than brush, though, and Crenn spat in return, a single golden dart spearing three of them at once with a sound like breaking sugarpane.

He'd shot this one with iron, right above the hip, and doubled back to find it in the middle of the road, scratching with maggot-white, waxen, broken fingertips, probably searching for a door or even a bit of free earth it could use to go to ground and escape. Crenn crouched, his hand sinking into the drow's hair, and he wrenched the thing's head back, exposing a wedge of pale throat.

No violet dapples of lightshield chantment on this one. Sunlight would kill it handily, but it paid to be thorough.

It hissed at him, baring sharp serrated teeth, and he glanced in either direction. No traffic on this desolate stretch of highway just now. His shoulder gave another twinge, and two drops of bright red blood hit the pavement. The drow writhed even more furiously, scenting nourishment so close.

Leading them away from both mortals and their other prey had required all the ingenuity and cunning the swamps of Marrowdowne had taught him, and more. He couldn't remember the last time he'd bled, or the last time he'd actually *sweated*. Not much could wring the salt out of a Half, but by God, misdirecting an entire Unseelie raid came close.

She'd escaped, though. The dog had carried her, and Robin Ragged had escaped.

Crenn dragged the knife across the drow's throat, his lip curling as an arterial gush of bluish ichor splattered on concrete.

I will cut your heart out, she'd told him, in that broken whisper it hurt to hear.

"Too late," he said to the rapidly decaying mess of drow corpse in the road. He yanked the arrow free, examined its head and fletching. No major warping, he could account for the slight curve if he had call to shoot later. Good enough, and his quiver would replenish itself by nightfall.

Was this how Gallow had felt, so long ago, after the mortal policemen had descended on shantytown and set fire to whatever they could? Had he felt the sick thump in his stomach as he contemplated what damage might have been done to a woman, especially one he might have felt...something...for?

For a moment Crenn's face twinged, as if his scars had returned. It was a new thing, to wonder if perhaps that might be best. If Robin looked at him now, she'd assume that the scars vanishing were Summer's payment for a betrayal. How could he explain that was only *part* of the truth? He shook his hair down over his face, a supple movement, as he turned. The moss among the strands had dried to verdigris crumbles, the tinge of Marrowdowne's curtains of green stillness finding the dry mortal sun uncongenial at best. It was habit, to view the world through a screen, shielding the scars from prying gazes.

Besides, every assassin sometimes needed a mask.

His arms ached, and his legs too. His boots were caked with dust and drying ichors, his leathers shedding more of the same. The eastern horizon ripened, tongues of orange and lateral stripes of crimson intensifying, a flameflower about to bloom. No hint of moisture on the wind, and he had traveled far enough inland that he couldn't smell the sea.

She escaped. Otherwise he would have heard the silvery hunt-whistles thrilling up into ultrasonic, the cry of prey brought down.

He turned his back on the bubbling mess of Unseelie, and set off along the side of the highway. Funny, after so many years, he'd finally made it to the mortal California. Land of milk and honey, where a man could get a job—that had been the dream, long ago, riding the rails with Jeremiah. They might even have made it if the Hooverville shantytown they'd ended up in hadn't been raided by the good citizens of a town uneasy at the thought of a collection of migrants on their doorstep.

The same old song. *Move along. Nothing for your kind here.* Even in Summer there were places a Half shouldn't tread.

And a few the fullborn wouldn't dare either. Like the fens' green curtains and hungry depths. He'd looked for a hiding place, and found it, retreating from the goddamn mortal world and all its problems.

Now he was thinking daring that green hell hadn't been as much of an act of bravery as he'd wanted it to be.

Crenn trudged back along the highway, mortal dawn rising over the low blue smears of distant mountains. Dust, sage, rock, and the ribbon of the road. As soon as he was far enough away from the drow's death, he could slip through the Veil into the lands of the free sidhe and begin to track her. She wouldn't be happy to see him, but sooner or later he'd prove himself useful. He'd spend the time he had to convincing her.

Because a girl who would face down Unwinter without a qualm, and spit in Summer's eye to boot, deserved all the protection a man could scrape together, and more. Certainly she deserved a hell of a lot more than an arrogant former Armormaster and a Half who spent his time hiding in treetops.

A woman like that could make a man immortal, or so close it didn't matter.

His breath came a little shorter and his palms dampened at the thought. The mortals at the carnival had dragged her from the sea, and she'd slept in one of their trailers. Standing over her in the dark, her black heels in his almost-trembling hands, Alastair had thought perhaps he could simply leave this entire fucked-up situation where he'd found it, go back to the swamps, and let Summer, Unwinter, and their playthings fight it out without him.

Then he thought of Robin Ragged spitting at the Seelie queen, and her determination as she flung herself into whatever lay in that white tower by the sea, the tower Crenn had brought her to.

What was a woman like that doing with Gallow, of all people? What could he have that she wanted? How did he *do* it? Even when Crenn had been unscarred, the other man drew them, those women. Sometimes beautiful, sometimes not, but always with that…spark. With something you couldn't quite put your finger on, a female magic entirely different than chantment.

A burring sound in the distance—an engine. Crenn put his head down, old habits dying hard if at all, and wondered if you could still travel for miles with a stranger in those horseless carriages. The last time he'd been in the mortal realm for this long, twenty-five miles an hour was high speed. Now they were almost as fast as elfhorses, but far less elegant. Exhaust-stink chariots poisoning the mortal air. How long before the sidhe would choke to death when they bothered to come through the Veil at all?

For a long time, the sound stayed the same, a blurred buzz neither further nor closer. Then, as the sun mounted higher and pavement shimmered in the distance under waves of heat, it drew close all at once, a roar like a wyrm's breath and hot wind buffeting the roadside.

A groan, a stuttering, and the great silver beast coasted to a stop not too far ahead, amber and red lights on its right side blinking.

Crenn lengthened his stride. The gigantic semi waited, rumbling idly, and a few minutes later, dust spumed, tires ground dry gravel, and Alastair Crenn had vanished into the cab.

THE DRIVER
6

Normally Bill Yonkovitch didn't stop for hitchers. Caution was the best policy, especially when hauling big loads over long distances. You never knew when luck might sour itself up like a bennies high gone bad, itching under your skin and turning the world into a funhouse distortion of paranoia.

Nope, best to stick to caffeine, safety, and keeping the cab clean. Maybe he didn't make as much by following the rules, but on the other hand, he'd been driving for years without a wreck, so that was good enough.

After Maria, he never wanted to be surprised again.

"Where you headed?" Bill scratched under the band of his baseball cap, squinting at the road.

The guy was out walking without a bag or anything, a shock of dark hair almost woolly-dreadlocked moving in time to his steps. At first Bill thought it was a hallucination, but he solidified at the side of the road and the brakes grabbed without any real direction on the driver's part.

Sometimes it was like that, even if a man didn't want surprises, the world conspired to force him out of his nice safe shell. Always best to grudgingly go along, because otherwise the road would choose another damn thing to throw at you down the way, one maybe not so pleasant or easily fixed.

"West," the man said, clearly enough. Hair hanging in his face, but he didn't look dirty. Sand crusted his boots, good well-worn Frye's brown leather. You could tell a lot about a man from his shoes. These had seen hard use, and he'd waded in something before trudging through sand—but he'd knocked them clean before he climbed into Bill's cab.

Which made Bill feel pretty charitable. Politeness was always good. "California coast, huh? You local?"

A flash of white teeth, under that mop of hair. "No. Thank you for stopping."

"I don't normally," Bill said. Was it nervousness, beating in time to his heart? The doctor said his ticker was fine. *Should last another twenty years or so,* he'd laughed, and Bill laughed with him.

You sort of had to, when they informed you how much longer your sentence ran. In front of the windshield, the gray road ran, and there was nothing to do but put the tires on it and speed along.

"Then I thank you again." The hitcher had a trace of an accent, maybe, which would explain the hair. You saw all types on the side of the road. A certain number of them were bad sorts, and you mostly couldn't tell unless you got stung. That was why Bill kept the Louisville Slugger with its lead core in the back, and the ax handle always tucked in its custom sheath on the left side of the driver's seat.

Now, despite the politeness, Bill was wondering why he'd stopped to pick the guy up. "The heat can really get to a guy out there. It'll make you crazy. Desert's nothing to fool around with."

"I'm used to it," the man said. "I lived in a swamp."

"Down south? That's wet heat. It'll drive you crazy too, but in a different way."

"Have you seen both?" The hitcher sounded genuinely curious.

It was nice to talk to someone every once in a while. "Oh, yeah. I been all over. Me and Betsy here." He tapped the dash, a proprietary movement. "Coast-to-coast. Can't stay in one place too long. Get itchy."

"Do you have a home, then?" Thoughtfulness in the soft baritone. Good voice. The man could do radio, if he wanted to.

Bill grinned. "Used to. Now I've got a mailing service and a sleeper cab. Better that way. Just roll all over the country. Rent a room when I feel like it, sometimes."

"Like a snail. Your home on your back."

"Some days it feels like it. You?"

"A house. In the swamp." A shrug. "But home is different."

"It always is." Bill nodded sagely. You often came across philosophers on the road. They were everywhere, from the tired utilitarian waitresses to some of the slow, dreaming Hell's Angels, the slipstream driving all thoughts but *make it big someday I'm gonna* out of their heads. Other truck drivers ran the gamut from materialists to downright spiritual—not to be confused with *religious*. The one poststructuralist trucker Bill knew had decided the Lower 48 weren't avant-garde enough and went to do short hauls in Alaska, where the crazy ran deep enough to suit him.

A sign flashed by—BARTON 10 MI. Now that was an asshole armpit of a town, he'd only stopped there once. "How far you going, son?"

"A long way. But the next town is fine, really."

"You may not want to with hair like that." *Not to mention, well.* These days you couldn't even give that sort of warning

39

without maybe hitting a touchy spot. "This part of the country's...well, you know."

"Just like everywhere else." A bitter little laugh. "You can't get away from it."

Which made his passenger a cynic, maybe. Or just a realist. "What if you could?"

"Don't know. Went somewhere a long time ago, because I was told it didn't matter there. The thing is, something matters everywhere. If it's not one thing, it's another."

This was shaping up to be one interesting conversation. Bill settled himself further in his seat, Betsy settling herself too, into a good even speed. It was a nice morning. "So where did you eventually end up? That swamp?" If he had found a corner of the South where things didn't matter, that was outright miraculous.

A place like that would be worth knowing about.

"Too soon to tell." Did the hitcher sound amused? "There's a girl, though."

"Oh, now." A deep rich chuckle worked its way up out of Bill's gut. He was putting on some pounds—long distances did that to you. Not enough getting out and walking. "I used to have one that felt like home." Maria's face, with the engaging gap between her front teeth and her humming in the kitchen. Waking up to that slow wandering melody had filled Bill with something very much like...well, he wasn't quite religious, so maybe *heaven* wasn't the word.

But it was damn close. Just like the opposite when he woke up one fine sunny morning and realized she wasn't coming back.

The stranger gave him a moment or two, then asked the reasonable question. "What happened?"

"She foreclosed. What about yours?"

"She wants to kill me."

Oh, man. "That's the best type."

"I don't blame her."

"Then, brother, pardon my French, but you may be fucked."

"No pardon needed, good sir." But the young man tensed. "There. You can let me out there."

"What?" Bill took his foot off the gas. "You'll have to walk through Barton, then."

"Maybe."

A few minutes later, the man brushed his hair back and reached for the door handle. He paused. "You are a good mor—ah, a good man. I wish you luck in finding your own home."

"You're sitting in it, son," Bill said, and made one last attempt. "Sure you don't want to ride a bit further?"

"Not today." A firm handshake, callused hand warm and hard against his own, and the young man hopped out of the cab. He headed for Happy Harry's Stop 'n' Sip, and Bill Yonkovitch never saw him again.

He also didn't notice the faint smear of gold on his hand, sinking into his own skin. Later that day, he bought a scratch ticket at a little stop-and-rob on the outskirts of LA. He didn't realize he'd won for three weeks, but by that time he'd already met an exhausted waitress in Nevada who almost passed out bringing him a chef salad. He took Deirdre to her apartment that night, slept outside in the cab of his truck, and when he woke up the next morning she'd left a note on the windshield with her number.

They lived a long happy life, childless in an RV, crossing and crisscrossing the States. And Bill, wiser than most, never picked up another hitchhiker.

That last one, he felt, was enough.

HEARTSBLOOD
7

A sere dust-choked afternoon found Robin holding Pepperbuckle's ruff, leaning against the sidhe dog's warmth and eyeing a patch of improbable green. Tiny winking gems of light coruscated around her, the damn pixies chiming nonsense and borrowed words from every language, both sidhe and mortal, as they fluttered. They darted close and away, their little mouths round O's of excitement as they hit the edge of her personal space, their daybleached globes of foxfire turning dark blue before they zoomed away again, laughing their tiny mad chuckles, as if her presence both dyed and tickled them.

Seen from above, the greenery was no more than a small divot in an endless sea of heatshimmer sand. It would glitter, a moment of emerald fire, before the eye found something else about the immensity of dun dust, rock, and greengray sage to fasten on instead. A mortal would forget it, or think it a hallucination, a mirage oasis, or possibly a stand of something spiny around thick sulphurous water.

It was, in fact, an oak tree. Sandy wilderness cradled it, the Veil curdling in thick folds around its thick trunk, and the fingers of its curve-bordered leaves caressed the oven-dry breeze.

Its branches sheltered a pool of greenery, light and dark moving in mellifluous leafshade, and its bark had a thick, smooth reddish cast, as if the tree had been poured instead of grown.

A heartsblood oak, a nail piercing the real and more-than-real, crouched in the desert, and Pepperbuckle had led Robin straight to it. It was as they approached, Robin's heels almost sinking in deep sand despite the chantments on them and her velvet coat-cloak flapping, that the pixies appeared, crowding thick as clotted cream. They showed up wherever the Veil was rent or curdled, tiny crowding things with gossamer wings and needle-sharp teeth. She was too weary to try to dispel them, and who would understand that they'd seen her if they went carrying tales? Nobody listened to pixies, and their language changed from one wingbeat to the next.

The giant redgold dog heaved a sigh as he stepped into the liquid shade, and so did Robin. She sagged and pushed the hood back, freeing her chopped hair with a grimace, and patted at her throat before she remembered, again, that her locket was gone.

Jeremiah Gallow had it. Was he dead, and the golden gleam in his pocket while he moldered?

What *she* had was black velvet, the pipes at her belt, and the small wickedly curved knife welling with its own translucent green poison. The boll Gallow had given her, stuffed in a pocket with a blue plastic ring. And Pepperbuckle, who led her to the tree and sank down to sit, his shoulders rising while his haunches dropped. The hound grinned, tongue lolling and his sharp gleaming teeth exposed, well pleased with himself.

"Good boy," she husked, scratching behind his ear just where she'd seen her sister caress stray dogs in their long-ago childhood, just where he liked it. He leaned into the touch, his dark-blue eyes half closing. "Best boy." She peered up at the tree's branches, moving in slow semaphore.

The milk had helped, but her throat was still a little raw. Rest would help even more, and oaks were good trees. Heartsbloods didn't have dryads lurking in their trunks, but they were sidhe all the same. Some said they spied on all that happened in their shade but never spoke, preferring secrets to blackmail. Others held that their movements were a language all their own, but even highborn fullbloods didn't live long enough to learn it.

A very few whispered that they reported to one sidhe only, but nobody knew *who*. Summer, Unwinter, or someone else, what did it matter? The important thing was, she could rest here, and so could Pepperbuckle.

At least, until dusk. Unseelie had to wait for true night before they could begin hunting her afresh during Summer's half of the year. It was small consolation that Summer might not have known Robin was still alive—or, more likely, sane enough—to be hunted, though.

Am I sane? She shuddered, scratching both of Pepperbuckle's ears now. The sidhe hound wriggled with delight, his head dropping. The milk had restored him, too.

The tiny chiming of the pixies made her wonder about the teenager in the small store, miles away by now. Why had pixies bothered to show themselves? It wasn't like them to take interest in a lowly Half, even if she was Summer's erstwhile errand girl. They'd intervened when she rode an elfhorse through a city to draw Unwinter away, too, and that had been strangely unlike them as well.

That was an unpleasant thought, and she shuddered afresh. Pixies clustered both of them, their glowspheres brighter in the liquid shade. "Go away," Robin murmured, but not very loudly. Conserving her voice was safest. The music under her thoughts, running wide and deep as a silent river, was full of piping chimes now, too. If she listened, maybe she could translate their chatter, but who would want to?

Best of all would be to climb into the branches and wedge herself in a convenient place. Her ams and legs ached just thinking about it, though the milk and creamer was a steady comforting glow behind her breastbone. In the end, she sank down next to Pepperbuckle, and the dog turned a few times before settling among the roots with her. Robin put one arm over his shoulders, grateful for his warmth, so different than the choking dust-dry mortal heat outside, and shut her eyes.

Sleep wasn't long in coming, but before it swallowed her completely she felt tiny pinprick-pats on her face, her throat, her wrists, her hands. The pixies didn't bite, they merely smoothed their tiny hands over her, their deep indigo glow sinking into her, a drugging calm. Pepperbuckle's eyes closed halfway, and the dog watched the shadows and the tiny lights with benevolent interest as the mortal wind rattled and rasped.

A heartsblood oak is a nail, and the mortal world runs around it like softened wax, slow but sure. The world outside that particular bubble of branch, bole, and shade blurred like dye on wet paper, and the tree carried its cargo serenely through a long, warm afternoon.

FAIRY GIRL
8

Go play, Jenny Markham's momma said, waving a skinny, languid hand. Both of her friends giggled, the slow slurring sounds that meant they were on their special medicine already, and Jenny's mother would be soon. Lanky, nervous Topper, who had brought the medicine in the first place, stared at Jenny. Sometimes Jenny's momma would let her stay inside while they took their medicine, but never while he was there, since Topper had once followed Jenny's momma from room to room, saying *How much, how much*, and pointing at Jenny in the corner with her only Barbie while a spring storm made the ceiling drip as if the house itself was crying.

So Jenny left the close, stinking living room, dodging piles of refuse out of habit, and didn't bother checking the kitchen for anything to eat. Hunger was a coal in her belly, but there was no school for spring break, which meant no lunch and no Mrs. Anderson, who let Jenny stay in her classroom during playground time, drawing on scrap paper and pretending her teacher was her mommy instead of the wan big-eyed woman with the marks on her arms.

Outside, golden sunshine bounced off the trailer roofs and

the cracked concrete, weeds now green-juicy from spring storms climbing in every crevice. Their own trailer was at the end of the road, huddled in front of a vacant lot starred with broken glass and windblown trash. Small paths ran through a tangle of blackberry bushes, their vines aggressively greening now that they'd received a good soaking or two. Jenny plunged into their embrace, small and quick enough to avoid being caught by thorns, and wandered, wishing there were berries on the branches.

Maybe she could eat the leaves. Or there was an old lady near the front of the trailer park who threw out a half box of doughnuts every Saturday night, for some reason. You could find all sorts of things in trash cans, if you had to.

The gnawing in her middle retreated a little, came back, vanished as she worked deeper into the tangle. She began to hum, an anemic half-forgotten pop song matching her lank dishwater hair and her dirty fingernails, her tattered blue jumper and shoes held together with reflective tape.

At first, breaking into the clearing, she thought she was lost, or had wandered too far. Then something zoomed at her face and Jenny ducked, a miserable little cry breaking in the suddenly golden-liquid air. She went down hard, knees and hands jolting on stony ground, almost biting her tongue in half. Tasting blood, she craned her neck to see what it was, but the thing zoomed away. It was an angry flushed red, like a landlord's face, and much too big for an insect, even a dragonfly. It wasn't a bird either, even though it flew.

Jenny rubbed her dry, aching eyes. She didn't remember this clearing. She *especially* didn't remember the tree in the middle, its reddish column growing out of lush grass much greener than even a golf course's clipped mane. The tree looked funny in more ways than one, but maybe it was just Jenny's rumbling stomach that made it seem that way.

There was something like a golden-copper horse lying at the bottom of the tree, and against its side was a sleeping woman in a black robe, like she was in a movie or something. Her short, artfully mussed hair was the color of the horse's coat, and her skin was flawless-pale.

The angry little red thing zipped back, along with others like it. They circled her, and the little girl cowered, covering her eyes. They buzzed around her, but they didn't dart at her face again, and when Jenny crept forward on hands and knees, miserably impelled, they merely hovered over her like a furious cloud. They were, as any idiot could see, little winged people, and Jenny knew what those were called.

What child doesn't?

Perhaps they didn't swarm her because she *was* a child, and her slinking approach was full of wonder instead of ill intent. It seemed to take forever to reach the grass, which smelled like crushed mint under her sweating palms. The woman kept sleeping, like she'd had some of Momma's special medicine in her arm.

The horse-thing's head curved down, resting over the woman's protectively. It was *big*, and it probably had some wicked teeth. Jenny crawled closer, suddenly very sure the horse-thing wasn't asleep but it was listening, eyes shut, very carefully.

She had to be a princess, this beautiful, beautiful woman. Sleeping under a tree with a beautiful animal, with bright-winged creatures all around. It was right out of a storybook, or a dream from Momma's medicine. Jenny crept close enough to look at the woman's shoes—black heels, shiny and perfect just like the rest of her. Even the draggled hem of the velvet coat was beautiful, each hole and fraying arranged just so.

Jenny stretched out in the cool shade, nervously glancing at the flitting lights overhead. They shaded into purple, then deep blue after a while, moving in patterns that weren't quite random. Hunger and thirst both forgotten, the child barely felt one of the tree's roots under her thin ribs shift slightly, and after a long while of staring at the princess who had suddenly appeared in a vacant lot, Jenny fell asleep too.

The oak's branches hummed sweetly, the bark resounding with a subliminal purr like a plucked string vibrating too low for mortal ears, a pressure felt in heart and throat and wrists. Outside the bubble of shade, the mortal world blurred. Slowly, so slowly, finger-roots of red bark, clotted with rich brown earth, rose to caress the bedraggled mortal child's form.

RIDE FORTH

9

Hunger or temperature didn't affect a Half much, not once they'd pierced the Veil over the more-than-real the first time. The first few heady gulps of different air, whether in the borderlands of the free sidhe, Summer, or Unwinter's ashen country with its splashes of crimson, perhaps changed something in those with sidhe blood. Activated something, like flipping a switch, turning on an electric glow in the guts.

When hunger did come for a Half, it was different than purely mortal emptiness. Maybe it was that Jeremiah wasn't dead after all, despite everything. Maybe it was Unwinter's poison, leached out of the long livid scar on his side and leaving weakness in its wake. There was a blowtorch in his belly, and his head was a lot lighter than he was used to.

Gallow followed Unwinter's straight, black-clad back through halls of black stone, their ceilings point-arched and Gothic-high. Cobweb curtains hung over some doors, sheer uninterrupted gray sheets, thick with whatever ancient dust fell in Unwinter's Keep. It wasn't the first time Gallow had seen these halls.

It was, however, the first time he'd openly followed an unarmed and unarmored Unseelie through them, the marks on his arms itching unbearably. He could strike, couldn't he? There was Unwinter's unprotected back. What was stopping him?

Not weakness, even though keeping the lance solid would require more effort than usual. And certainly not chivalry. Self-interest, maybe. The poison might simply be abated, not removed. Once Unwinter's venom worked its way into a wound, it was over. The only surprise was that Gallow lasted as long as he had.

There was another reason not to strike, one he tried not to think about. He needed all his wits about him right now.

Well, whatever of them he had left. Gallow scrubbed at his face, stubble scratching against his palms. A flicker of chantment would erase the rasp, but he preferred actual shaving. The scrape of a razor, a trace of cold iron chill-hot, was a mortal ritual.

Daisy had liked him clean-shaven.

Stairs rose before Unwinter, who glided upward at the same even pace. Maybe Gallow was dreaming, one last paroxysm before the poison killed him completely.

Or maybe this was Hell. Would so mortal an idea as the afterlife accept a being with a half share of sidhe blood? If sidhe had no souls, as the Pale God's wise men had thundered, did that mean Half only had, well, half souls?

Whatever you have, you know who it belongs to now. Keep moving.

Up, and up. From Unwinter's dungeons they climbed, Gallow's legs aching even as the chilly, dust-laden air moved past him in little feral licks, caressing his face and hands. Small crackles of dried blood, mortal dirt, and remaining traces of sickness dropped away, melting before they hit the grit-dusted stone floor.

Just like a mortal, stinking up the place. There was no banister, so Gallow leaned against the stone wall as his legs pumped,
carrying him after the mop of thistledown hair and the glinting silver fillet. Leather scraped, almost cringing from the
inimical chill of the wall. Funny, this was just like following
a Father through the halls of the orphanage so long ago, dread
weighing his limbs and the adult not even condescending to
look back. *Of course you'll follow*, the rigid black-clad back said,
and of course, Gallow did.

Another long hall, its left side opening up through a frieze
of pierced stone—a gallery, looking over an immense space
below. There was no sign of drow or barrow-wight, any of the
fullblood highborn sidhe who waited upon Unwinter, or even
a guard. You could maybe think the whole Keep was deserted,
except for the thrumming in distant halls, the air full of whispers and mutters, silent currents mouthing every exposed edge.
A quiet, deadly fermentation.

Unwinter paused at a junction, took the left-hand path, and
did not glance back at Gallow, who hurried to keep up. His
stomach trembled on the edge of a growl, an embarrassing
mortal noise.

Longing thoughts of charred meat dripping with spicy,
smoky barbecue danced through Gallow's head. Beer so cold
it made the teeth ache, or pungent yellow cheese—which led
him to that best of things, full-cream milk, a balm and full-
ness all at once. Sticks of butter, not the pale clots of fat sold in
supermarkets but warm yellow solidified sunlight, still smelling faintly of the hay and the glossy sides of the healthy animal
who made it.

When the sidhe before him finally halted, Gallow did too,
swaying slightly, his shoulder hitting the wall again. A chill
grated down his side, spreading from the stone.

Weak. I'm weak.

Unwinter turned, very slowly, and a cool bath of dread slid down Gallow's back. Not so long ago another sidhe had led him over hill and dale, to the roof of a mortal building, and Puck Goodfellow's intent had been murderous.

There was no shortage of murder flying around lately.

Unwinter's hands, each bearing an extra finger and each finger bearing extra joints, hung loose at his sides. Each finger and both thumbs were armored with rings, jewels colorless and otherwise throbbing with nasty sharp gleams. *"Were you thinking to slay me, Gallow?"* Thin, cruel, attractive lips—even though he was Unwinter, he was still sidhe, and that meant beauty. A high gloss of cold loveliness, a razor against numb skin. The crimson light living in the cold red orbs of the Unseelie lord's eyeballs sharpened, the hair-thin black capillaries in his bloody sclera moving ever so slightly.

It really was very much like Summer's ageless black gaze. *Her* eyes held dusty lights, stars and constellations no astronomer would ever decipher; Unwinter's held the last gleams of a dying sun. Sometimes those among his favored companions bore the bloodspark for a moment or two, in moments of high emotion or extremis...but Unwinter was the only sidhe who permanently bore the bloody gaze.

"I was." No point in lying now, Gallow told himself.

"And yet you refrained."

"It seemed impolite." He didn't have to work to sound exhausted, or sarcastic, either. Really, when you got to the point of not giving a fuck, why bother?

The cold grinding noise of Unwinter's amusement rumbled just under the audible. He spread his flour-pale, fluidly articulated hand against the door, a slight caressing motion that might have sparked nausea if Gallow hadn't been so used to the way sidhe joints moved. The rings twinkled, the glitter of lights in a drowning mortal's gaze.

Gallow blinked.

A shadow crawled over the back of Unwinter's hand, there and gone in a moment. He forced his aching eyes to look *underneath.*

Hard, evil-looking black pinpricks marched across Unwinter's skin, each radiating hair-thin cracks. The center of each prickle was a raised bump, a needle-tip of leprous green. "You're plagued," he said, flatly.

"*Yes.*" The single word made the hallway shudder and flex slightly. "*There is only so much will can keep at bay, Gallow. Even a will such as mine.*"

They said it was will alone that kept his ash-and-flaxen lands from sliding deeper into the Veil, just as the flint knife plunging into changeling chests kept Summer green and bountiful. Gallow's throat had gone dry, or perhaps he just now noticed it. He searched for something to say that wouldn't remind Unwinter he had a good reason to kill one small, irritating Jeremiah Gallow, and failed to find it.

The Unseelie lord saved him the trouble. "*You took what is mine, and slew one dear to me.*"

Well, he couldn't argue with that. Killing Unwinter's parlay might not have been the best move in that particular situation, but it was the only one he could have made.

Story of my life. "Yes."

"*Walk with me, just a few steps further.*" Unwinter pushed the door, which quivered and scraped its way open, deathly silent.

Outside, fine smears of ash fell from a slumbrous, umbrous sky. Unwinter's light was either the sere cold shine of a white winter sun, no warmth to be found in its glow, or the bruise-dusk of a blizzard with ice on its back. Black, lace-starred mountains, their sides splashed with fuming, smoking crimson hellholes of dwarven furnace vents or the mouths of greatwyrm dens, reared in serried edges on the horizon. A narrow obsidian walkway led away from the door, the ash soaking into its surface with tiny puffs of clawed steam. A mutter in the distance was the Dreaming Sea, touching even this cold shore. Above, pennants snapped and fluttered on the wind—black cloth, its edges gracefully fringed by moth-chewing.

Wait. He's not flying the red flags. What's this? Gallow followed as Unwinter strode onto the walkway, each step accompanied by that crackling scream of frozen, compressed air. Finally, Unwinter halted, and rounded on him.

Jeremiah tensed. Now they were getting somewhere.

"*I will die,*" Unwinter said, as calmly as if he were ordering an execution or a breakfast. "*But not before I have had my vengeance, Half. Do you understand?*"

Not really. "Here I am." He almost added, *Do your worst,* but that was just a step too far, even for a man who didn't give a fuck if he lived or died.

Except if he died, who would play this insane ten-sided game to keep Robin safe?

Unwinter's lips peeled back from his white, white teeth. The crevices and grooves between them were threaded with crimson, the wide bloody smile of true amusement indistinguishable from a pained grimace. "*Indeed. Look upon my realm, Jeremiah Gallow. Look.*"

He did.

After a long moment, Unwinter spoke again. He told Gallow, softly and calmly, what he wished the Half to do.

Gallow couldn't help himself.

He began to laugh.

KNIFE
10

The slow dead glare of a desert afternoon cradled a sad, sorry collection of broken-down tin shacks. They looked just like Hooverville shanties, except larger and longer.

Mortals had grown richer even in their poverty, it seemed.

A sign at the mouth of the group announced it as BUENA VISTA TRAILER PARK, but there was no vista, buena or otherwise. Just tired huddled tin cans in a scraped bowl crowded by weeds, gutted cars on blocks or flat tires, sunbleached children's toys scattered in random approximations of yards.

His skin tingled. He lifted his head slightly, and the pressure against every inch of him grew sharper. The instinct of a predator, following invisible clues to his flagging, toothsome prey.

Of course, the fact that he'd taken a scrap of velvet from her ragged coat probably helped, as well. No reason to make instinct work any harder than it had to. He lifted the fabric to his face again, inhaling deeply. Spiced pear, cherries, a russet thread, a wash of deep evening-sky blue. The salt-sweet tang of mortal blood, all mixing together to make up Robin Ragged.

The tugging led him through a tangle of indifferently paved streets, each one more sunscorched and sorry than the last.

Blackberry bramble clustered at the edges, their fingers thick and juicy even in this arid waste, free earth seeking to reclaim the blot upon its back. In short, it was just the sort of in-between place a sidhe would be drawn to, though the mortal dwellings were rancid and ramshackle. It would offend a brughnie to see the disrepair, and dryads would sniff at the lack of trees. Pixies might gather in the blackberries on a solstice or equinox, and greenjacks or jennywillows might make their homes in the dandruff of mortal refuse spreading out from the bowl, avoiding the rusted appliances that reeked of cold iron but finding much castoff overgrown furniture acceptable. There would be mortals to fox and misery aplenty to grow drunk upon for any sidhe who cared for such things.

Crenn stepped lightly, his shadow a pool at his feet. High noon buzzed and blurred with insect life among the brambles. There were no gardens, and the houses were shut tight, no mortals visible though he could hear stealthy movement in many of the tin rectangles.

He followed the tugging to the very edge of the bowl, each corrugated shack turning its back on the empty land beyond. Past the ragged border, sand and sage reclaimed their primacy, but the edges were lined with those blackberry vines, a green wall.

The tingle-pull became a thrum. He slipped through the nominal idea of front yard this last domicile at the end of the crazy-cracked approximation of a street possessed, and in another moment he would have been gone completely.

Except the door flung itself open, the ragged screen door pushed wide almost in the same instant, and a lean young mortal, his scent fuming with sicksalt disease and the furious yellow metallic tang of some drug, staggered out into the hammerblow of sunshine. A threadbare flannel shirt fluttered, and he was starred and spangled with crimson.

"Little giiiiirl," the mortal crooned, his wide brown eyes glazed with whatever he was high on. "Little *giiiiiiirl*, your momma wants you!"

Crenn halted, caught in midstep, all his weight on one foot and the other hovering a few inches above weedy earth, paused like a cat sighting an inattentive bird.

The mortal inhaled. "*Jeeeeeeennyyyyyyyy!*" he yelled, weaving drunkenly down the steps. "Come heeeeeeere, you little biiiiitch!" The gleam in his left hand was a claspknife, and the crimson on him was fresh mortal blood, reeking of iron and salt.

Below that, the brassy scent of death. He had been at grim work, this drugged mortal apparition.

Crenn considered this, and might have gone on his way, following a hunter's certainty. But the mortal saw him and stopped dead, breathing heavily, nostrils and ribs flaring synchronously. Rail-thin, he moved like a pixie-led traveler, quick jerking movements not quite connected to each other. The drug, whatever it was, smelled powerfully adulterated, his body jittering as it sought to consume whatever its rider had subjected it to.

"Whotha-fuckare*you*?" the mortal spat, waving the claspknife for emphasis.

Crenn gauged the distance between them. A single mortal, even hopped up on an ugly substance, was very little threat. And yet, Robin had come this way. Had she met this welcome as well?

He set his booted foot down, carefully, and simply regarded the mortal, who wove unsteadily down rickety porch steps. The screen door banged shut, rebounding and quivering, sending weary darts of bright reflected sunlight dancing across yellow, dying grass, and a lopsided blue car crouched in the almost-driveway.

"I *said*," Spittle bubbled on the mortal's lips, and he enunciated with care now. "*Who* the *fuck* are you?"

Crenn shrugged, a loose liquid movement, and his hand itched for a blade-hilt. "A stranger," he said finally, measuring each word. Another sidhe might well decide to ill-wish the mortal for his rudeness, or investigate the signs of bloody brutality on him. Alastair, however, had no urge to enter the dark cave of the long rectangular aluminum shanty. "Passing through."

The mortal crow-cawed with laughter, weaving another few unsteady steps closer. *Don't,* Crenn wanted to tell him. *Go on your way, whatever mad way that is, and whatever you've done, the punishment will be less than if a sidhe takes notice of you.*

It was already too late. The mortal studied him for a long taffy-stretching moment, head cocked as if he too was listening to faraway music piercing the Veil from some corner of the more-than-real…

"JEEEEENNNNYYYYYY!" he howled as he lunged for Crenn, the knife gleaming, cleaving air with slow sweet sounds.

Crenn stepped aside, half-pivoting, and his booted foot flicked out, catching the weedy mortal in his midriff and sending him stagger-flying back into the crumbling porch. Wood splintered, more blood spattered, this time from broken ends scraping the thrashing mortal body. "*Jenny you biiiiitch, you biiiiitch!*"

Does he think my name is Jenny? Crenn shook his head, his hair swaying. It didn't matter. Nor did whatever crime he'd committed inside the dark cave. What mattered was finding Robin.

And yet…was there anyone alive in that slumping, glittering, tired old shack? Someone who could perhaps use aid? The blood on the mortal was fresh, and not all of it was his.

Crenn hesitated as the mortal moaned and thrashed even more. He had to find Robin.

What would Gallow do? He was the one her gaze followed, the one Robin flung herself into danger for. If Crenn wished to...

He swore softly, a vicious curse in the Old Language that tore another chunk from the mess of splinters and moaning mortal that was the porch. One of the posts had pierced the mortal's back, jetting from the front of his belly, slick with blood and a battlefield stench of ordure.

Nothing stank quite like human bowels, not even in the rotting recesses of Marrowdowne.

Crenn leapt lightly, balancing on a broken spar. Underneath him, the skinny mortal moaned for Jenny afresh. Bile touched the back of Crenn's throat as he tore the screen door off its hinges—the damn thing was a nuisance. He plunged into the darkness beyond.

A few moments ticked by, full of the whisper of wind on dead, blasted grass and throbbing green blackberry vines. The mortal in the ruins of the porch twitched, coughed up bright blood, and the knife dropped from his paw. He exhaled, a long final rattle, and had ceased to move by the time Crenn, pale under his dark hair, rocketed out of the stinking abattoir inside. A few paces away from the shattered porch Crenn leaned over, in the hot sunshine, and retched. Nothing came out—his stomach would not give up its cargo so easily—but still.

The wind, now heavier, stroked his hair and leathers, touched his fouled boots. It carried distant sirens drawing nearer—some of the stealthy movements in the other tin rectangles were watching, perhaps.

Alastair Crenn wiped his mouth with the back of his hand, and shook his head. His hair swayed, the last bits of dried moss crackling and crumbling green, and he stamped his boots, chantment flickering. The stains were easy enough to shed, and after he did so he ran along the side of the house, following the tugging along his nerves and muscles, leading him onward.

Even Gallow wouldn't have been able to help them, he thought, and suppressed another flare of nausea.

Whoever Jenny was, he hoped she wouldn't return.

ROBIN'S ROAD

11

Dusk fell in sheaves of indigo, starred with the hard dry points of diamond stars. Robin gained both feet and wakefulness in a single lunge, struggling up out of a nest of warm safety, her hands thrown out like white birds as if to stave off a blow. The oak tree quieted, its branches shivering with unease or just a warm liquid wind full of the promise of rain.

The simmering smell of minty crushed grass, almost as fragrant as Summer's shaded hollows, rose around her in veils; her toe caught on something in the almost-dark and she stood for a moment, teetering on the edge of a fall, before the lightfoot and quickstep chantments in the heels woke, righting her with the help of her natural sense of balance. Her hair didn't swing heavily, her head curiously naked, and she ran her fingers back over the ragged, chopped mass before she remembered cutting it in the carnival trailer while her nameless hostess slept.

They had dragged her from the sea's embrace, and been burned by the Unseelie for their pains. Just another instance of sidhe spreading death and destruction, the poison of a Half caught between two realms and at home in neither. Robin exhaled sharply, silently, as her pulse returned to normal and the unthinking terror retreated.

The nudging at her toe was a small discolored skull sinking into the crushed grass and rich black soil, vanishing almost as Robin peered at it. The tree hummed, and Robin cast a glance over her shoulder, gauging the sound.

Pepperbuckle rose a little less expeditiously, shaking his fine coat, his tail dipping, then wagging vigorously. He yawned, pearly serrated underteeth gleaming wickedly, and the music under Robin's thoughts took on the slow sonorous fluting of the desert wind against worn rocks.

Tiny balls of pixie-light cavorted in the branches, some of them darting down to circle her, their glow turning deep incandescent blue when they crossed the border of her space, into her cloak of breathing chantment. After circling, they laughed, giddy as schoolchildren released for the summer, and flitted off to chase each other in the branches once more, while a fresh crop descended to her level. They sang, snatches of mortal obscenities and sweet chiming songs in sidhe slang, and every once in a while one of them pronounced a few syllables of the Old Language and brightened, faltering in midflight and falling, sometimes recovering itself before it hit the ground and sometimes winking out, consumed by the oldest and truest of tongues.

Pepperbuckle nosed her hip. The heartsblood oak shivered, bending slightly as the Veil swished around it, and she suddenly knew, without a doubt, that one of her pursuers was close.

Robin took stock. Her throat no longer ached or rasped, but letting out the song here might destroy the oak and send her tumbling through the Veil in a most unpleasant fashion. Best to save it for when she really needed it, although it could fail then if she *had* injured herself by screaming helplessly, hoarsely, before she ran out into the sky from the tower and fell into the Dreaming Sea.

Don't think about that. Little prickles all over her, underneath the black velvet, as if goosebumps were trying to break through her skin and not quite succeeding. It was past, she'd survived it, and she was relatively...

Well, still relatively *sane*, hopefully. Would it occur to Summer to visit the tower again and see its broken stub rising like a jagged tooth, or a hole in its sheer white side, and would she guess Robin was still alive? The Queen had promised her life to Jeremy Gallow, but if Robin had... done something to herself, that couldn't be considered Summer's fault, now could it?

Next time, Summer might take extra steps. *If* she knew Robin was still alive, or suspected Robin wasn't driven to madness by the...

The mirrors. She shuddered, rubbing at her upper arms, and Pepperbuckle made a low sound, not quite a whine or a word.

I don't have just me to look out for. Robin dropped her hands. Shook them out, planted her feet in the soft earth. It gave resiliently under her heels, not quite as dirt really would, like almost-plastic stone. The sense of a pursuer, very close, perhaps tracking the heartsblood oak patiently through shifting layers of the Veil, taunted her.

Where would they be safest? Another night of running in the mortal world would simply exhaust them both. She half turned, gazing at the pixies—they'd never treated her in this fashion before. Spying on her for someone? But who would take the time to listen to scatterbrained little wingflicks, even if you could convince them to stick to a task for more than a few moments?

She shook her shorn head, as if to dislodge the question. Better to think about things she could *do*. What was possible, right at this moment?

Her mouth tasted of crushed mint, the softness of leftover cream, and a sharp brassy note. Blood, perhaps.

Or fear, that constant companion. Once, she'd thought maybe you could outgrow being afraid. Then, as something that could be called adulthood settled on her at Summer's Court, she realized it grew with you, twining like a vine through blood and breath and bone.

The fullblood could feel it, too, certainly. But mortal fear, Robin thought, had to have a flavor and a shapeshifting ability all its own. A half measure of sidhe only made it stronger, maybe. Just as it made muscle and bone more durable, and gifted a measure of breathing chantment.

Pepperbuckle leaned against her. Robin's left hand, caught in his ruff, squeezed unmercifully, but he didn't seem in the least troubled or pained by her grip.

Summer was closed to her, and there were none among the free sidhe who could or would shelter her. Even Morische the Cobbler, who had made her shoes, wouldn't grant her any aid—they were at quits, the crafty, vicious little sod and Robin.

Let me go, and I shall give thee hooves which will not falter.

Which left running through the mortal nights until she was brought down, or doing something nobody would expect of a Summer sidhe.

Put that way, the answer became almost ridiculously simple.

She found the edge of the heartsblood oak's influence, the lush grass fringing like seaweed as different layers of real and more-than-real flowed past, turning over, thickening. She braced herself on one foot, extending the toes of her right foot out of the oak's sphere. A cool, dragging pressure, a current against her leg. Pepperbuckle's deep, inquiring whine.

"You don't have to follow me," she whispered, not trusting

her voice, but the hound made a short chuffing sound, as if he considered her ridiculous.

Perhaps he did. In any case, her fingers refused to let go of his ruff and he hunkered down slightly, anchoring them both.

The pixies sent up an unhappy, chiming racket, but Robin took a deep breath, her planted leg bending just a little as she prepared herself. She whistled, a high drilling noise you didn't need a throat for. Pepperbuckle tensed, and when she jumped, landing hard on her right foot, the impact threatened to send her sprawling. He crowded behind her, vital and warm, and they spilled onto a quartz road under a bruise-dark sky, dusk instantly becoming thick night under tangled, thorny branches.

The cold struck her, all along her velvet wrapper, and Pepperbuckle snorted unhappily. She staggered, her heels tiptapping on the milky surface of a road arrowing straight through the knotted, gnarled, black-barked trees.

She coughed, and the cold retreated. It was only the first few moments, she knew, before she adjusted to the change. Temperature didn't bother a Half much... but this sensation was different than purely mortal chill.

Pepperbuckle butted against her, and she steadied herself against his warm bulk. He blew out a breath that turned to icicles, chiming as they fell, and tiny crackling slithering sounds crawled between the trees on either side.

Robin Ragged raised her head, slowly, and gazed willingly, for the first time in her life, upon Unwinter's ashen lands.

PHILOSOPHICAL THOUGHTS
12

The Steward was a tall, thin sidhe, his bone mask sheer and blank where the eyes should be. Whether he *was* blind or not seemed academic; his head certainly seemed to behave as if he *could* see. The mask's beak shaded thin lips, far too wide for the head they rested on, and when the Steward infrequently spoke, the sharklike ranks of his teeth showed like a series of locked doors standing to attention on a blank street. He did not often need to bare them, for it was understood he carried Unwinter's authority inside the Keep.

He stood in the small round room while Gallow ate at a small round table stacked high with roast fowl, gelatinous confections, brughnie-baked bread with its soft interior and crisp-cracking crust, and the fruits of Unwinter's field—thornapple, the tart almost-bitter chokeberry, damsons from the borderlands carefully carried to the Keep in featherstraw cartons, the black grapes that would not produce *lithori* but instead could be squeezed with chantment and sidhe fingers to coax out a thin trickle of bloodwine. Pale butter, leached of its sunny color by the chill but still good, and cold blue milk that coated his throat.

Gallow ate, and ate, and ate. Not to gorge—very soon he'd be running, and you couldn't do that weighed down. No, he ate to replace flesh melted away by the poison's wasting and to store energy for later use. Goblins could consume until they bloated, trolls and dwarves were prodigious eaters, and the great wyrms swallowed livestock whole during their infrequent feedings. The fullblood ate mostly to please the palate, but a Half…well, it varied. Sometimes Gallow thought it was more the *idea* of nourishment that mattered, when he bothered to indulge in any philosophical thoughts.

The Steward's dusty black robes reminded him of Robin's long coat, and Gallow tried not to think about it while he chewed and swallowed, mechanically. The idea that behind that blank bone shield was an old, crafty sharptooth sidhe watching his lips and throat move was similarly uncomfortable.

The end of hunger came quickly, between one mouthful of bread and the next. His stomach shut like a door, and new strength filled him. His side didn't ache, and the scar under his armor was a white line, not livid and bulging with fresh colorless venom. He took one last swallow of bitter dark ale, though now it tasted of ashes and brass, and stood, scraping the ancient wooden chair back along stone flags. Some mad urge made him push the chair back in, surveying the ruins of the table. It had never occurred to him before to think of where the leftover food from sidhe feasts went.

At least he could be sure this wasn't a meal of sticks and broken stones, glamoured to break a mortal's dreams and teeth at once.

The Steward's beaked mask nodded once. *"Dusk approachess."* His tongue, a purple, lizard-forked flicker, caressed the sibilants.

"I know." Gallow suppressed the mortal reflex of a belch, though it might have been amusing to see if that noise would cause a shadow of distaste on that long mouth and pointed chin. Blue veins stood out on the Steward's cheeks, a tree-branching map. His hands were gloved, the sixth fingers vestigial and oddly curled, more like fiddlehead ferns than phalanges.

"It musst be dussk pre-ccissely."

"I know," Gallow repeated. "Take me to the Gate."

For a moment he thought the sidhe would bridle at a mere Half issuing a command, and the marks itched and shifted on Jeremiah's shoulders, running down his arms, teasing at his wrists. A single death to fuel the lance, before the game began.

The Steward's head cocked, as if he could hear the thought. He pointed with one too-long, black-gloved finger, and across the small round room a high-arched door creaked, opening with a dusty groan. His teeth came out from behind those bloodless lips, sharp pale bleached bones under a grinning rotten moon. *"Thiss way."*

The sidhe glided across the room, passing Gallow on a chill draft that reeked of dust and some colorless burning fume. An edge of the black velvet robe almost, *almost* touched Gallow's knee.

If it was an insult, it was a fairly judged and well-earned one. Gallow suppressed a sigh. He didn't even *want* to kill the goddamn sidhe.

Or so he told himself.

Robin.

He couldn't think about that, now. This was the last toss of the dice, the last hand in the game. Win or lose. Double or nothing.

Either way, Unwinter would protect Robin. The lord of the

Unseelie had promised as much, on his own truename and Throne. Sooner or later his hunters would bring her in, and maybe Unwinter would even explain to her.

Or not.

Jeremiah's hand rose to his chest, and he drew the burning cold medallion free as they walked. The Steward's gliding quickened, as if the sidhe could tell what he held.

These halls were larger, and less dusty. The same thread of bustling activity ran parallel to their silence; they moved in a deserted bubble. Doors reared up, were opened, passed away. The ceiling and walls drew away as the passages became larger, and finally, acres of polished glassblack stone rang under his boots and the shushing of the Steward's robes.

The great gates of Unwinter's Keep stood open, and the bridge over the murky moat stretched threadlike over the fluid underneath, also glassy and smooth. Gallow wasn't fooled— the Watcher in the Moat was capable of blinding speed, and if the tentacles didn't get you the sheer horror of the thing probably would. More than one idiot attacker, just after the Sundering, had discovered as much.

"*I am to answwer any quesstionss.*" The Steward's tone plainly said he hoped for none.

Well, Gallow had a few, but there were only one or two that needed answering. "The pennants." Gallow pointed vaguely upward. "Black."

No reply. The bleached-bone unface regarded him, the mouth closed tight. Of course this sidhe wouldn't give anything for free, especially without a direct question.

"What do the black flags mean?" Gallow persisted.

The sidhe made a low creaking noise. Dust puffed from its robes, and Gallow realized the creature was laughing.

After a few moments, the mouth bubbling with blue-tinged

saliva at its corners, the Steward inhaled wetly, tongue flicking out once to test the air. *"Foolissh Half, do you not know?"* There was no pause for any answer Gallow might have made. *"My lord Unwinter is no longer patient; he ridess to war."*

Ah. Gallow didn't have to ask against who. A plagued Unwinter had nothing to lose, especially with Summer weakened as well.

He lifted the medallion, and the Horn, perhaps sensing what was about to happen, twitched as it unfolded, its curve elongating. It was one of the few things older than sidhe or Sundering, that flute-lipped instrument, and its shape was of no geometry a mortal could look upon without queasy revulsion. It was whispered that Unwinter himself had been the only sidhe to escape its deadly call since the first dawning of Danu's folk, when mortals were merely a bad future-dreaming.

Silver-glinting, curled and chambered, the Horn grew heavier, neck-chain thickening as it took its true shape. The Steward hissed and fell back, and Gallow didn't even feel good about the way the other sidhe ran pell-mell for the interior of the Keep and whatever precarious safety the black lacework bulk of stone could provide. He tipped the Horn back and forth, watching the play of light on its surfaces, as he stepped over Unwinter's threshold and onto the bridge.

To give the ancient thing a blast of living breath was to call the Wild Hunt in its full strength, both Unseelie and, more importantly, the Sluagh, the ravening unforgiven. The smaller horn-whistles the knights carried were copies, and awful enough, their ultrasonic cries chilling every living thing, even those that could not hear it. Unwinter had not ridden the full Hunt in a few hundred years, and he'd been about to wind the Horn on Gallow himself not too long ago.

Or at least, he had been before Gallow had knocked it out of his hands and run for his life. And more importantly, for Robin Ragged's.

Attempt this, and we are at quits, Unwinter had said quietly, coldly. *If you succeed, very well. If you do not, just as well. But in either instance, I will watch over your Ragged, and give her every care and protection I may offer.*

How long that care and protection might last with Unwinter plagued was a different matter. Still, the promise was better than he thought he'd get, and Gallow found he didn't give a fuck how this fit into Unwinter's plans or war with Summer. The two of them were ancient, the Sundering their goddamn war, and this was probably just a sideshow. Not so long ago Jeremiah had told himself he didn't care if he died, as long as Robin was safe. Told himself that just as Robin wasn't a usual faithless side, he wasn't either.

Here was his chance to prove it.

He touched his lips to the flute-bell of the Horn. Inhaled… and lowered it, spending the breath uselessly. He closed his eyes. Funny, he'd been ready to die, or if not ready, at least resigned. The poison now seemed like an easy out, but of course it couldn't ever be *easy*, could it.

Not for Jeremiah Gallow.

Do you really expect to pull this off, Jer?

Behind him, Unwinter's Keep held its breath. Were they watching him from the slit windows, peering from the casements, sidhe highborn and low crowding for a glimpse? Was Unwinter in one of the towers, looking down?

The urge to turn around and make an obscene mortal gesture passed through him, drained away.

He took a step onto the bridge. Another. A third. Raised the Horn again.

In every battle, you had to give your name.

"I am Jeremiah Gallow," he whispered into its smaller mouth. Then, the irrevocable words. "And *I will master you.*"

Then, quickly, before he could lose his nerve, he sealed his mouth to the Horn, and exhaled.

Hard.

THE SLUAGH
13

A silver nail pulling a golden thread, a thunder passing through ears and heart and chest all at once, a wall of noise so great it was almost soundless.

It rolled through Summer, that sound, a trembling through the green hills and the smoke-shamed orchard where Summer's apple trees lifted their gnarled, ever-blossoming limbs. Summerhome quivered on its hill, the green-and-white stone flushing icy blue for a single crystalline moment. From the graceful spunsugar mountains to the white-sand shores of the Dreaming Sea, from Marrowdowne's sinks to the high heaths where the giants and trollkin passed their slow, lumbering days, a single precise shiver passed, shifting every sidhe, awake or asleep, just a fraction of an inch. In the greatest of her halls, bolt upright on the low bench that served her as a throne, Summer raised her golden head, and the Jewel upon her brow flashed, an emerald star, as if it had not been drained and darkened by the assault upon her lands.

In the lands of the free sidhe, from the trashwood groves just a breath of the Veil away from mortals to the deep bramblecaves where the scions of unhappy fullblood unions huddled—say, for example, the son of a dryad and a troll, or a satyr's leering clovenhoof get—pixies thickened, following the sine wave of disturbance through tavern and waste lot, greenbelt and forgotten land clinging to the edges of urbanization. In the mortal realm, a thrill ran through the blood of any being with a share of sidhe, no matter how small. Some, artists or musicians, had nightmares; others seized upon whatever work was to hand and redoubled their efforts. Tired mortals with only a drop of sidhe blood found new strength surging through their veins, and with the sudden jolt came a nameless fear, one that caused shivers or breakdowns, dreams or a moment of *déjà vu*. Standing on the crushed-mint grass near a hungry-humming redbarked oak, a Half sidhe with worn mortal boots and a hoop of cold iron in his ear, hidden under fat snakes of matted dark hair, staggered as he attempted to leap onto the trail of his prey.

Do you hear?

The sound rippled in concentric rings through Unwinter's ash-starred land, from the Dak'r Woods where a Half girl in ragged black velvet, her white hand buried in the ruff of a goldenred dog, suddenly clapped her other hand to her ear and folded down, hunching as an amazing black bolt of dreadful pain lanced through her skull, to the Ash Plains where the white flax and the occasional stars of crimson poppies bent under a sudden freezing lash, cinder-smears falling from a black sky mixed with diamondprick snowflakes. In the knife-sharp cliffs above the Keep and along the jagged teeth of the mountains that held the rest of the land from sliding deeper into the Veil the great wyrms stirred in their hot slumbers, the smaller ones slithering for the mouths of their caves, their blunt or fringed or narrow noses lifted to test the cold, clear breeze. The Fell Moragh and the Harrhall, the deep luminescence-coated tangle of the drow barrowtown of Usnaragh, and the stones of the ancient doorways into the mortal world, blood-refreshed at every hunt, jumped with tiny specific movements, thudding back into place as the sound-unsound settled into a reverberation felt in tooth-root and marrow.

Did you hear that?

The sidhe whispered among themselves. Naiads, their long hair raveling on the surface of sea or river, pond or lake, bent their pretty heads together. Dryads gathered in knots, hushed, and for once satyrs did not chase them but stood solitary sentinel, horned heads upflung and broad nostrils quivering. Kelpies and selkies hesitated, between horseform and biped shape, their wicked teeth gleaming as they snorted and stamped; among them, night-mares or elfhorses along the shores of the Dreaming Sea—which touches all shores, always—tossed their manes but did not neigh. Greenjacks and jennywillows flitted from branch to branch, liggots swarmed into any hole they could find, brughnies drew back into the shelter of whatever hearth they claimed or cleaned, and in the sky above every portion of sidhe land, whether Unwinter, Summer, or free, the gebriels and harpies took wing, cloud-dogs and bird-women not rending each other's flesh but simply winging hard among birds and other flitting airborne things. Giants and trollkin stamped uneasily on the moors, and deep in every dwarven cavern the Red or the Black of the earthfolk, and the Outcaste besides, halted in their creation of whatever beautiful thing they had conceived. Hammers raised, tongs slipping, beards quivering, they *listened*, and the great hush in the halls of every mountain was swallowed by the slipslithering of the wyrms as they moved restless and fuming.

What is it?

Highborn fullblood paused in their crystalline halls, or halted in their business. Elf-maids older than the mortal idea of history shivered, their true age revealing itself in a single moment of transparent loveliness touched with unthinking wisdom as their hair fell free of braids and ribbons; elf-knights both Seelie and Unwinter paused as their armor woke with the glow of chantment chasing, cups of *lithori* or bloodwine falling from graceful hands. The Half paused, and more than one sank to the ground, hoping whatever it was would pass them by, a deep chill flashing through the mortal part of their blood and bones.

What is it?

Barrow-wights clustered at the entrances to their dank cold burrows, the bleached gold of their jewelry flashing with rich sunglow for a bare moment, their noseless faces flush with pale skull-light. The drow and trow bared their curving teeth, hags and skinnocks and gytrash and robber leprekha and every other manner of sidhe halting, heads lifting, listening, listening.

Do you not know?

Dark corners lit themselves with foxfire, as if pixies had decided to lead astray every being in the sidhe lands at once. The low cobweb glow twisted, spun itself into ghostly patterns, almost, *almost* coalesced...and collapsed back into the mothering earth or moldering stone, vanishing like dewdrops at noon. Then some few of Danu's folk sighed with relief, but if there were others about who cared for them, they were chided.

Hide. Hide now, hide quickly.

Shutters slammed, doors closing, dryads fleeing for their trees, naiads flickering back into the depths, the Dreaming Sea turning to glass as its inhabitants withdrew from the dangerous surface, lake and forest gone quiet-placid, drow barring their burrow-gates, dwarves shrinking not only behind their great clandoors but also into their individual houses, some even bolting their bedroom doors and retreating to their narrow pallets. Harpies and gebriels and birdlike things plummeted, seeking the safety of nests, and only the pixies remained, uneasily flitting from one corner to the next.

Pennants ceased their motion over Summerhome and Unwinter's Keep as the wind itself died, dropping the bannercloths like old rags. Giants stumped for their chimmerpearl castles and trolls retreated below bridges or into stoneform, withdrawing. Flowers sealed themselves into buds, and in Summer's orchard, the drift of white blossom arrested itself, petals hanging in midair, waiting.

What is it? Some few of them asked. *Why are we hiding?*

The wiser replied, *Shhhh, hold your tongue, stay still.*

One sidhe alone moved, crossing the bridge over Unwinter's glassy moat with long strides, the Horn falling from his nerveless hand and melting into its medallion-shape, quivering with anticipation. From hill and dale around the Keep the foxfire gleams rose, and they did not collapse.

To wind the Horn was to call the most ancient of Hunts from its restless sleep. Since before the Sundering only one sidhe had done so, for only one sidhe possessed a will harsh enough to bind the ravening, unforgiven dead to a command. It was whispered that once, long ago, when the Horn fell to earth, he had been the only one brave enough to wind it, and the only one canny enough to escape the host it called from whatever unquiet depths housed the aching remnants of every angry thing lost in the depths of Time, so old they had lost even the slumber-dream of death.

Jeremiah Gallow's stride lengthened into a lope, and he plunged into the woods around the Keep, thornbranches shrinking from him, his breath a plume in the chill air. Around him, silvery huntwhistles lifted their chill cries, but these were not the thin copies Unwinter's knights and huntmasters carried at their breasts.

No, these were the horns of a skeleton army, its rotting host knowing neither pain nor fear, nor weariness, nor anything other than the imperative.

To *chase*, and to *catch*.

Movement boiled in Gallow's wake, and his lope became a canter, then a run.

Shh, the wiser sidhe said. *I will whisper it, but only once.*

He had blown the Horn, and the one thing every sidhe without exception feared was on his heels.

The Sluagh is rising.

The Wild Hunt had begun.

IN MORTAL DARKNESS
14

Pete Crespin worked dispatch, and it was a thankless fucking job even at the best of times. Some of the girls felt like they were helping, coordinating, they joked with the cops and EMTs and firemen. *Our boys*, they called them.

Those motherfuckers, Paul would think, *out there like cowboys*.

He should know. He'd been one of them. Then a rainy night had stuck him on deskwork, and he'd taken the dispatcher classes without much enthusiasm. It was a surprise to everyone, he suspected, when he passed the exams, and kind of an affirmative action when he was hired into the overwhelmingly female dispatch pool. Maybe they wanted a cripple to round out their compliance with federal laws.

He settled back in his wheelchair, running a practiced eye over the screens. There was the usual crop of fender-benders and ditch-divers, the spring rains greasing everything up and driving everyone crazy. You'd think, with the melt happening every year and the storms following like clockwork, people would have gotten used to it by now. Instead, they had the attention span of gnats or something, because each turn in the seasons produced a massive fucking freakout. Snow? Freakout. Rain?

Freakout. Hot weather? Freakout. Tornado watch? Extra-super-double freakout with sauce.

Morons.

Just before he was due to go on lunch, there was a brief flurry—a couple shootings on the west side, a possible jumper on the East Bridge, and a rash of skids turning into fender-taps. He worked through the first half of his break, even though you weren't supposed to—hungry dispatchers made errors. Fatigue crept in on padded feet, poisoning the brain.

At first he thought the silence was everyone listening to him. The last call was the jumper on the bridge—they had him safely talked down, ready to be wheeled to Mercy General and sedated. Tomorrow there would be the unpleasantness, since it wasn't technically against the law to attempt to end your own life, but there could be a raft of charges like endangering others on the damn bridge. Adding legal, court, and ambulance fees was, in Crespin's opinion, just a way to force the jumper to pick a less public and more efficient method next time, but what did he know? Once they were rolling to the hospital and traffic safety was cleared, his job was mostly done. Then he waited for the next call...

...And waited some more, finally flicking the brake and pushing his chair back. A deathly hush had fallen over the entire 7A dispatch fishbowl.

Wendy, her corkscrew curls hanging limp instead of artfully mussed, peered over the low, temporary cubicle wall. "Hey, Pete. Is your line live?"

He toggled it, heard the tone in his headset. "Sounds fine. Yours?"

"It sounds fine, but—"

"Is anyone getting calls?" This from Christina of the mellow voice and ample hips. She had the flawless creamy skin some fat women were blessed with as well as a cheerful serenity, and if Pete had been ambulatory he might have asked her out on a date. He'd never liked the chubby ones before, but there was something about them that nowadays seemed like a good deal. Softer, less hungry than the thin ones. More forgiving.

"Just a lull." Jenna the Butch said, from her expansive desk in the middle. "They happen sometimes. Who's up for break?" She'd been in the force too, maybe got tired of the unrelenting boy's chatter in locker room, break room, duty room, roll call, over the airwaves. It soaked in, toxic testosterone, and there was only so far a woman could go to make herself one of "them."

The fact that Pete would give just about everything to swim in that poison again was beside the point. Jenna's tight thin-lipped mouth spoke volumes, but she didn't go out of her way to be Pete's buddy the way some cops did. It had irked him at first—weren't women supposed to *care*? But then he found out he liked being treated as if he was just another male intrusion into a female cloud.

Treated, in short, as if he was normal.

"Me," Pete said, finally. "Unless someone else wants to go."

"Me too." Rhonda, all the way over on the other side of the fishbowl, stood and stretched. You could hear her joints popping all through the room.

That wasn't normal, either.

The silence turned thick. Pete ran his hands along his wheelchair's hoops, a thoughtful motion. His nape crawled—what his old partner Darcy would have called *hinky as hell*.

Darcy was a good ol' boy, and some of the admins called him *Mr. Darcy*, and he'd never caught the joke. Pete hadn't either until one of them patiently explained that there were books by a chick named Astin, and Darcy was a gentleman hero in one of them. It was funny because he was a slob, but it was the slob's presence of mind that meant Pete was still here today and not six feet under like the slob himself.

That night. The bullets, the rain, the coughing gasps as Darcy radioed for backup and ended up bleeding out halfway in the front seat of the cruiser, his bulk heaved up like a gigantic graceless fish—

Creeeak. His wheelchair wheels squeaked a little. The silence was fucking unnerving.

"This is bizarre." Wendy leaned on the top of the half wall, blinking rapidly.

"It happens." Jenna had her supervisor hat on, and it made her goddamn insufferable.

"It's not just quiet here," Pete found himself saying. "Outside, too." Even the rain had stopped.

More heads began popping up, women standing, some stretching, others tilting their heads to listen. Pete took an internal vote and decided he didn't need to pee—he didn't flood himself with coffee the way he used to on the force, and it had done wonders for his digestion—and found himself wishing he had his service revolver and two working legs instead of a concealed-carry permit and one and a quarter. Although "working" might be too generous a term for his right leg still receiving nerve impulses. *You're lucky*, they kept saying. *You can stand with a brace if you need to. For short periods. Lucky.*

Yeah. The bullet hadn't done it, complications from the damn surgery when they fished it out had. At least he didn't need a catheter, he had enough nerve feedback to know when he was about to piss himself.

"Stay at your stations, ladies." A thread of unease worked its way into Jenna's tone. "We could get a rush."

Like at the grocery store. Pete suppressed the urge to open his big fat mouth, and stayed where he was. His lunch was in the breakroom fridge, the fussy little bento box he'd learned how to make from the book Sandy had left, all about rice and fish and arranging things neatly.

Don't think about Sandy, for fucksake. Brooding on his ex-wife was best done at home. But your brain jagged all over the place in situations like this.

Situations like what? It was Darcy's voice he heard in his head, the drawl turning it into a comedic slur. *Like whuuuuuuuuuut?* With a waggle of his bushy eyebrows, just before he belched or released a bomb from the other end.

Situations, Pete Crespin thought, where you knew you were going to get shot at, but not soon enough to do any good.

A faint beeping was a call coming in. Christina's lovely, radio-quality voice purred through the standard greeting, then a pause that lasted too long.

Pete realized he was holding his breath.

Then the entire place lit up. Every line, even the doubles and the silents and the shunts and the overflow. The squealing, ringing din made several women leap to their feet, tearing at their earpieces or headsets, and a chorus of salty language that wouldn't be out of place in a precinct locker room at shift change rose. Pete half turned his chair, meaning to go back to his cubicle, and paused, staring down the hall leading past the breakroom door and the water fountain. The last stretch of said hall held printers on one side, cubicle half walls on the other, and terminated in a window looking out on the front of the building. An expanse of grass that had just begun growing again as the days got longer, a few ruthlessly trimmed shrubs, and the fountain in the middle of the paths, like a goddamn college campus. It had just been turned on for spring, and nobody had poured dish soap in it for the entire time Pete had worked here.

Pete rubbed at his eyes. Stared, his jaw dropping.

The fountain was glowing. More precisely, thin luminescent wisps of steam were thickening as they swelled upward, clotting and condensing around…what? Something held in steam, the vapor describing the borders of an object, nothing else.

Pete rubbed at his eyes again. *What the fuck?*

Just like after the accident, they found out he was allergic to one of the pain meds and the world became a sideways-sliding distortion of itself, nurses and doctors all vacant-eyed, gap-mouthed rotting corpses bent on tormenting him. In his ravings, he'd only been able to kick his right leg, a crippled bug seesawing on its back, and they'd tied him down while he screamed himself hoarse.

The mist rose from the grass now, too, instead of just the fountain. Pete opened his mouth to ask if anyone else saw it, shut it. There was no way.

No *way*. They'd have him in the looney bin so fast, and it wouldn't be just sidelong looks or having to use the handicapped shitter, he'd end up with an assful of meds and…

He kept staring. The shapes coalesced. Humanoid. The mist stretched, became firmer, wrapped around them. They rose from fountain, lawn, garden, and concrete, and they just *kept coming*.

"Holy *shit*," someone whispered, and Pete realized it was him.

They leapt forward, some running, some riding big bulky steam-animals, filthy droplets splatting the window as they passed, the mist describing just enough of their faces to turn his heart into a clot of senseless meat inside him and his throat into a pinhole. The phones were going nuts, but nobody could get a clear signal; Jenna was yelling for a reset, and Rhonda's piercing scream from the other end of the room was a flash in the auditory pan.

Rhonda's cubicle had a window view. So did Sharon's, and

the other Jenna's, the wispy just-out-of-college girl with her big stoned eyes and bad skin. Were they watching this shit go down like he was?

It was, Pete decided, probably time to go home and take out that fifth of Wild Turkey he had stashed in the remodeled cupboard—*for a rainy day,* he thought, with enviable calm—except to do that, he'd have to wheel himself out into the parking lot, and those...those *things*...

A sharp lancing numbness spread through his skull, down his left side, the hand turning into a claw and his withered leg twitching spasmodically. His heart pounded, pounded, and Pete Crespin closed his right eye—the left one had fallen shut on its own.

The verdict pronounced a week later by the overworked coroner's office was that he'd had a stroke, but Sarah Thornton, who had come around the corner from the breakroom to see what everyone was screaming about, always privately thought—though she would never dare to express this—that with his grizzled face twisted and his left side all scrunched up, it looked like the old guy had died, quite plainly, of fear.

PART TWO

VENGEANCE MINE
15

She stepped out of a disturbance in the Veil, head held high and the fringes of her feathered mask trembling just slightly. Her hair, a shade caught between platinum and gold, was looped, braided, and coiled with periwinkle ribbons; it made her at least a foot taller and her dress was not of the latest Seelie court fashion but of an older style.

One might even call it *ancient*. One single braid of her beautiful hair held a single golden flower, a work of exquisite dwarven metalsmithing twisted into a bead by a fury-hot chantment.

Her fan, held in the manner of a truce envoy, clattered slightly with pixie wings dipped in light, glittering metal and encrusted with spunsugar glitters—dewdrops frozen by chantment, requiring a fullblood's numinous aura of glamours to keep them whole and unmelted. Her deep-blue mantle, the cloth figured with stylized maned creatures roaring silent-fierce, brushed the floor. Into the knife-edged chill of Unwinter's throne room she stepped, eschewing the normal politeness of appearing in the entry hall so a steward, high-ranking of course but perhaps not the chief of them, could inquire of her business.

The great blackstone hall rippled, ringing with the echoes of a horn-cry, and she flicked her fan once, precisely, and let her sleeves fall forward over her long, velvet-gloved hands, each with six phalanges. The graceful curve of her wrist had been accorded many plaudits at Summer's Court.

Perhaps too many, considering.

In the center of the chamber, blue flames crawled over stone-wood, slowly caressing the gray logs into ash. Around the fire-pit, runes etched into the floor shifted, their shape growing more angular as the chill deepened, steam rising from one of Summer's creatures *here*, in the sanctum of a different power.

The fullblood female looked toward the Throne, gasflame-blue eyes peering through the mask, and regarded its deeper shadows without a betraying flinch or shiver. Two red gleams were all that could be seen, the high curved spikes of the Throne damp with rusted red but not weeping.

Not at the moment.

The room was empty, yet it felt crowded, the air flirting uneasily over this new arrival, mouthing her with slow indignant brushes. No word of greeting or dismissal rose from the deep well of shadow in the Throne's sharp embrace. Only the sense of *presence* and cold intent announced that Unwinter was, indeed, upon his throne.

And listening.

"Lord of Unwinter." A light, feminine voice, smooth as silk and cloying as cream. "Lion of Danu, Favored of the great Wyrms. I greet you."

The flames crawling in the pit made a low sibilance, a dissatisfied sound.

She waited, this metal-haired sidhe, and after the long pause of two creatures who measured age in geologic spans deciding whether the silence was thoughtful or simply because one considered the other unworthy of a reply, she drew in a sharp breath and spoke again. "I come bearing a gift."

That earned another long crackle-fire silence, but the shadow in the throne's recesses gleamed as it shifted. Unwinter's armor, dwarf-wrought and supple, nevertheless made the grinding of ice rubbing against itself as he leaned forward slightly. He wore no helm, and his pale hair was much lighter than hers, and finer besides.

"And what gift," he said, finally, *"would one such as you bring me, Feathersalt?"*

Ilara Feathersalt drew the feathered mask aside with one elegant hand, let it drop to her side. The face revealed was drawn haggard-beautiful, as only a sidhe's could be. The exhaustion graven on her features only made them finer, her cherry-red lips drawn tight and bruised love-hollows under her bright, bright blue eyes, their pupils acutely triangular instead of round. "Are you uninterested, my lord?"

The small red sparks in the Throne's deepest gloom winked out, and she drew in a sharp breath.

"I know where it is," she said in a rush. The words bounced around the cavernous hall, fell into the firepit, made the blue flames flare and the runes around the edge speed up, purple instead of blue spreading through them as if, like pixies' glow-globes, they simply reflected. *"Glaoseacht."*

Her lips and tongue shaped the sound, the Old Language dripping through the syllables, and the word burned between them, expressing several things at once. The sound was a razor edge, a handle that cut the wielder, a humming made when a crystal cup-rim was stroked just right, the shiver passing through a windowpane—a reminder that it is still, essentially, liquid—before it shatters.

A brisk breeze slid through the hall, the tendrils of heat

rising from the sidhe woman turning visible before they froze, falling with little tinkles to the floor and vanishing.

"*Ah.*" Unwinter's tone was thoughtful, nothing more. "*Have you come to curry favor, then? Or to mislead?*"

"Neither." Her lips drew down again, bitterly, before her expression smoothed. "We are alike, my lord Unwinter."

He did not sound as if he would be easily convinced of any kinship. "*In what way?*"

"*She* has stolen from both of us," Ilara Feathersalt replied. "And we will both have our vengeance."

Unwinter considered this. "*What is your price, my lady?*"

"I am no merchant, my lord. I do this because it will please me to see the Glass in your hands."

"*Then why not bring it to me?*"

"I dare not attempt liberating such an item from its holding place alone, my lord." A graceful shrugging movement, her mantle rippling. "As you would no doubt not trust me to approach you with it clasped before me."

A soundless shudder passed through the Keep, dungeon to spires, the floor rocking a few millimeters and stilling almost immediately. Unwinter leaned forward, and his own gaunt-beautiful face, his paleness tinted with the blue of a frozen corpse and even more wretchedly attractive because of it, swam into view. He examined the Summer fullblood from top to toe. "*What did she steal from you, Feathersalt?*"

"That is my concern."

"*Is it? I have heard there is a knight she has paid much attention to of late, a dark-haired lord among the merriment of her Court who used to star his locks with gold.*"

The sidhe woman said nothing. Her gaze held Unwinter's, and for a moment, the two ancient, ageless creatures held a thin humming line of force between them. Seen in this attitude, the similarity of sidhe was underlined—the beauty of a cheekbone-curve, the glamour of weariness, the daggered edges of armor or mantle fashioned with the same aesthetic geometry.

Unwinter lifted a mailed finger, and a door opened. His highest-ranking steward, the blind bone-masked robed scarecrow, glided in.

"*Make our lady Feathersalt comfortable in the West Chambers,*" Unwinter said gravely. "*There is one I will send with you, my lady. We await an arrival.*"

"I will wait one day," she said, haughty, chin up and her fan trembling slightly. She was not quite as unconcerned as she wished to appear.

"*By all means,*" Unwinter said very softly, "*leave without my permission. You will never be granted another audience, no matter what artifact you claim to know the resting place of. I have not forgotten where your true allegiance lies.*"

"Allegiance." Her laughter, an elf-maid's careless rill of amusement, turned the flashing motes of ice in the air to blue petals, forming just under the ceiling and turning the hall into a bower. "We are Danu's chosen, my lord. We serve only ourselves."

Unwinter settled back into the gloom as she followed the Steward, her step light as a leaf and the robed creature's soundless. When the door closed, the petals turned to ice, and plummeted instead of drifting, shattering on the glassine floor. The perfumed smoke they released was whisked away with a cold, bright exhalation.

"*Speak,*" Unwinter said quietly, privately, "*for yourself.*"

A MAN SHE COULD
16

Alastair Crenn jolted free of the heartsblood oak's bubble, his mortal boots hitting concrete and the world contracting and loosening around him as dusk and dust both swirled. Passing through the Veil made time as well as space jump and bend in interesting ways, and had he less sidhe blood it might well cramp his belly to leap so cavalierly in the direction instinct tugged and told him Robin had taken.

Unfortunately, as soon as his feet left the ground, something had *shifted*, and he realized he'd been just a fraction of a second off. Late or early, it didn't matter. He hung suspended in the flux; sometimes you could get back on track if you focused, desperately, on the trail you were following.

Instead, the awful drilling whistle hadn't finished echoing through the real and more-than-real. It yanked him sideways, spilling him out on weed-cracked concrete, the breath squeezed from his lungs with an inelegant huffing noise. He landed catfoot-soft, a chainlink fence to his left rattling snakelike, uneasy. Crenn hopped like a marsh-bird, the lightfoot blooming under his soles in case he needed to leap, and found himself next to a weed-choked vacant lot probably full of pixies on summer nights, the neglected street to his right holding only burned-out hulks of warehouses. Firesmell still hung in the air, faint and fading; mortals wouldn't smell it, but a sidhe could almost hear the flames and shouts. Something had happened here, high emotion tearing and curdling the Veil. Riot and burning.

Overhead, the hard bright points of stars winked in and out of rents torn in scurrying cloud. Crenn turned in a full circle sunwise-deosil, either to shake off pursuit or to aid his thinking and clear the noise from his head. You could always mark the sidhe-touched—a single item worn inside out, an undone seam or selvage edge unraveling, a circling or turning, all the old ways to shake off pursuit. Mortals had forgotten, of course. At least, most of them had, and sidhe mischief wasn't what it used to be. With so much cold iron and exhaust poisoning the very air, opportunities were fewer, and rationalism meant the Folk weren't propitiated like they used to be. Crenn had heard some fullbloods bemoan the boredom, and others plan fantastical vengeance. They said *When the mortals are gone*, just as mortals had said *When the Depression ends*, in the faraway time of his youth—a fanciful event that might or might not happen, a pixie-led pipe dream.

He could still hear it, faint and faraway, a high cruel silver note filling the unheard corners of dusk. Crenn knew the pale imitations, the silver Unseelie huntwhistles.

This was something else.

Either Gallow had winded Unwinter's Horn, or Unwinter had regained it. If the Unseelie lord had reclaimed his property and used it in this fashion, it could only mean he was bringing down the Half who had thieved from him.

Well, good. Let Gallow finally rest in a stew of his own making. Alastair Crenn's business was finding Robin.

I shall cut your heart out, Alastair Crenn. And his own reply, given afterward when she could not possibly hear.

Too late.

How, by Stone or Throne, had that selfish prick drawn such a woman into caring for him? It was a mystery.

Crenn knotted his fingers through rattling chainlink, shielded from cold iron by the mortal half of his inheritance. He almost shut his eyes, wondering why he wasn't turning around to find another rip in the Veil to slide through, picking up Robin's trail again. It was an uncomfortable thing when a man didn't know his own mind.

What was he thinking? Surely he didn't *owe* Gallow anything. It was the Half bastard's fault Crenn had been scarred in the first place. Or at least, wounded so badly the scars lingered.

He'd told himself as much so often he almost believed it.

And yet.

He could all but see Robin, her coppery hair dark with rain, her summerdusk eyes wide and mistrustful, softening only when she glanced at Jeremiah Gallow. For Alastair Crenn, who drugged her with shusweed and delivered her to whatever vengeance the Queen had waiting, there would be no softness.

Robin, head held high, had actually *spat* at the ruler of Seelie, and plunged into the darkness of her own accord. With a woman like that at his back, what couldn't a man do?

In the swamps of Marrowdowne, patience brought Crenn everything he needed. He could keep after her, begging for scraps, or he could do something... better. Something worthy of her.

What are you thinking, Alastair?

The air chilled. His eyelids raised from half-mast, heavily, and he looked through the chainlink. The blood drained from his face, he could *feel* it sinking from cheek and forehead, and his fingers spasmed shut.

The echoes of flame and riot around him intensified, cricket-chirping in a deadly silence. In the middle of the field, where the Veil curdled heaviest, thin threads of mist rose, smoke describing shapes rising vapor shouldn't be able to form. A chill crept up his muscled back, and behind his hanging hair, shaken over his eyes out of old habit, Crenn's irises turned briefly bright springleaf-green before fading into their usual darkness.

The Sluagh were rising.

Which meant their prey was close.

He could, he supposed, just let them hunt Gallow down. It was what the bastard deserved.

On the other hand, a man Robin Ragged would look kindly upon might not do that. Instead, he might do something foolish, like try to help a cornered animal escape the Hunt. Or, if Gallow had winded the Horn...

That was ridiculous. There was no reason for a Half to do that. It was far, far more likely that Gallow had committed a fatal misstep. Helping him was suicidal. It was idiotic. It was the single worst thing he could do if he wanted to survive.

It was also, probably, the one thing he could bring to Robin Ragged, to gain a slight welcome.

Like a cat offering a half-dead vole. You're not seriously considering this, are you?

He watched the shapes rise, the unforgiving dead clothing themselves in steam and chill, gathering form and substance from proximity to their prey. The hunted one, sidhe or mortal, was close. He noted the way the gossamer smoke streamed from them, yearning, vaguely northwest.

"Gallow," he whispered, unable to help himself.

A powdery-white bloom spread through them, and one or two turned their smoke-draped heads in his direction. They intensified, and his heart began a high hard elfhorse gallop inside his ribs.

Well. That answered that.

At the very least, Crenn would be able to tell her how he died.

He was running beside the chainlink fence before the thought faded, and when it ended he cut across the road. Sooner or later he'd be able to turn northwest, and as long as he followed the thickening of the Sluagh he would eventually find his way to their prey. He might even, if he were blessed, get there too late.

The thought made him speed up, the ground-eating lope a Half assassin could keep up for a very long time, and he hoped his legs wouldn't give out.

He also hoped the Sluagh wouldn't take an interest in *him*, as well.

A COWER, A SONG
17

Her hand had gone numb, knotted in Pepperbuckle's ruff. The wind, full of those dancing speckles of ash and knife-edged chill, licked at the edges of her velvet robe. Some needle-chantment had mended the worst of the fraying and holes, and now she looked no less ragged than a ghilliedhu girl or a minstrel. She was glad of the hood, too, since her chopped hair no longer kept her neck warm. The redgold was too distinctive, even if it looked like she'd hacked at the strands with a knife.

Which she had, as a matter of fact.

Robin shivered, looking up at the pile of lacy black stone. It rose, spire upon spire, and from many of the towers black pennants snapped and crackled in the rising wind. The Road had crept downhill and out of the tangle of the Dak'r, and perhaps it was because of that awful, chilling sound in the distance that she was allowed to pass unmolested. Certainly the thorn-dark woods, the foliage of ash-white, deep umber, and the occasional flash of scarlet, had turned silent afterward, and the sense of unfriendly eyes upon her had faded significantly.

The drawbridge was down. The moat, its sluggish, opalescent

water calm as a slug's leavings on flat dirt, looked placid enough. Robin sought to remember every scrap of legend or tale she'd heard of the Keep and Unwinter's cold realm, and decided there was no use in having a moat if there was nothing in the water to fear.

"What do you think?" she whispered, bending slightly. Pepperbuckle's blue eyes, a shade or two lighter than hers now, gazed calmly upon the open cobblestones of a bailey behind the throat of gate-and-portcullis both open. It was a very large maw, and she a very small morsel indeed.

His ears flicked. That was all.

"I don't suppose you'd wait here for me." The last of the shusweed numbness had left her throat, but she still didn't dare speak loudly. The words purred, rough honey at every edge, as if the music below her thoughts needed less than the act of singing to release it.

Would she be rendered mute, unable even to speak for fear of unleashing destruction on the world? It might even be a relief; if she couldn't speak, she couldn't get drawn in.

Oh, you know the sidhe would find a way, Robin.

The hound didn't move, still as stone. Not tense, simply... watchful.

There was some comfort, she supposed, in such steadfastness. She had done what no Half dared to attempt and succeeded so handsomely the evidence wouldn't leave her side, even when she stepped over the shifting borders into this gray, cheerless place. Unwinter even seemed to suit Pepperbuckle—or he was merely larger now, and shaggier against the cold.

She considered the drawbridge afresh. She'd come this far. Setting her feet upon that tongue of black timber and metal, dwarven-wrought and sturdy but still a slim hair over the moat's sheen, seemed perhaps a bit *too* far.

A shadow grew under the portcullis. Thin and tapering, with branchlike fingers and a high-crested pale head, it glided forth, pausing imperceptibly before stepping onto the bridge. Robin swallowed, dryly. Her presence had been noted.

With any luck, this sidhe would tell her to go away.

But to where? Summer? The shudder passing through her might have been mistaken for faltering.

The crest on the sidhe's head was a wide fan-expanse of bone, lacking eyes. The mouth was a cruel slit, the teeth serrated-sharp, and the sticklike sidhe in black velvet much finer than her own glided to a halt some ten paces away. A steward, then, sent to greet her.

Pepperbuckle's ears pricked fully now, and his ruff stood up around Robin's hand, fur brushing her wrist, a stripe raised all the way down his back and along his fine tail.

"Ragged," the creature breathed, the word a hiss even without sibilants. "You are ex-sspected. Allow me to welcome you, and esscort you into the Keep."

Her throat was dry. There was no way to avoid what came next. "I . . . I come as a messenger, to the lord of these lands."

"You come as a ssupplicant, my lady Ragged." The scarecrow bent slightly at his middle, with a creaking. The bow was accompanied by a spreading of its pale, multifingered strangler's hands. Had it once been a drow or barrow-wight? *"And my lord wisshes wordss with thee."*

Oh, no doubt he did. Many words, and perhaps a death or two.

Robin gathered her courage and stepped onto the bridge. The moat-water rippled once, its oily sheen intensifying, before it turned smooth and placid again.

※

The hall was vast, and she couldn't stop shivering. She didn't dare examine the firepit, its cold blue stone-eating flames trammeled by the runes flowing at its lip. She didn't care to look closely at the Throne either, its high piercing spires tipped with frozen, rusty stains. Robin stood just a few paces inside the door, which the bone-frilled, eyeless steward closed behind her with a sound like river-ice cracking. Pepperbuckle's tail did not wag, tucked securely under his hind end, and he leaned into her, his warmth a comfort and a reminder all at once.

Overhead, dusty flags hung motionless. Tiny slivers of ice sometimes worked free of their edges and fell, vanishing in midair with tiny crackles. No Summer sidhe would be comfortable here.

She didn't even have the song to protect her. What if Unwinter decided she was a loose end that needed snipping, or an insult? They said he gave shelter to the desperate, the unclean, the outcast, as long as they *obeyed*. She'd caused him a great deal of trouble and cost him the lives of no few of his followers, and even if he was disposed to listen to her before he gutted her...

Her breathing heat sent tiny questing fingers of steam up, a halo shouting she didn't belong here. Her acceptance into Summer's ranks had been sealed with a soft pressure of the Queen's lips against Robin's damp forehead so long ago, with Puck hungrily gazing on.

What did Unwinter do? Would it be painful?

"*Robin.*" A soft, hurtful voice. "*Robin Ragged.*"

Her eyes flickered, her gaze roving to find the source. The Throne's recesses were too dark to pierce, even with sidhe-sharp eyes. Pepperbuckle's ears flattened against his graceful head, and his fur was tipped with tiny condensing droplets.

One moment, nothing; the next, a tall broad-shouldered sidhe-shape separated from the Throne's shadow. He stood, armored from shoulder to spurred foot in blackened dwarven-made metal, pale hair held down by a plain silver band. Wearily attractive, with a sharp nose and dark eyebrows, his cheekbones gaunt blades and his lips blue as a drowned man's, he took another step away from the Throne and stood at the rim of the dais leading to it, the steps of knife-sharp almost-obsidian laced with delicate traceries of frost.

They looked like doilies, the kind elderly women in trailer parks put under knickknacks, crocheted by hand or bought in packets from catalogs full of cheap gadgets meant to stave off age or decorate empty loneliness. A mad red urge to bray a giggle or two threatened to block Robin's throat, but she swallowed hard, tasting the peculiar copper of fear and anticipation.

Four in, four out. Keep breathing, Robin. And if he wants to kill you, you may as well try to sing.

She put one toe behind her and bent the other leg, an approximation of a Court courtesy, bowing her shorn head. When she regained her balance and looked up, he hadn't moved, his boots spreading veins of ice across the stone. The steps rang as his weight shifted fractionally, and she flinched. Pepperbuckle made a low whining noise, pressing ever closer.

"You are in no danger, Half." Each word carefully, precisely measured.

Robin found her free hand was a fist, to match the one wound in Pepperbuckle's ruff. "I beg to differ, my lord." Her voice sounded strange, even to herself, and the runes marching quietly along the firepit's rim flared into ruddy gold for a few moments.

A millimeter's shift of that cruel blue mouth. At least he wasn't showing his teeth. Was it a smile? Did she *amuse* him?

"Our last parlay was interrupted." His mailed left hand rested

109

on a massive hilt at his side, the colorless icy jewel in the pommel holding a single bloody spark at its center to match his crimson eyes. Unwinter took another step, descending from the Throne. Would her blood dew its sharp spines?

They said he used to hang prey from his castle's sharp stabbing spires if the hunt had displeased him. Courage brought you a quick death. Almost painless.

Almost.

Robin began to feel strangely lightheaded. *Breathe, damn you. Four in, four out.*

"That was not my doing." She measured the words carefully, sparing herself breath between each one. Her voice seemed to be holding. That was good.

He took another step. "*Indeed.*" A long pause. Hot blood thundered in her ears, in her wrists and throat.

I should be begging him to take me in. I should have a pretty speech prepared. If the song burst free here...

Thoughtfully, lingering over each syllable, he spoke again. "*I expected you.*"

"Did you?" Her heart kept pounding. If this kept up it might explode and she would be free of the entire mess.

"*Where else do you have to go?*" His right hand lifted, made a slow graceful sweeping movement, and Pepperbuckle cowered even more desperately against Robin, almost knocking her off her feet. She made her knees stiffen, with a physical effort that almost made her sweat. "*But soft, there is a question I would ask thee.*"

"My lord?" If she spoke very quietly, her voice didn't do anything strange. Time, and a little more milk, would heal her fully.

He took two more steps, reaching the level floor of his thronehall. Another two long strides, straight toward her, and Robin braced herself. His spurs rang, icy rowels striking musical notes from the glassy floor, and the air under his feet flash-froze, crackling in agony. His hand lifted, and she saw a familiar gleam hanging from those armored fingers.

"Have you come here for the Gallow, little bird?"

No. I'm here to save my own miserable skin. Robin opened her mouth to tell him as much. But that glint of gold swung, stopped the breath in her for a long moment.

It was her locket.

The gold one, the one with six strands of mortal hair closed in it with the strongest chantment-lock a Realmaker could muster. Three of them were redgold, a faded copy of Robin's own hair. The other three were pale floss, the numinous color only very young mortal children wear. Her gold locket, the one her fingers leapt to her throat to find, helplessly.

The locket Jeremiah Gallow had taken.

"Is he still alive?" She almost swayed, caught herself. *Why did I just ask? Stupid, silly Half bitch, you can't stop yourself from showing you care.*

Unwinter's corpse-blue lips became a curve. He smiled, and she got the idea he was deliberately keeping his teeth behind them. *"Would you plead with me, for his life? At the cost of your own?"*

She struggled with herself, briefly. "I have the cure," she said, numbly. "I can trade it to you, for—"

"He is beyond your saving, little dove." The smiling grimace intensified. *"He has used what he stole, and his fate is beyond either of us at the moment."*

The noise, in the woods. It was the Horn. Oh, God. Robin swayed again. "You..." If Unwinter had called the Hunt on Gallow, why was he standing *here* instead of riding to lead it? "Then—"

Unwinter held up his right hand, and she closed her mouth so quickly she almost clipped her tongue with her teeth. His lips skinned back, and she saw his teeth, the spaces between them veined with crimson. *A bloody mouth to match a bloody gaze*, one of the ballads said, and now she knew why.

"Yet if you could aid him, little winged handmaiden that you are... Would you do so?"

"Yes," she heard herself say. "Yes, I would."

Unwinter's smile widened. Robin stared, fascinated. He halted a respectable ten paces from her, and the cold was a living thing, an invisible current radiating from him. *"You are Half,"* he said, musingly. *"You wish for vengeance."*

There was only one possible answer to *that*.

"Vengeance upon Summer." Quiet, and very flat. The edges of her words flashed as they left her mouth. Her hand slipped free of Pepperbuckle's ruff as the dog hunched further down, curling around the back of her legs as if to hide behind a single birch sapling facing a hurricane. The hound's ice-starred coat was redgold, just like her hair.

Just like shards of blood-edged amber scattered on a marble floor in Summerhome, a statue of a mortal boy broken into a thousand pieces.

Had Sean still been alive and trying to draw breath inside that prison, before Puck tipped it over?

Robin-mama, the little mortal had called her. She had taught him the names of the constellations in Summer's fragrant night sky. All the stars of Summer's dusk, and the hound cowering behind her now was all that remained of a laughing, chubby mortal boy who smelled of salt and dust and sweet perishable youth.

"Yes." *Who's using my voice? She sounds...*

Cold. And furious.

The firepit creaked. The runes raced around its rim, the flames cupped inside grew rosy for a brief moment, and the stonewood logs underneath gave out a high note of stress, miniature tectonic plates shifting.

"*Yes,*" Unwinter echoed, gazing down at her. Robin tipped her head back, unwilling to look away. If he wanted to strike her down, she'd at least stare him in the face while he did so.

Any revenge *he* had planned had more chance of working than something Robin could attempt on her own. Was that why the fear fell away, and clarity took its place? If he wasn't going to kill her, she might as well ask for details. "What do you have in mind?" For a lunatic moment, it was almost as if she were addressing Gallow, or another Half, a simple question between equals.

"*You shall fetch something for me,*" Unwinter replied, in the very same tone. His right hand rose with slow, oiled grace, heavy, supple armor whispering as it shifted with him. He glided even closer; the cold made her eyes sting and her cheeks redden slightly as if just-slapped.

"I shall?"

"*Yes.*" One finger—the longest on his mailed hand—extended, and hovered a bare inch from Robin's velvet-clad shoulder.

So cold. So cold it *burned*, that almost-touch. "What might that be?" Ice fringed her lashes, was collecting cold and soft in her shorn hair. If he stayed this close she might become a statue herself, coated in freezing.

Was this how it had been for Sean?

"*You,*" the lord of the Unseelie told her, his frozen breath redolent of myrrh caressing her upturned face, "*you, little dove, shall chip free Summer's Jewel.*"

BETTER THAN TO TOUCH
18

Unwinter had entrances everywhere, and the exits were only marginally harder to find. Thrashing through the fringes of the Dak'r was more trouble than Gallow needed, even if every sidhe in that dark, thorny tangle was likely to be cowering instead of looking to cause one former Armormaster some grief.

So he'd turned hard left—sinister, widdershins, against the sun—as soon as he left the bridge, plunging down a gorse-clad slope. Little flashes of crimson retreated as he passed, the flowers pulling back into themselves, shying away from a Summer sidhe...or from what he fled.

He didn't need to look to see the traceries of heavy white vapor rising along his tracks. He hit the bottom of the slope, hopping across a tiny rivulet of dead-white, foaming liquid that probably ran off the moat, and his body obeyed him without heaviness or weariness, without the dragging pain or fever. The lightfoot bloomed under his boots, the vivid wellness of a sidhe warrior beating in time to his heart and pounding footsteps, muscles waking and singing without weakness.

It was goddamn good to be back.

Still, he paced himself. Going flat-out would just tire him, and he needed time.

After all, he had to figure out how to escape the Sluagh. Unwinter would hold the rest of the Unseelie from chasing him, but hadn't given him any helpful hints. Just the one sentence. *You must master what you wear, Half.*

Easy for *him* to say. On the other hand, Unwinter's reputation for fairness was pretty well earned. Not many fullbloods would overlook what Gallow had done, between stealing from the lord of the Hunt, challenging him, *and* killing one of his boon companions.

Unwinter, Jeremiah decided, was actually a pretty righteous sidhe.

Jeremiah Gallow loped along the other side of the rivulet, instinct burning and buzzing under his skin. There was an exit very close, unless his memory misled him.

There. Another slope rose sharply, the rivulet pooling at its foot, and set into the hillside, blending into the gray turf and choked by finger-thin bramble branches with long wicked rose-blushed thorns, was a door of weathered wood. It was already opening, sensing his need, and he splashed through runoff moat-water, ignoring the sudden knifing chill against his ankles. His hobleaf boots could handle whatever fluid the Watcher swam through, and to spare.

He gritted his teeth and slip-scrambled up to the door's lip. He had no time to brace himself, shouldering aside the wood and throwing himself into the darkness beyond.

His stomach turned inside out, his armor ran with ice, his breath dropped out of him with a grunt before he landed, legs buckling and instinct tucking his shoulder so he could roll and make it upright, still running, on uneven concrete.

Where am I? He slowed, his stomach deciding it wasn't going to turn itself inside out *just* yet, and glanced about.

A large rectangle of concrete, pieces heaving up here and there where the ground had swelled or buckled underneath. It looked familiar, and he realized it was a foundation pad for a doublewide. More flat pale spaces at regular intervals, and a few bulky, overgrown shadows were abandoned trailers that hadn't been taken off their legs yet. Headlights flashed along the south corner, behind a chainlink fence woven with plastic strips, its top festooned with coils of razor wire.

If it had been just-Unseelie hunting him, the cold iron in the fence might have been a comfort.

He veered southward, toward the headlights. Crossing streets was like crossing rivers, it might slow his pursuers down. The air smelled familiar, a cold breath of river, engine exhaust, a damp spring wind a little warmer than it should have been.

Huh. Now that's *weird.*

His feet beat the earth in a quickening tattoo, he *leapt,* hobleaf boots striking hissing sparks from the razorwire as the strands flexed, and it was a joy to feel his body responding with the cursed sidhe speed and grace again.

Contemplating suicide was one thing. To have a poison crippling him, turning him into a worm-crawling idiot...that was something else, and the best way to describe it was *unbearable.* All sidhe had pride, and a mortal man might have some too. His own had been tormenting him ever since Daisy died. He should have been able to protect her. He should have been able to protect Robin, too, or at least somehow been less of a blundering idiot.

He might be able to salvage this entire stupid tangle, if he could just figure out how to escape—or master—the Sluagh.

Details, details. He landed hard, brakes squealing as he

darted into traffic. This looked like a major artery, and he narrowly avoided being run over by a red Toyota, his knee kissing the fender with a metal-crunching sound. Up and over, the marks on his arms and shoulders and chest running with flame, and all he could think of was Robin, standing head high and shoulders back, facing down Unwinter for the sake of a stupid Half who had fallen for her pale copy and not the original.

An alley opened up, he dove into it, bouncing back and forth between brick walls to gain height. A rooftop—he was over the side in a trice, skidding to a stop with his head upflung, his irises incandescent green for a moment before he shut his eyes, listening, his entire body a taut string.

For a few moments, nothing but the soughing of tires on damp pavement, a string of curses from the well-bottom of the street he'd left behind. A familiar mortal song, and one that might have made him want to smile...

...if a single clear, chill, ultrasonic note hadn't sounded in the distance. West and south, maybe at the north edge of a graveyard or the middle of a potter's field, maybe in a culvert or at the end of town where someone had dumped a body long ago. There were many places one of the unforgiven, angry dead could linger, and their rage at the manner of their deaths was surpassed only by their thirsting to run to ground their quarry, who had stirred them to a bastard simulation of life.

Gallow checked the sky. It felt like 10 p.m. or thereabouts, if his internal clock hadn't been knocked out of whack by almost-dying locked in Unwinter's dungeon.

Christ. I don't even know what day it is. He couldn't even tell how long he'd been trapped in that stone cube. It couldn't have been very long, right?

Now was a fine time to wish he'd asked a few more questions, but he doubted Unwinter knew or cared what year or month it was in the mortal world.

There was one silver lining, he supposed. He finally recognized the city he'd landed in. Maybe Unwinter had something to do with it, guessing Gallow would choose the closest exit, or maybe Gallow himself had been thinking about it and turned the door to somewhere he was familiar with.

In any case, this was home ground. It was Daisy's city, the place he'd worked construction in, playing at a mortal life. He knew its alleys and geography, its secret places and its heights. He had a good chance of using the terrain to keep himself out of the Sluagh's clutches until dawn, if he was lucky.

After that, he was going to have to get creative.

Midnight found him in the shadow of the Gaffney Bank Building downtown, a brick facade he remembered repairing about a decade ago still holding up fairly well. The gray bulk of the second-largest of the city's cathedrals, Saint Ignatius's, was a few blocks away, and the ultrasonic hunting-cries were circling.

He skirted the pay-for lot behind the bank, pausing only to look at the anemic pine trapped in a concrete round near the attendant's hut. It was a sorry, scrawny facsimile of a tree; he remembered its sapling newly planted when the lot had just been paved, level and black-sealed, the stripes fresh. Back then urban-renewal dollars had been flooding the city from the federal teat, and Gallow had been fresh from Summer, waiting until he could approach Daisy at the diner. Waiting a decent interval, to hopefully dissuade Summer from thinking Jeremy had left for a mortal, had been agonizing.

In the end, it hadn't mattered.

His skin chilled, an atavistic shiver all the way up his back. The lance woke, tingling painfully, almost coalescing in his hands. Gallow turned, slowly, hobleaf soles sliding over pavement differently than his workboots full of the dust of mortal construction sites. The chill—and the lance's danger-warning—rushed over him in a blinding sheet.

Not even Unwinter was this cold.

The pavement near the pine tree exhaled white vapor through its cracks. The veils rose, steam condensing on invisible surfaces, and in the flowing, flooding ribbons a female shape turned slowly, sniffing.

The chuffing noise—invisible, rotting lungs making a mockery of breath—sent a bolt of loathing through Gallow's belly.

Sometime after the lot had been poured, someone had met a violent death here under the pine tree. Not every murder made for a restless spirit—but *this* one had.

She turned, floating in the steam-veils as if caught in a water tank, the spirit exhaling from ground that remembered shed blood and pain.

And *rage*.

The ruin of the face was visible even through the shifting scarves. She'd been bludgeoned. Gallow's gorge rose. The tales of the Sluagh were bad enough.

This was somehow worse. He remembered when this lot was *built*, and someone had killed a woman right where he'd worked. Maybe right where he'd stood and ate lunch, or joked with one of the purely mortal workers.

"Christ," he muttered, and the thing cringed furiously, its blind eyes lighting like live coals, tumbling forward on shredded hands and knees toward his breathing, living warmth. Its head lifted in a mockery of human movement, and its queer sniffling turned into a sharp, singing inhale grinding past torn vocal chords.

Next, it would throw back its almost-visible head and shriek, and the Sluagh would know he'd been sighted.

A clatter, a familiar shout and a scattering flash, a snowdrift of crystalline glitters hanging in midair, bright as a photographer's strobe. The lance sprang into being, its handle rasping against his calluses, and its blade swept harmlessly through the thing, Jeremiah dragged forward as the sluagh-spirit grabbed the blade and pulled it inward with her almost-visible hands. The sparkles pattered down, stinging, and her gutted face flushed red for a long awful second before collapsing, the lance's keening choked off as it fled back into the marks with a jolt.

Jeremiah, blinking, staggered backward. A horrid draining sensation filled his arms, and the new arrival grabbed his arms with strong, familiar fingers. His rescuer had flung a handful of salt through the dead woman, disrupting her hold for a few critical moments.

A glitter of furious dark eyes, a shock of dark hair with moss dried and flaking away, and the ever-present pair of hilts rising over his broad shoulders. *What the fuck?*

"Idiot," Alastair Crenn greeted him, with a not-quite-unfriendly shove. "Don't you know better than to touch, if you're stupid enough to call for them? Come, Glass-gallow, let's away before it screams."

LOVE-TOKENS
19

Crenn had time to be thankful that he'd found a grocer's and navigated its confusing fluorescent-lit aisles for a carton of salt; the blue paper canister was oddly familiar despite all the intervening mortal years. It wouldn't hold a flood of them at bay, but a lone sluagh could be mazed for a short while. Gallow had almost been sucked into the steam-scarf embrace, stabbing at the thing with that pigsticker of his as if he expected it to do any good.

They ran side by side, Gallow in red armor sidhe-light and silent, and Crenn himself glancing over his shoulder frequently to check their trail. If not for the armor, if not for the old, threadbare anger smoldering in Crenn's chest, it could have been the long long ago, both of them in the flush of youth and invulnerable, running for the joy of it because they'd figured out how to work a few poor chantments, the best Half children could do before they were brought into the sideways realms and their sidhe blood kindled.

The interesting thought that maybe they might have both been happier if they'd stayed in the goddamn orphanage, with its brutality and purely mortal cold, occurred to him, as it sometimes did, and was discarded just as quickly. Normally it made his scars ache . . .

But Alastair Crenn was no longer scarred.

He slowed Gallow's headlong speed by the simple expedient of yanking on his arm, breath coming high and fast. "Easy, there. Don't exhaust yourself yet." *It's a long way until dawn.*

Gallow slowed, their footsteps brushing pavement in eerie unison. "Robin," he said, hoarsely. "Have you—"

Crenn swallowed, harshly. "She was alive, last I saw." *Go on. Tell him the rest.*

"Is she *well*?"

Her gaunt wan face, her chopped-short hair, and her hoarse husky broken voice . . . Crenn struggled with a lie, opened his mouth to give it voice. What came out instead was closer to the truth than he liked. "I don't know."

"Summer." Gallow said it like a curse, pointed swiftly. "Up. Let's get some height."

Crenn nodded. "There were Unseelie." Lamely, as if it would matter. "She escaped. That dog of hers."

"Wonder where she got him." Gallow hawked dryly, as if to spit, and a cool spring breeze ruffled past them. "So what does Summer want?" He plunged into a malodorous mortal alley-way, leaping lightly and catching a fire escape ladder with a muffled clatter. Crenn followed, the iron almost-burning as he reached the top and hopped over onto a flat roof. His mortal half insulated him, but—

Crack. He went down hard, rolling out of instinct, and when he shook the blow out of his head the lancepoint was there, glittering, an inch from his exposed throat.

That was one thing about Jeremiah. He was fast and ruthless when he made up his mind to be.

"I said," Gallow repeated quietly, *"what does Summer want?*

124

Since you're her little errand boy now. You took word to the dwarves, didn't you."

Did he perhaps remember Crenn's presence as he thrashed and burned from the poison on a small dwarven cot? It had taken some doing, to persuade them to let him in, let alone persuade them of Summer's gratitude long enough to get Robin out of their clutches. "Wasn't my idea." Crenn lay very still, the damp rooftop slightly gritty underneath him. Stars peered through shredded rips in orangelit clouds, struggling through the veil of citylight and turning Gallow's form into an indistinct bulk, underlit by the lance's quivering moonfire. "I'm here to help, Jer!"

"Oh, sure. Help me right into a new trap." A sneer lifted Gallow's handsome lip. Either Findergast the dwarven healer had given him a hell of an antidote, or Unwinter had released him from the poison. Both prospects were equally disturbing. "What does she want, lapdog?"

Crenn shook his head, wished he hadn't. His hair fell back, and the lancetip hovered closer to his skin. "I just saved your life, Gallow, and this is how you thank me?"

Gallow bent slightly, peering at him. "Looks like you've been paid for whatever you did," he said, softly. "Look at you, all good as new. Is it a glamour?"

What? But the ghosts of his old scars flamed, and Crenn swallowed harshly, acutely aware of the hungry, humming sharpness so close to his Adam's apple. "The Queen didn't ask if I'd find this payment acceptable. You know how it is, Jer. She sends a bird, and we fall over ourselves to obey because she's *Summer*. Not all of us are lucky enough to run away."

"So she paid you for something. Since it wasn't bringing me to Court, that leaves only one thing." Jeremiah tensed. The lance gave a little eager quiver, a hunting dog scenting blood. "What did you do to Robin Ragged, Alastair? *What did you do?*"

Whatever Crenn might have said was lost as a thin ribboning ultrasonic cry lifted just a few blocks away. It keened on, and on, thrilling up and down a register mortal ears couldn't precisely *hear*, felt more inside the skull than through the eardrums. It was the sound copied by the small Unseelie hunt-whistles, all patterned on the nauseatingly beautiful curve of Unwinter's Horn.

Prey sighted, prey sighted!

The salt had worn off. The sluagh in the parking lot cried out again, the sound fading into a cold, clutching, ringing emptiness before it was echoed from other places, some near, some far.

The dead, the Unseelie say, *always find their own.*

"I don't want *them* to get you," Crenn said. It sounded as if he'd just realized as much, and perhaps he had. "Even you don't deserve that, you faithless bastard."

Even with the edge to his throat, he couldn't be conciliatory. How much of a simpleton was he to believe Robin would look upon *any* of this kindly?

I'm saving someone she…cares…for. That has to count for something.

"Why not? You think if I'd been with you when they were burning the Hooverville, you wouldn't have been shot and set on fire? You blame me for coming back every day and trying to chantment the goddamn scars off you? You blame me for taking you over the Veil, too? For the Enforcers not taking you on? You wanted to be at Court, I brought you, and I did more than you know keeping the fullbloods' mouths shut over your *misfortune*. It wasn't my fault you got your goddamn *feelings* hurt and ran off to Marrowdowne!"

How long had Gallow been sitting on saying that? Crenn pushed the anger down, and for once, it went quietly. *Go ahead, Gallow. Stab me if you want.* "Maybe we should have this talk later, huh? Unless you really want to argue while *they're* singing themselves closer and closer to your idiot self."

"Now might be a good time to make sure you can't do me— or Robin—any more fucking mischief."

"She's the reason I'm willing to save your worthless hide," Crenn barked. In a few seconds he was going to slap the lance-blade away, maybe take a hit to the shoulder and maybe not, but *definitely* take out Gallow's knee with a flicker of a kick. Then he might decide to turn around and leave the bastard to sit and simmer in his own dirty diaper, for God's sake. He'd go back to tracking Robin; he was a fool for thinking Jeremiah would be anything but a raging jackass even while the worst nightmare possible under a sidhe or mortal sky bore down on him.

Gallow opened his mouth, maybe to tell him to go to hell or maybe to give a name before he plunged the lancetip downward, but a new sound intruded. A rushing and a clicking, little pebbles under a rolling spring tide in the Whispering Harbor, where the slim swan-ships lay at anchor, forgotten but not fading.

"Half, and Half," a low male voice said, as a cloaked shape melded free of the darkness. "The vengeful spirits draw close, I suggest we repair elsewhere to have you exchange love-tokens."

Gallow was already moving, the lance rising into middle guard; Crenn gained his feet in a rush and both his blades rang free. The Sluagh sent up its cries again, and now they were in a more definite circle.

The longer Gallow stayed in one place, the smaller that circle would become, and eventually it would draw choking-close and they would have him.

The Sluagh would *feed*.

"And just who are you, sir?" As usual, Gallow was quicker off the mark, while Crenn moved to the side a single step, to give both of them freedom to attack—and to back Jer up in case shooting his mouth off led to trouble.

It felt, again, familiar. So familiar he wanted to curse and kick something.

The sidhe-shape pushed his hood back, a head of dark, oddly spangled hair rising from the shadow. A long nose, and mailed shoulders under the draping velvet cloak, no betraying glimmer to give him away in the shade beneath the bulk of a silvershimmer HVAC unit.

"One who is willing to aid you, if you will allow it," the new-comer said. "First, Gallow-glass—for you see, I know you—I ask you, politely, where is Puck Goodfellow? And," he added magnanimously, flexing long gauntleted and gloved fingers as he stepped free of screening, rippling dark-glamour, "I suggest you tell me while we run."

PROTECT AND SERVE
20

The radio squawked like a pimp caught between two different protection rackets, fuzzing so bad with static Adkins started swearing. Normally he was pretty mild-mouthed, but that sort of sound was enough to send anyone into a paroxysm of obscenity, and Officer Paco Melendez's hands tightened on the steering wheel. Number 79, the most busted Rocinante ever ridden by a pair of Sanchos in blue, wheezed along with the defroster fan working at max.

It was a damp night.

"Mother*fucker*," Adkins snarled, staring out the window. His collar was too tight, creasing the papery flesh of his chicken-shaven neck. "Even the goddamn radio's busted. This is what I get for riding with *you*."

"Likewise, I'm sure," Melendez murmured. Sticking the rookie with the bad car and the bigot was classic. It didn't even rate an eyeroll, by now. You learned to expect the worst, and going through Academy just put the bloodclot cherry on top of that particular shit-sundae. If you ended up with any optimism left, it was of the Murphy's Law variety. Unless you were sub-normal, in which case, you got promoted to desk work.

Heavy fog always made things a little weird. The weather report hadn't said anything, and Melendez *hated* that shit. Would it have been too much to ask that bleached blonde on Channel Six to give a word of warning?

"Shitfucking cocksucking piece of made-in-China *shit*," Adkins kept going, tapping at the radio with one blunt finger in cockeyed time.

He was goddamn near a poet sometimes.

Later, Melendez would sometimes think about right before it happened. He would try to explain it to himself—maybe he'd seen a flicker in his peripheral, or maybe he'd heard something other than the burring of the car's engine, or maybe it was a full-body shiver like you sometimes got. His mother used to call those *brainshivers*, saying it was your body pushing a button to get everything to shake and settle right. Just like flicking a pillowcase so she could fold it in thirds with her cripplequick work-roughened hands.

The truth was, he sometimes admitted if he was most of the way through a bottle and staring out his apartment window, there was no warning, nothing. His foot simply jammed down onto the brake without so much as informing the rest of him, the entire car shook and shimmied, Adkins almost hit the dash since the bigot bastard wouldn't wear his seatbelt, and the radio sent up an unholy screech as the dark figures darted across Pallacola Avenue, one-two-three. Broad-shouldered male shapes, but the last one had something on his head—something like feathers nodding and waving, the outlines blurring as he moved with catlike grace.

"Wha*fuck*?" Adkins spluttered, and Melendez gripped the wheel so hard his knuckles turned white. The radio went dead, the engine ticking along with its usual choppy rumble. The headlights dimmed, and all of a sudden, Melendez was very certain he didn't want them to go out.

"Did you see that?" Adkins demanded. "Like the goddamn circus is in town."

"I saw it." *Problem is,* Melendez thought, *I don't know what exactly I saw.*

"Wearing feathers. Think there's something up?"

"Didn't hear it on the radio."

"Should we call it in?"

Melendez shrugged. "We're not even getting static. We should go back to base and have them—"

A horrific squeal erupted from the radio and the car rocked on its indifferent shocks when Melendez leaned over to turn it down. The fog thickened, the headlights dimming further, and Adkins shifted uneasily, which made the car rock a little more.

"Kid?" Adkins almost-whispered. "I've got a bad feeling about—"

What happened next, Melendez didn't care to think about, no matter how much alcohol he consumed.

Something hit the windshield with a soft thud. Adkins let out a little-girl screech, choking off halfway as the thing's face smeared against the glass. It wasn't precisely *solid*, though—the fog coated it in runnels, twisting and fluttering to show the edges of a ruined face leering at them both.

No. Not at them both. Leering at Adkins, who inhaled sharply. Almost as if he recognized it.

"Jesus Christ," Melendez whispered. "You're seeing this, right?"

The tongue came out, thick moist condensation spreading along the glass with a rasping hiss. The engine labored, burping along, and a sudden sharp stink wafted through the car's interior. Somewhere between the sweet foulness of rotting flesh and the loose bowels of a junkie, along with an acrid yellow scent Melendez later found out was *fear.*

131

Adkins's breathing rasped too. He sounded like he was running a hard mile, and all of a sudden Melendez had the idea that his partner might have a heart attack sitting in the passenger seat of Number 79.

That got him moving. He pressed the gas pedal, the tires chirped, and Adkins screamed again, a high hopeless noise, because it wasn't just the one face.

The fog had turned to *people*, clustering the car, the sound of their queer sniff-chuffing breath blanketing both engine noise and Adkins's yell that had somehow turned into words.

"*I didn't mean it!*" he kept screaming, and Melendez had a sudden vivid mental image of the windshield shattering and the fog-things pouring in, wrapping around Adkins in thick cheesecloth veils—he mashed the accelerator against the floor, and Number 79 summoned up a deep coughing roar, belching black exhaust the fog-things crowded around, running their wasted, steam-cloaked fingers through the fringes and shuddering, hissing their displeasure.

He didn't remember the rest of the wild screeching ride to the precinct, and when they got there it was to find confusion, everyone shouting about radios and weirdness, Dispatch screaming their heads off about their network going down, and Adkins blundered for the locker room without even double-signing the car in. Melendez did it for him, and waited for him to come back, but he never did.

No, Adkins went back to his own apartment in Falida and hung himself. The inquest wasn't quite hurried, but Melendez wasn't called upon to testify to more than "Yes, he was there that night the radios failed, no, he didn't say anything, it was our first ride together, I don't know." Suicide rates being what they were in the force, the case was closed.

Six months later, Shorty Greggs in Vice told Melendez about

Car 79—back when it was new, it had been Adkins and his old pal Harry Krjowiscz's, and there was something about a perp not surviving the ride to lockup. Neither officer was charged, of course, but the whole thing had been...

I didn't mean it! I didn't mean it! I didn't mean it!

Well, Melendez didn't want to think about it. The job went easier if he didn't, and he was the first one in his family to finish high school, let alone get ahead. His mother was always so proud of her son the officer.

There was one thing, though.

Paco Melendez, for the rest of his career, never worked on a foggy night.

OTHER MEASURES
21

Summer's orchard drowsed under a hot golden afternoon. Its fringes were fleecy with drifting blossom, flashes of round fruit crimson as the Queen's lips and almost as delectable—or so the bards said—peeping through the fragrant cloud. Their trunks were still solid, their roots still holding fast, but on the edges something had changed. Instead of the deep-graven lines carving sleeping or contorted faces into the green-tinged bark, there were shallow slices, some of them oozing golden-red sap.

A black, smoking path cut through the trees, a blot on a trembling face. It was the remnant of Unwinter's incursion, and the Unseelie had torn down branches and feasted on gushing sapblood, set torch to the deep grass and tree alike, and the pyre-breath from that treachery and later deaths still fumed in a solid column. The miasma hung straight, no breath of wind smearing at its edges. No pixies crawled among the blossoms or veered among the fallen fruit, drunk on heady ambrosial fumes. Early in the full flush of Summer's renewal and reign, her slice of the sideways realms should have been throbbing with activity, growth and rejuvenation spreading into the mortal world as well. Nymphs should have been dancing, and music should have floated from the towers of Summerhome.

The pennants hung limply from those high green-and-white spires, and the castle had lost much of its welcoming quality. Its battlements were sharper now, noontide sun glittering from razor edges. The great Gate was still open—the Queen did not have a moat guarding her fastness.

Her beauty, the bards said, was enough. Who would wish any ill upon Summer?

In the center of the orchard's blackened streak, a chunk of weathered blue stone crouched, curiously clean. No ash or dirt clung to its rough rectangle, and its solidity made the rest of the bleached, drained surroundings look even more faded.

A dark-green mantle brushed the withered grass. She swayed gracefully into sight, Summer's brightest blossom, a high cage of fragile bones lifting from her shoulders and cupping her golden head. Golden hair had been coaxed through them, tied artfully with scented ribbons, and on her forehead the Jewel, Danu's gift to Her chosen one, gave out a low stuttering glow.

The red scarf at her wrist was joined by others, knotted up her arm to the elbow. A dozey, sicksweet fuming of harvest incense followed her steps, rippling in her wake. Summer's face was...not as it had been. Instead of the laughing, carefree nymph she sometimes affected, or the icy grandeur of remote, impossible beauty, she looked...

Not *old*, certainly. Not quite haggard. Perhaps it was only the responsibility of ruling Danu's folk that weighed upon her, giving her a gravity of step, of expression. Perhaps the matted snarls under the surface of her rippling golden hair needed the bone-fingers to keep them from forming afresh. Perhaps her weakening—for it was whispered in far and dark corners that

Unwinter's breaking of her boundaries had cost the Queen dearly—was temporary.

Her Armormaster Broghan the Black, Trollsbane himself, stepped proudly in her wake as well. If the foulness offended his aristocratic nostrils, he did not show it.

She halted at the altar-stone, her hands hidden in the mantle's long sleeves. The robe was heavy, as if she felt a chill. Normally the first third of spring was a time for divesting oneself of layers, of showing the loveliness of ageless flesh and glamoured tints.

"Broghan," Summer said softly, "where is it?"

He paused, then cleared his throat. "I . . . my Queen, I do not know. The call was sent forth."

"I sense them, lurking. Come forth." Her tone was icy. "And bring your charges."

One moment empty, the next moment full—a space in the fabric of the Veil rippled, and a long thin gray form slid through. It rippled, heavy and oily, pouring itself along the ash-choked ground, and rose from a cloudy pool, its cloaked and hooded hunchback form firming as the pool shrank. Two gray glints showed from the darkness of its hood, and its long gloved fingers twitched.

"*Hail, Danu's chosen*," it murmured in a lovely, clear, fluting bell-voice. In the mortal realm it could wear many guises, all of them benign.

What else, indeed, would a childcatcher look like?

A mortal child, hearing such a voice, would also hear promise. Enticement. Laughter and carnivals, and warmth. The gray cloak would close about them in some deserted place, and after a jolting ride through the Veil, they would arrive in Summer, to a warm welcome indeed. A changeling would be left behind, a placemarker in the mortal world, and all the delights of Seelie were open to the children of mortal salt and brief blossoming.

The other half of the coin was a childcatcher's returning of a sleeping mortal to its home and family, most spending their lives saddened by a loss they could not quite remember, chasing the glorious fleeting almost-memories in different ways— sometimes through art, more often through drugs, each hit promising a return, however temporary, to their charmed captivity.

The changeling, of course, had a different fate. Many had been called home to Summer and the flint knife, since the treachery.

Many indeed.

Summer paused. "Well? Where is it?"

"*My liege.*" A note of uneasiness, in the bell-tones. "*There are none left.*"

"That cannot be." Summer's smile had set itself in stone. Her chin lifted slightly. "There were hundreds."

"*There are none left.*" The childcatcher made a soft movement, expressing regret in the face of the inalterable. "*No changeling, sleeping or waking, tarries among the mortals.*"

Summer's sleeves trembled slightly. Below them, certainly, her hands were fists. Those soft, snowy hands held a harp so gracefully, or caressed an elf-knight's cheek, or stroked the shoulder of an elf-maid or dryad. *When Summer takes a fancy, she takes an equal amount*, some whispered.

Never very loudly, and never in her presence, of course.

Not until recently.

"Where did they go, then?" She smiled, winningly. "Where, in the wide wide realms of here or there, did they go?"

"*They went,*" the childcatcher said, "*where we may not.*"

A soft rumbling ran through Summer, from the sinks of

Marrowdowne where green-clad giant hulks settled a little deeper in the mire, to the borders of the Free Counties. The rolling hills shuddered once, a mere millimeter's worth of movement, and birds took wing from thrashing treebranches.

"Unwinter," Summer said, softly.

"*Perhaps.*" The childcatcher's approximation of a shrug was more definite now. "*We do not know. There are none ready in the Slumbrous Caves, my liege. It will simply take time.*" Those caves, where the buds of changelings swelled in mist-wreathed bulbs along walls of unformed dreams, gray flitting moths swarming each bulge...how could they be empty?

"Time." A bitter little laugh. "Of course."

But it had already vanished, stepping back through the Veil to their peculiar drowned slice of the sideways realms, full of whatever gas they breathed instead of air. Theirs was an ancient contract, and as far as they were concerned they had fulfilled its terms exactly.

Perhaps they judged Summer too weak to hold them to account if they had not.

"Broghan." She did not turn. "How many mortal children enjoy our hospitality now?"

"Ah." He coughed slightly. Another Armormaster might have guessed she would ask, and been ready with an answer, but he had not. It was a high honor to wear the glass badge, and those who did often shared the Queen's bed. Perhaps Broghan the Black was learning the lesson that a high honor carries a high price. "Six, Your Majesty."

"A bare half dozen." Summer's slender shoulders did not drop or rise. She turned, with slow, terrible grace. "Well, bring them hither, then."

"All of them?" His eyebrows did not rise.

"Yes, Armormaster." Her tone did not waver, but something

in its depths warned she was losing patience. A sharp breeze ruffled the branches. "If I cannot have the changelings, I will be forced to use other measures. Unwinter's foulness knows no bounds."

"I shall gather them at once, oh Summer." Broghan bowed, a fine flourish at the end of the motion, and hurried away.

Summer studied the altar's stone face. Faint lines etched into its surface had once been deep and broad, the Pattern changing at a glacier's pace. Some said the first trees in Summer's orchard were dryads who stopped to study its loops and whorls, and remained, staring until they forgot any other sight. Others held that the Pattern was traced by Danu's slight movements as the goddess slept, unaware of the Sundering in her beloved first-chosen folk. Who knew?

Summer, left alone, turned her scarlet-draped wrist up and pushed back the fabric with one red-lacquered nail that sharpened, scraping painfully.

The hard black boil on her pale, flawless wrist had spread, vein-branches gripping ageless skin. The delicate traceries of black exhaled a fetid breath no matter how she scrubbed with rose-attar or fresh mugwort with pixie-sprinkled dew.

Nothing could permanently damage Summer. She was eternal, the first among the sidhe, and the Jewel Danu's mark upon her chosen favorite. Or so the bards said. Other, darker songs told of First Summer sickening and the Sundering that followed *that* fair queen's untimely death, but those were not sung even on moonlit nights. Not for a long, long while.

Some might have begun to hum them again. The sidhe were a fickle collection of creatures, indeed.

"I am Summer," the Queen whispered, her carmine lips barely moving. Her other hand patted a small bag hanging at her waist, secured with a filigree chantment-chain that sparked, sensing her attention. The small glass ampoules inside did not clink together, and she'd thrown away the rag Robin had wrapped the cure in. Watching the coruscating fluid inside them, the treasures brought her by Jeremiah Gallow before he turned on her, soothed Summer. She would not use one just yet.

Not until Braghn Moran brought her Puck's head and the free sidhe's treasures, the pipe and knife. Just to be sure.

ONCE A SERVING-MAID

22

A door bound with dark metal opened, its clockwork hinges tick-tocking, and the Steward glided through. Robin stepped nervously in his wake, the tiny clicks of her heels loud in the hush. There were scurryings and a raft of other small noises in the rest of Unwinter's Keep, but none of his other subjects appeared to Robin Ragged.

She was, actually, quite grateful. Her teeth kept wanting to chatter, and faint traces of Unwinter's myrrh-laden breath lingered in her hair. The black velvet cape-coat steamed, her living warmth melting the furred ice-diamonds of his presence as well. Between that numb freeze and the sunny, sweetened malice of Summer's Court, there were the anarchic free sidhe, but she didn't care much for them, either.

The more she thought about it lately, the better hiding in some disused corner of the mortal world sounded. If she could just be left *alone*, really, anywhere would do.

This particular hall was so high it appeared narrow, like all the others, its ribbed ceiling festooned with metallic, lacy cobwebs. On either side, stone rectangles rose table-high, most with a thick coverlet of dust. In the middle of the hall, however, six crystalline blocks, innocent of dust or cobweb, sat atop curved stone spines.

Pepperbuckle slunk beside her, pressing as close as he could and still walk, her knee bumping him every few steps. The horn-fan head of the Unseelie in front of her didn't move, and she sensed no disapproval emanating from his thin frame. Instead, a freezing soft excitement, like snowflakes on bare metal, spread out from the Steward in waves.

There were forms inside the crystal boxes. Robin blinked twice, reaching to touch the matted elflock—not hidden under her hair anymore, and the bone comb and two pins could be seen under the chopped-short mess. No tingle of glamour ran down her skin, and the outlines didn't waver.

They were real.

Breath left her in a rush. Three glass coffins on either side, and in each one a homely little sidhe creature lay with eyes closed, their small hands lax at their sides. Some had vestigial sixth fingers, all had pointed ears poking through their silken hair, whether dark or blond. Four girls, two boys, buckteeth and freckles, most in pajamas and one in jeans and a Cubs T-shirt.

She reached for Pepperbuckle's ruff.

They were *changelings*. What was Unwinter doing with them? Or did he somehow know what Robin had done, the unforgivable act she'd committed with her own blood and her Realmaking talent? Was this a threat? If she didn't do as he wished, would he—

The changeling closest to her, in red-striped footed pajamas, twitched.

Robin choked back a cry, and Pepperbuckle bristled. The Steward paused, his bone fan tilting as he half turned.

Cracks runneled the crystalline box, little sparkles of dia-

144

mond dust puffing up as the changeling contorted, curling in around its narrow chest like a spider flicked into a candleflame. Robin forced herself to inhale, digging her heels in sharply as Pepperbuckle growled, the sound thrumming and splashing uneasily as the crystal spiderwebbed into cracks.

"Ah," the Steward hissed. "Sso sshe is forced to mortals, now." His grinding chuckle puffed dust out through his robes, and he continued on, ignoring Robin's hurry to catch up.

Forced to mortals? Robin had never heard of Unwinter sending out changelings. He had...other methods, of keeping his slice of the sideways realms from sliding further into the Veil. So these were Summer's? But why keep the changelings, if—

Another crackling sound filled the hall's listening depth. Another crystalline box spiderwebbed with cracks, the tiny form inside convulsing and drawing all its limbs together.

"She's killing the children," Robin whispered, horrified, unable to help herself. The childcatchers wouldn't be able to find the changelings in Unwinter's realm, but Summer could use the flint knife on mortal flesh, too. Mortal corpses couldn't be buried with a sapling spearing their frail chests, but the shedding of their blood carried its own power.

"Yess." The Steward did not halt. "My lord ssusspected sshe might."

Oh, God. But Robin shut her mouth, concentrating on her breath. Four in, four out. Pepperbuckle paced uneasily next to her, his proud head drooping. He didn't like it here any better than she did. At least they both had company, and she was further grateful the hound had decided to stay with her.

He'll end up dead, Robin. Like everyone else you care about.

"So he took the changelings." Her own voice took her by surprise.

"My lord," the Steward replied, "hass losst patience." The final sibilant covered another cracking, another convulsion. Robin's stomach twisted.

It was going to happen anyway, she told herself. *You knew what happened to changelings. If she'd sent Sean home, his changeling would have been buried, or burnt, or heart-stabbed.* The mortal children were returned alive, but so many of them chased the memories of their time at Court with the crude fire of drugs or pain, it hardly mattered. Every time a mortal brushed up against the sidhe, the mortal suffered.

Robin was just as guilty as Summer, really. The only problem was, someone couldn't be called *guilty* if they had no conscience, could they? Summer was a highborn fullblood, no mortal dross in her blood to grant something as stupid, as petty, as *mortal* as regret.

Innocent as a cobra. Did a snake rejoice in the suffering, after it sank its fangs in prey?

She heard another creaking fracture, and tried not to look. Her chest hurt, a swift spike through the traitorous part of her that couldn't forget and stubbornly refused to change.

Robin looked anyway.

This changeling had been left for a female child. It wore a worn but well-washed blue dress trimmed with white eyelet lace, hemmed neatly many times. Small white ankle socks with more of that lace, and brightly polished Mary Janes. Changelings were often troublesome. Some mortal parents, however, considered any child a blessing, no matter how... strange.

The Steward waited at the far door. Was he impatient?

Had Unwinter ordered her brought by this route?

You shall chip free Summer's Jewel.

As if he thought she'd need convincing.

Robin's chin raised. The lovingly polished little shoes danced against the stone as the body contorted. A changeling was only a placeholder left in the mortal world, soaking up enough of *something* to make their sacrifices nails driven in to keep the Veil from carrying Summer away. How many times, going to and fro in Summer, had Robin walked over a space held fast only by a changeling's death?

Pepperbuckle halted, looking over his shoulder at her, a flash of blue iris. The familiarity—Daisy, checking if her big sister was watching; Sean, brave enough to stray from Robin's side but slyly glancing for reassurance—warmed her clear through, a clawed heat.

If Unwinter's breath could numb her, it might be better.

Her footsteps tapped as she hurried to catch up with the Steward. For a moment, she thought he was about to close the door and leave her in the hall with the crackling, creaking crystal coffins, and the thought poured a river of prickles down her back. Pepperbuckle hurried at her side, his claws ticking against the floor as well, but he did not look away as he paced, trusting her to steer him along the center aisle.

The Steward simply indicated another dark, narrow door with a bow and glided away as if on rollers; opening said door had taken much of Robin's remaining stock of bravery. After the last few days, the Ragged thought very little could surprise her—but the round room in the heart of Unwinter's Keep with a cheery fire and two comfortable, wide leather-backed chairs, a small table holding a clear fluted decanter of *lithori*, and two priceless diamond-glittering glasses might have.

If it had not, the slim sidhe-shape standing before the fire, her pale-blue mantle of an ancient cut and her almost-platinum hair dressed high and curling with chantment ribbons, would have. For a brief terrifying moment Robin thought irrationally that it might be Summer, come to strike at her even *here*, but that was ridiculous.

"Ah," Ilara Feathersalt said, in her most dulcet tone. "A familiar face."

The greeting, not direct but still gracious, was polite enough. Robin braced herself. "My lady Feathersalt."

"You were the personage Unwinter was expecting. How... interesting. I thought it would be someone...taller." An elegant lift of the highborn's lip, but she indicated the chairs and the *lithori*, glowing fragrant in the decanter. One of her braids held a twisted golden nugget, swaying as her head turned.

"I thought the protection my lord Unwinter promised me would be armed." Just on the edge of insult, but not quite stepping over—even, all things balanced. Robin took a cautious step away from the door, and Pepperbuckle paced through the opening behind her. He examined Ilara from top to toe, sniffing twice, then blew out a gusty sigh and paced close to the fire.

Ilara's laugh was a beautiful ringing sound. She wasn't glamouring; Robin didn't deserve such display, being a lowly Half. Still, a mortal man looking upon her would have been dazzled. She was a paragon of fullblood beauty, fair creamy skin, the high cheekbones, the sweet mouth pale instead of carmine—of course, she wasn't at Court—and her grace as she turned back to the fire, leaving Robin to seat herself if she chose. That gold bead swayed afresh, and Robin remembered Braghn Moran had worn many of those dwarven-crafted flowers in his dark hair, to match his lady's coloring.

"Protection. Aye, a Half might well wish for such, where we are bound." Ilara merely sounded thoughtful now. She had never done Robin a service, or a disservice either. Of course, Robin was Half, and below her notice.

"And where is that?" Robin did not sit. She gripped the back of the nearest chair, wishing she could share some of the fire's warmth. Pepperbuckle turned, silently, toasting both his flanks and watching her with his wide blue eyes.

Ilara pointed at the hound. "Are you certain of him? He looks a Summer creature."

It was a fair question. *Is he one of Summer's spies, you mean? Like me?* "Certain enough."

"And you, held in high regard by our gracious Queen, this is how you repay her trust?"

Robin's husky laugh burst free, and the fullblood stiffened cautiously. Of course, Ilara had seen Robin sing a song or two at Summer's bidding.

And seen the results, as well.

"You find me amusing, Half?" Ilara's golden eyebrow raised. If it was an imitation of Summer, it was a good one, and perhaps unconscious. Still, one couldn't ever be sure. Ilara's beauty had been compared to the Queen's one time too many, and Robin had witnessed the Feathersalt leaving Court very early one cotton-fog morning, stepping into a pumpkin-carriage with her gossamer veils close-drawn. Braghn Moran had taken the golden flowers from his hair, since Summer's gaze had turned upon him, and Ilara had perhaps decided absence was best.

"I find the idea of Summer's trust, or trusting Summer, a jest in and of itself." Robin suddenly longed for Gallow's voice, salted as it was with mortal speech. Keeping everything even in a conversation with a sidhe was habit, and one she'd used for so long she hadn't realized how much she liked plainer words.

Ilara studied her for a long moment. One of Pepperbuckle's ears stayed pricked in the fullblood's direction. He did not sit, just kept turning, silent and graceful as the sidhe creature he was.

Robin gazed at the fire. Was it wood from the thorn-tangles of the Dak'r, or mortal wood hauled over a threshold for Unwinter's guests? He must have Unseelie here, sometimes, or envoys from the dwarven clans. He had a Court of fullbloods too, boon companions that rode with him during the Sundering and Unwinter's Harrowing. They didn't gather in his Keep, but they obeyed his summons. And he had to have attendants, didn't he?

"Then you are wiser than most." Ilara drifted to the closest chair and settled herself, her mantle spread with pretty grace as if she were sinking onto an ivory bench in one of Summer's glades. "Do you know what Unwinter sends us forth to fetch, Ragged?"

"A knife."

The fullblood smiled slightly. She was much thinner than Robin remembered, and the almost-haggardness of fine-drawn sidhe-wasting upon her had its own attractive sheen. "Oh, indeed. But not just any blade. We shall be fetching the last tooth of a wyrm so massive Danu Herself rode forth to hunt it."

I thought that was a fable. Still, every fable that survived had a germ of truth at its center.

"I should sing you the story of that battle, but then you might sing me a tale in return." Ilara's soft laugh mixed with the fire's merry noise, and she slid a velvet-slippered foot from under her mantle, toward Pepperbuckle, as if to caress the hound with her toe.

His low, thrumming growl, ears suddenly pinned back, shook dust free of overhead beams. Robin's hands tightened on the chair-back. At Court, a beast who did not know his betters was soon taught.

We're not in Summer anymore. It also occurred to Robin that she could, just possibly, do any highborn fullblood she chose an injury at this point, without worrying too much about the consequences. Knowing you were probably going to die in the near future pretty much eradicated the fear of revenge.

Funny, the thought just made her tired. "I save my songs for when they matter most, Feathersalt."

Ilara's shrug was a masterpiece of nonchalance, but her irises flamed with hot gold for a moment, shading to ice-blue before the glow died away. "Then I shall be plain."

Stone and Throne, finally. "Please do be."

"First Summer carried the Fang for ages before the Sundering. Then some fell blackness sickened her, and we all ailed likewise. I was there, the night First Summer died. So was the Fatherless."

Robin almost started at the mention of Puck, a pinch in a sore spot. Her palms remembered the crowbar clutched in them, and the stamping time it beat as bones crunched and sidhe flesh split. She let go of the chair-back with an effort. *Stone. How old is she?* Robin's shoulders ached, she forced them to relax. "A black night indeed," she murmured, as tradition demanded.

"Oh, yes. The handmaiden at First Summer's side took Danu's Jewel, and Summer was reborn. But the Fang, well. It was given to the Fatherless, and hidden away by his cunning."

Robin considered this, her hip pressed against the back of the chair and the hilt of Puck's own knife digging in. It was a relief she had left Puck Goodfellow twisted past recovery on a rooftop, she decided, and yet another relief knife and its belt were hidden under the black velvet. "You helped him?"

"No." The soft reminiscing tone turned chill, and Ilara Feathersalt's irises flashed again. "I was a young maiden overlooked in a corner, then. The neglected may witness much, if they know to be still and silent."

Two can keep a secret, if one of them is dead, Robin recited to herself. Ilara probably also meant that Robin had seen her own share of secrets, being a mere Half and thus of little consequence. The insult was, again, merely reflexive, and merely for balance. Of far greater weight was the information.

Did Ilara guess Robin had seen her leave Court not so long ago? The golden bead all but dared one to mention Braghn Moran. Often, a knight carried a lady's favor into battle.

Maybe a lady could do the same.

The highborn continued. "I overheard, and I followed, and I know where the Fang is hidden." She shifted slightly in the chair, as if uncomfortable. "I shall guide you, and even protect you, and we shall bring it to our lord Unwinter."

Except he wants me to take it somewhere else instead. I see. Robin nodded. Had the Feathersalt come to Unwinter with her knowledge, or had he somehow found out? "Very well, then."

"This only leaves the question of when to start." The fullblood glanced at the decanter of *lithori.*

You think I'd drink something you were left alone in a room with, highborn? Robin bared her teeth. It wasn't a smile, and the expression would never have crossed her face at Court. "The sooner, the better."

HORNS
23

The bone-frilled Steward carried his proud scarecrow self into the Great Study, careful not to disturb the ice-crusted dust on either side of the narrow safe track. He was one of the very few, servant or otherwise, allowed in this dangerous sanctum, and his lord had placed paths for such visitors.

Shelves of leatherbound spines frowned on every wall, both shelf-lumber and book-spine chased with chantment to keep the cold and damp at bay. The massive astrolabes—seven in all, each with a sharp-spined finial weeping trace amounts of red, spun lazily or furiously, depending on the corner of Unwinter the lord's attention lingered upon. Well-oiled joints made a soft whispering, but the film-eyed drow who attended the astrolabes were nowhere in evidence. Usually, the drow who wished release from a crushing burden shuffled blindly in the study's quiet, their pinpricked fingers twitching in time to the spinning, and every once in a while one fell upon the spines with a sigh, bones cracking softly as its body folded in like a spider flicking into a candleflame.

Such mercy waited for any of Unwinter's subjects who requested it.

The Steward waited at the very edge of the safe path, his robe pulled back to avoid the dust. Under its hem, the hooves were plainly visible, gloss-varnished with a bloody tinge. Sharp edges had almost worn through the velvet pads cupping them, but the elaborate black-silk knots on its gaiters were still firm.

High overhead, a cushion of white ice-freighted air held a tall sidhe frame clothed in simple, dusty black. Unwinter's thistledown head, its silver circlet glinting in the harsh white snow-glare from some source overhead that nevertheless escaped the eye, was bent over a large tome, held effortlessly before him though it was as long as his torso. The age-darkened cover, innocent of jewel or stamp, was the simplest to be found in any highborn's manse. Onionskin pages rustled as Unwinter's gloved right hand twitched a single, supple finger.

The slender, empty space on the shelf before Unwinter yawned, bleak and black as ink. It had not been touched since the Keep was dragged from the Veil's depths, the night of the Sundering. Only a will such as Unwinter's could have performed such a feat, they said.

The Steward waited. Moments ticked by, each elastic when compared to the mortal world, where they had definite beginnings and endings. Of course, even mortals know Time is subjective to a degree. Just *what* degree, though, is a matter of much debate.

Unwinter continued to page idly through the book. The astrolabes spun, some furiously, others barely moving. All whispering, as they had since his pale hand had set them in motion with flicks of elegant, already-wasting fingers.

Finally, Unwinter spoke. "*Steward.*"

"My lord." The black-robed scarecrow did not bow, but his every line expressed submission, from the bone frill to the way its thin lips kept the crimson-grimed teeth well covered. Here, his voice lacked the weight of his master's authority.

"Have you made much study of mortals?"

"My...lord?" The Steward considered the question, his head twitching slightly in ways no human cervical spine could emulate. "My...dutiess...do not permit."

"There was a mortal king, long ago even as we reckon." Unwinter's finger flicked, more pages riffling as they turned. The angular script, eldritch ink flaring with light as his gaze touched the page, sent dappled reflections toward the high ceiling. *"When he rode to his last battle, he burned his Keep to the ground behind him."*

Silence held the last sentence. The astrolabes did not pause their spinning, but two slowed and another one began to revolve more quickly. It hissed a bit as it did, a slight mechanical noise, and Unwinter tilted his head.

"Iss...that your will, my lord?" The Steward's tongue, dead white, flicked nervously out, tasting the air, and retreated with a rasp.

"If it was, servant, would you obey?"

"You raissed me from the depths, and gave me vengeance." The Steward bent slightly at the waist, leaning a fraction more toward the end of safety. "I do your bidding, and yourss alone." It paused, and when it spoke next, the words quivered under their own weight. "You are my King."

For once, Unwinter did not chastise such a title uttered in his presence. Instead, he closed the book with a snap, and in the echo, a thin silver thread of sound rose, piercing the Keep from spire to foot. The Steward flinched, his hooves scraping through the last threads of their cushioning. A corner of his robes swayed past the edge into the hungry space beyond, and Unwinter was suddenly *there*, his slim gloved fist striking the scarecrow's midsection, knocking him back into safety, along the groove worn in the dust.

The Steward hissed, a sound of surprise but not pain. Its neck craned again, and its breath whistled high and hard. "My lord…my lord…" Its relief was palpable.

Unwinter stepped onto the path and halted, his ringed fingers spreading. Pale ash-sparks whirled about him. The armor came, flowing from the Veil, closing around Unwinter with soundless grace. Greaves and thighplate clamped themselves home, spurs sparking against the Veil's drugging, dragging pull. Spiked gauntlets closed over his hands, and the breastplate made a hollow sound as it unfolded over Unwinter's chest. More than the armor was his *size*, the shadow of his will peering through the appearance of an elegantly slender sidhe lord, broadening the shoulders and lifting the head. Crimson sparks lit in the depths of his pupils, and the spikes at his shoulder-armor bloomed with painful tiny noises, their tips fresh-wet with red. The cloak blossomed from them, a waterfall of crimson so deep it was almost black, exactly the shade of the last wringing of blood from an exhausted mortal heart.

His chin lifted, and Unwinter's great helm spread in segments, closing over his weary thistledown head. Twin bloody sparks settled in eyehole darkness, and he towered over the Steward, who lay supine, the top edge of his bone frill against the cold, unforgiving floor. It was as well that he did not have eyes, for the moment before the helm closed showed…

In any case, the helm closed fully about Unwinter's pale head, and the astrolabes whispered, whispered, cheated of fresh prey.

"*My faithful servant,*" Unwinter said softly. "*Take more care.*"

"Yess, my lord." The Steward lay still as Unwinter passed overhead, his step light as a frostbitten leaf. The lord of Unseelie halted near the great doors, one ajar and the other creaking as it began to slide open for the first time in many a long year, sidhe or mortal.

"*After I leave...*" Unwinter paused. "*Burn only this room, Steward. If you so wish, you may remain in the flames, and perish at last.*"

"My lord." The creature drew its arms up, and its legs, folding inward. "My lord, my lord, my King."

Without eyes, one cannot weep. Yet the thankful sobs of a creature receiving a reward for much long weary service echoed against the Great Study's walls.

Unwinter did not look back. Once more, the silver unsound pierced the Veil. The Sluagh was in the mortal world.

And it had not run its prey to ground just yet.

AN IDEA
24

The roof was the worst place in winter, and in summer sometimes it baked the nod right out of you. In spring, though, when the pothead gardens began to bloom—and those hippies knew how to grow *everything,* man—it was the best. The storms came in, but there was a special little sheltered corner Henry McDowell had found, dry even during the worst lightning-and-thunder duos. It was chilly sleeping outside, but you didn't really feel it once the nod hit, it just made the couple of manky blankets he'd found in the Dumpster behind the Savoigh Limited seem more like...

Well, like camping. Like when he was a kid, out at Bright Lake, Mom and Dad singing in harmony and his sister laughing like she used to. Those had been the best times. Later, everything just drifted.

Henry was just starting a good one—you didn't smoke it if you wanted the hit to last, and finding a vein was still easy for him—and he itched all over. Maybe that was just the blanket, though. It had to be near 4 a.m., even the sound of traffic from Camden Avenue was muted and faraway. His eyes opened on their own as he drew the needle out, the sting in his arm turning to warmth. The itching would crest in a couple minutes, and after that it would be the deep soft nothingness he lived for.

A rattling sound scraped his ears, and he stiffened, drawing the blankets up. Nobody came up here, it was safe, so why did he hear footsteps? They were light, crunching against the dust and bits of gravel that had somehow gotten up here, and now he heard voices, too.

"Rest. They'll cry again soon enough."

"Yeah." Breathing, harsh and light. "Braghn Moran. I know your name."

"And I know yours, Gallow."

"I ask the price for the aid you give."

"Very simple. Tell me, where is Puck Goodfellow? For that information I will help you as well as I may until this hunt is finished."

"Ah." A heavy, rasping cough. The breathing began to even out.

Now Henry could see them—three shadows, all tall, one of them with a weird outline, like a dress, and a glittering helmet. He made himself as small as possible, and kept still. The warmth began, spreading up his arm. When it hit, none of this would matter.

"The Fatherless is dead." There was a green gleam—looked like eyes.

Wow. Seriously weird. Or maybe he was nodding already? He had to be. His chin drifted down, jerked back up. He'd never heard voices in the nod before.

"This is...heavy news, indeed. You are certain?"

"Very. If you don't believe me, ask Unwinter. He was there."

"Ah." A long pause. "His head? Was it taken?"

"There wasn't anything of it left to take. The Savoigh downtown is where it . . . happened, you can go and see for yourself."

Henry twitched. Well, of course the voices would talk about the Savoigh. He'd just been there, rooting around in the dumpsters for anything good.

"This is distressing news indeed."

"Only if you're looking to avenge him, Moran."

A third voice broke in, not sharp but a little impatient nonetheless. "Save your breath for running. It's a long time until dawn."

"You do realize a Half cannot hope to escape the Sluagh."

"We'll see."

Henry's chin dipped again. It was spreading all through him, the nothingness, and he was glad. If he was going to start seeing things every time he shot up, though . . .

"When they take you down . . ." The third voice trailed off. "There is someone who should know."

"Then you'll tell her."

"I will."

"Come. We must away. Two Halves, and knight—they shall sing songs of this, indeed."

A weird chill passed through Henry McDowell. Ice-spikes jabbed at his ears, fighting with the glorious abyss he'd injected himself with. He closed his eyes, trying not to whimper, and maybe he succeeded, for his chin fell again and he was gone. The three shadows vanished with a rattle and a soft sigh, and a little later, fog crept across the roof in thin tendrils, almost-caressing the drugged mortal's knees. He wasn't awake enough to feel the chill.

When he woke at midmorning, shadows, voices, and fog were all mostly forgotten. Instead, he had only one thought.

Got to get another score.

Two years later, when he overdosed in Amberline Park, he saw little spots of gem-bright light zipping among the tree-tops... but he was dead before the chiming, clamouring pixies, drawn to his curious exhalations and the scent of opiate torpor, crawled over his hands and face.

Then, dissatisfied, they winked out.

AIR AND DREAM
25

Crenn leapt lightly, reached down, and grasped Jeremiah's hand in both of his. A heave, a slight sound of effort, the rustle of lightfoot chantment, and Gallow *flew*, landing with a whisper across the alley and a story up, the fire escape rattling a little. Crenn followed, having to bounce from the brick wall a couple times. Next time they climbed, it would be Gallow's turn to fling him, both of them conserving energy and moving more quickly than they could separately. Braghn Moran disdained their methods, flickering in and out of the Veil—but never too far, ahead or behind, lest the disturbance bring the Sluagh right next to them.

It bothered Crenn. It bothered him a *lot*. The last time he'd seen Moran, the fullblood had been Summer's favorite, dragging a changeling toward the flint knife on the very day a white bird had summoned Crenn from Marrowdowne.

They paused on another rooftop to catch their breath. Gallow looked none the worse for wear. It was less likely that the beardless bastard Findergast had given Jer a *hell* of an antidote; far more likely, then, that Unwinter had removed his poison.

Unwinter was there, Jer had said. It would be just like Gallow to get in a lucky shot and kill the Fatherless. Puck was a canny opponent, but once Gallow started waving that goddamn pig-sticker around, *someone* always got hurt.

"So," Crenn said, his hand on Jer's shoulder. The leather armor underneath his palm was supple, chain-stiffened, and chased with subtle, effective chantment. Not like Moran, whose cloak couldn't disguise the lines of Seelie plate beneath. It was a wonder the knight didn't clank when he moved, but sidhe-armor was whisper-soft, when the wearer wished it to be. "Puck, dead?"

"Yeah." A faint misting of sweat on Jer's forehead. He was pale, under his mortal tan. "Then Unwinter...well."

"He let you..."

"He's got a use for me."

"Does he, now."

"So he said." Jer glanced at Moran, who had paced across the roof, scouting the next part of their route. He could no doubt hear them. "What about that?"

Crenn sighed. "Summer." The word made Jer's expression flick between disgust and grudging acceptance; Crenn didn't want to guess which was meant for him. "I'll tell you again. I am *here to help.*"

"With that cute new face of yours, sure." Gallow's fingers tensed, as if he felt the lance beginning to take form in their grip. "Why would you help *me*, Alastair?"

Because there's a redheaded girl, and because... He settled for something Gallow might conceivably believe. "Nobody kills you but me, Gallow."

"Touching," Bragn Moran said from the roof-edge, a soft cutting word. His hair moved oddly, even for a sidhe's. "It is too quiet. We must move."

"If the Fatherless is dead, why should a Summer knight

promise us aid?" Crenn addressed the air over Moran's dark head.

"A Summer knight promised an *Armormaster* his aid." The correction was addressed to the air over Crenn's own head, impoliteness balanced against impoliteness. "And his reasons are his own."

"The Queen of Seelie has a favorite." Crenn's hands itched for the twin hilts over his shoulders. He'd feel a lot better about this if he was back in Marrowdowne with the knight in his sights and an arrow to the ready. "A dark-haired lord who fetches her meals."

"A knight may wear a chain not of Summer's making." The knight did not move, staring over a slice of tall tenements reeking of poverty. "A Half should not concern himself with his betters so."

His lady left Court, didn't she? I remember hearing something about that. Crenn found himself glancing at Gallow again. Just like old times, seeing if the other man believed the line of twaddle they were being given.

Gallow's chin lifted slightly. His irises flashed green, precisely once. Cool spring wind riffled uneasily across concrete canyons, stars of mortal light in every window. It used to be candles—in the orphanage, the hissing of gaslamps had followed dreary dusk. The first light bulb he'd seen ... Gallow had been there, too.

They had both thought it was magic, before they knew anything of the sidhe.

It was almost a relief when Jeremiah glanced at him, one dark eyebrow lifted a fraction. No, Gallow didn't believe this story, but he wasn't going to challenge it. Just like they wouldn't challenge a fellow hobo with the glint or glare of volatile madness on him. Days spent on the lookout for a scrap of food or

165

tobacco, nights spent sleeping in shifts, because *young* meant *vulnerable* to the stiffened, angry fellow travelers. You could lose a lot, skidding the freight.

Gallow regarded him steadily, and Crenn did not look away. Perhaps so long spent in the swamps, where he didn't have to keep his face neutral or care who saw his grimaces, had made him easier to read.

Or maybe Jeremiah was feeling the bite of Memory tonight too. That particular bitch had sharp teeth, and Crenn could never decide if the sidhe had too much of it, or not enough, or maybe just the wrong kind. Never forgot a grudge, and if they sometimes repaid a kindness with misuse it was their right, as Children of Danu, first upon the green earth and blessed with beauty and viciousness mortals could barely dream of, and long, long lives to boot.

Except the evanescent pixies. Whether they were a symptom or just the Veil taking brief chattering life, Crenn couldn't decide either. He'd watched their dances over Marrowdowne's sinks, the same flickers and glimmers that would lead a mortal astray, shaping swamp gas into globes and spirals and firing it with their own burning chantment. If they were immortal, winking out in one place to be born again in another, or if they were simply so brief and delicate frost or sharp edges killed their tiny humming bodies, nobody could tell.

If you watched them for long enough, you might see a mad sort of sense in their patterns.

Just like mortals.

"Alastair."

He'd only heard Jeremiah Gallow sound this serious once. A very long time ago, when the other boy slipped through the dormitory and stood at his bedside, whispering, *I know a way to get out. Wanna come along?*

"Jeremiah." It was his own voice, from long years ago, both mortal and sidhe. *Okay*, he'd said that night, and the whole world opened up.

"Did you harm Robin?"

He shook his head. "I would not harm her, Jeremiah Gallow. Ever." *Not now.*

"You delivered her to Summer." It wasn't a question.

"And I foxed an entire Unseelie raid to buy her time to flee, afterward." Crenn shook his head. No use in explaining, even if Jer would believe him. "He's right. We'd best get going."

"I shall write a song about this," Braghn Moran commented, brightly. "Three Halves and the curst plague. We have much larger concerns than the Ragged, sirrahs."

"A knight serving two ladies," Gallow replied. "That's a pretty song, too. No doubt the Ragged could sing you a fine one, were she so inclined."

For a moment Crenn thought Jer had gone mad. Almost-insulting a highborn was one thing.

Outright threatening one, even with the name of a Half girl, was another.

Miraculously, the knight didn't take offense. "I have heard that little bird sing, Armormaster; the spectacle did not move me. Her mortal half must have been exquisite, though. A brief blossoming, soon over, but Puck Goodfellow brought the result to Summer. Now she is flown, Summer and half the sidhe dying, Puck Goodfellow vanished and Summer seeking him, and Unwinter breaching borders that have stood since the Sundering." Braghn Moran turned from his vista and took two steps, his loose graceful hands well away from the greatsword hilt at his side, the sunny jewel trapped in its end giving one colorless gleam. "I have many thoughts on the most ragged of robins ever to perch upon Summer's finger, and you should as well."

Crenn's throat had turned dry and slick. The iron hoop in his ear warmed, a comforting heat. "Say a word against *that* lady, Braghn Moran, and it will be your last."

"I? I say nothing, I merely express thoughts. Children of air and dream, no ken to balance their kenning." Braghn Moran shook his head slightly, and the chiming was from his hair, some kind of metal in it shifting and sliding with dull, angry, wet gleams.

A high chilling silver note bounced up from the well of the city, spread. The balance of night had tipped imperceptibly toward dawn, and the Sluagh felt it. They could not pursue in broad daylight, but they could still watch, and when night fell, unless their prey had kept moving, the knot would be tied about it.

Even the mortal sun brought no rest to those hunted by the ravening dead. More than once their prey had fallen, heart and lungs both giving out from sheer exhaustion, and risen in steam-veils as the vicious host took temporary clinging life to worry at the vacated corpse with their smoke-pearl teeth.

A shiver raced down Crenn's back. By all rights he should leave Gallow to it, and track Robin to wherever she had wandered.

Instead, he clapped Jeremiah on the shoulder. Not too hard, but not too softly either. "Time to move, old man." He bared his teeth, Gallow smiled back, and for that moment, the past was the present again, an endless loop.

STRANGE WEATHER
26

The lights came that evening. Jadek Kosminksi's grandmother had known what to call them.

Here in the new country, though, he was *American*, and his mothertongue had fallen away like dried mud during the difficult years after he left. The black coats and secret voices did not follow him, because now he was in this brand-new country where they were soft and placid and shiny, even their faces. His cousin got him the holy American visa, and his other name, his *old* name, was left in the chalky mud and the wide-open fields with snow clinging to their edges, and the graves they made you dig out on the steppe before you got a tap to the back of the head, just one, and in you fell.

Jadek didn't think about that. Now he was Jimmy Kamens, apple pie and cheddar cheese, and he drank the milk-weak vodka they had here only in secret. He had a good job, a steady job, and he had lasted at it far longer than anyone else they had hired.

Nights in the gate-hut attached to the wall—brick for the first six feet high, then chainlink and razorwire, just like the black holes in the old country where people vanished—were peaceful. Sometimes some teenage kids tried to scale the wall in search of kicks, sometimes a tourist got lost, and occasionally the cops called ahead, bringing in a live one.

Although even the cops didn't like to visit Creslough at night. They thought maybe the crazy was catching. During lockdown Jadek would patrol the front segment of the wall, from one corner to the other, and no further. A crumbling concrete path ran along the front, but the side and back walls pressed against a thicket of spiny bushes, firs with their bottom branches lopped to discourage climbing, and swampy muck that could grab a shoe if you weren't careful. Even in the height of summer the water seeped up from God-knew-where, exhaling dampness and a nose-numbing collection of rotting halitosis. Some deep parts of it probably stayed green even during winter, but Jadek could only suspect as much. Going into that mess was a bad idea, and he'd had enough of bad ideas to last a lifetime.

On a night like tonight, with a raw spring breeze rustling in budding branches, he should have felt just fine, especially with a slug of vodka in his strong black tea. He rationed it carefully—one shot per night, just after his midshift break. They called it *lunch*, as if he did anything but sit in the gate-hut and eat his two peanut-butter-and-Vidalia-onion sandwiches. Anything else in the middle of the night gave him heartburn, just like Uncle Vladek, who had disappeared when Jadek was eight, the year before the crossing.

Baba Jala had been shot during the crossing, and every time Jadek thought about *that*, his left calf twitched. There was still a sliver of bullet buried in the muscle mass, not worth digging out now.

The breeze fell off, though, and fog crept in, thick and cold. It smelled of salt, and rotting vegetables. Jadek—

No. It's Jimmy now.

Jimmy Kamens opened the window a crack and sniffed, cautiously. Something familiar, teasing at the edges of memory. Was it iron? No, another metal. Something else.

He took another slug of vodka tea and nodded. Yes, tonight he would stay in the gatehouse, even if the cops rolled up. You were supposed to get out and check their ID, but that smell made him uneasy, made his neck tight and ticklish, just like lying facedown in the frozen, snow-crusted mud, the cold burning against his child-round cheeks, and hearing the footsteps. Booted feet stamping, and the sound of metal clinking, and the jokes they made as Baba Jala's body flopped against the hard-packed snow.

She'd been caught crossing the road, and they probably knew there were more hiding in the bushes, but it was too cold to go hunting outside their nice warm towers. So it was only the white glare of spotlight and the chatter of machine-gun, the *pockpockpock* of the bullets hitting the road, Jadek's calf stinging and his mother's breath whisper-sobbing next to him as she watched her mother's body, shapeless under layers of coat and cloth, contort.

When he was older, Ja—*Jimmy* realized electricity had been intermittent in the city, but the searchlights at the borders never went out. He never shared that observation with any cousin. They didn't want to hear about the old country, or about an old woman facedown in the ice-sharp mud.

That was fine. Except the fucking fog smelled just like that night, right down to the breath of green from the pines. Sometimes, in winter, they exhaled from one horizon to the next, and the wind carried that cold, verdant sigh even further.

Fog all but boiled down the road. Jimmy checked the door. Locked, old-fashioned bolt pushed over all the way and the deadbolt thrown too.

When he looked out the window again, the breath slammed out of him in an onion-and-peanut huff.

Tiny lights flickered through the condensation—blue, then green shading up into gold, zipping in tiny circles, coalescing into almost-patterns. A wave of blue went through them again, a somehow benign deep jewel-tone. The fog moved, following the tiny lights, thickening and thinning across the road like streams of sour cream dropped into borscht. Almost as if the lights were...coaxing it. Directing it.

Don't look, Jadi. You'll make them angry. Baba's voice, from behind the locked door of the old country. *Don't look, but don't ignore.*

The crazy *was* probably infectious. Maybe it leaked out of Creslough Asylum like radiation from nuclear plants. Invisible, deadly, you had no idea, then *pow!* Too late, and you were seeing lights in fog and hearing your dead grandmother's cautions, and smelling her borscht, a warm good smell mixing with snow, and ice, and mud, and the sudden reek of shit when an old woman's bowels gave way, and—

Jadek decided it would be best to look into the tea mug, a big, blue cappucino-bowl with a half-broken handle. He knew it was chipped, but he hadn't studied it before. Not closely. The exact contours of the chip, the white ceramic underneath no longer pristine but grimed with dirt and skin-oil, its jagged edges, the way the glaze had flaked outward from it. There were spiderweb-cracks throughout the glaze, too, and he studied those. The steam drifting from the shimmering black surface didn't thicken, didn't coalesce.

It went by in a rush and a clatter, a soft female laugh that made Jadek's hard, sagging paunch quiver a little in time with his chin and a skittering against the gatehouse's windows. Thousands of tiny fingernails tapping, drumming, and a chill ringing tone like a wineglass stroked with a damp finger. It stroked the inside of his skull, too, that ringing, and the smell became the fragrant warmth of Baba Jala's hugs, with the sour tinge of old-woman smell a child could know as *safety*.

You shouldn't have brought an old woman, the man with the rotting teeth at the crossing had sneered at them. *They're onto us now.*

No. That was a closed door, one he never opened. He was Jimmy Kamens, and he stood guard at Creslough, though most days he drove home in his old yellow sedan and wondered which side of the wall the crazy was *really* on.

The ringing faded. Jimmy's heart thundered in his chest. The tea had cooled, but he took it all down at once anyway, and by the time he finished the long deep swallows and gasped for breath, he could explain the fog and the lights. Something scientific, electricity in the air, water condensing, just weather. Strange weather, in this damp little pocket of an American city. There was no history here from the old country, and the things Baba whispered about when she tucked him into bed and could be persuaded to tell a story could not cross the ocean and find him.

Nothing could.

He repeated it until he believed it, and found he was wet with sweat. He managed to raise his bullish, balding head, peeking through the window.

No fog. No lights. Just the turnoff from Spindler Road and the hum of faroff traffic, the vacant lots on either side strewn with trash visible in the harsh yellow streetlamp glow, and the distant stars of the city casting up an orange stain into the night sky.

"Nothing," he told himself. "It's nothing."

Then he realized he'd spoken in the harsh consonants and

throatcut vowels of his mothertongue instead of good solid English, and he bit the inside of his cheek so savagely it bled. Tea, vodka, and copper slick-coated his throat, and he just managed to get the door open before heaving out onto the pavement, a steaming mess of Wonder bread, blood, onion, and peanut paste. He slammed the door and locked it again, and he did not see the little spatters of light as the pixies, briefly interested, swarmed the alcohol-fuming vomit. Some turned curiously toward the door, but the steel plate at its foot burned their tiny fingers and they retreated, chiming.

They were gone by the time the undigested puddle turned cold.

MERRY CHASE
27

Sliding through the Veil in a fullblood's wake was a good way to turn your stomach inside out, even if you were Half. The few times Robin had been allowed to trail Summer's passage through the layers of real and more-than-real, the nausea had turned her pale and shaking.

This time, with her arm over Pepperbuckle's shoulders, it wasn't bad at all. Something about his steady warmth soothed the cramping, and if she shut her eyes she didn't see the blurring of several places and unplaces at once that could drive a mortal without a half share of sidhe blood into catatonia. Ilara Feathersalt laughed once, a cruel tinkling sound sending a shiver through both Robin and the hound, and it was probably because she'd done some mischief, appearing casually to a disbelieving mortal or spreading ill luck along the edges of her wake.

Motion stopped with a jolt, and Robin's eyes snapped open. She leaned against Pepperbuckle, his warm vitality tickling her hand, his fur soft even through the velvet coat-cloak. Mortal darkness pressed against them both, deep in the shade of a clump of ragged bushes at the foot of a wide field, greening rapidly after a winter's sleep. At the other end, a large building rose, golden light winking through some of its windows.

Robin took stock. The Feathersalt stood tall and slim, her face and hands glowing faintly. Her platinum hair rippled in smooth waves, but the ends knotted into elflocks and that one chantment-blasted gold bead shivered uneasily. Robin blinked, peering at the fullblood; the glamour rippled, sensing her attention.

"Do not gawk at your betters, Half." The words were cool and haughty, and the Feathersalt's chin raised. "There." She pointed, a graceful lifting of one silken-clad arm. "The knife is there, and *you* will go in to fetch it."

"I will?" Robin examined the building. Brick or stone, a wide roof, and something that spread chills down her back.

"Mortal blood means less danger for you."

That would be a first. "And you're going to simply stand here while I do so?"

The fullblood shook her head slightly. "No. I—and your hound, there—shall be leading the guardians left here a merry chase."

"Guardians." *Of course it couldn't be easy.*

"Did you think Summer—*or* Goodfellow—would leave such a prize undefended?" Ilara cocked her pale head. She gestured, the blue-velvet mantle shrinking on her frame, the sleeves melting and the skirt pulling itself free of the ground. Dainty pale-blue leaf-shoes curled around her feet, deceptively thin and probably loaded with lightfoot and other chantment. She shook her gloved hands, five fingers and a thumb loose and elegant, chantment beginning to spark between their tips.

Pepperbuckle's ears pricked, and his eyes fired blue in the gloom. His ovoid pupils flared, tiny blue sparks in their very center, and he looked back at Robin, craning his flexible neck.

Robin *listened*. A faint, faraway grumbling, like a mortal subway. It made her think of Parsifleur Pidge, the poor Twisted woodwight she'd thought to leave the cure with at the start of this whole mess.

Dead, now. Stabbed by barrow-wights and turned to dust by Robin's voice, just one more casualty. How many more would it take?

The thudding grew closer, rippling through the Veil. Tiny dots of light began to sparkle around the small, ragged copse— the pixies, sensing a disturbance in the curled and clotted fabric of the mortal world? The building shimmered once, and Robin took a deep breath. Whatever was in there was likely to be nasty.

Whether it was nastier than Unwinter, or Summer, remained to be seen.

"Pepperbuckle," she whispered. "Run them ragged, boy. And keep yourself safe."

"Safe." Ilara's soft laugh held an edge of ice, though not nearly as sharp as Unwinter's. "There is no *safe*, little Half."

There had better be. Robin didn't bother replying. She simply stepped through the bushes, twitching her black-velvet cape-coat's long flow past clutching branches, and set off across the soggy field, chantment tingling along her calves as her shoes kept her from slipping.

Because if I come back out and you've hurt my hound, you're the first one I'm stabbing.

NICELY JACKETED
28

Everyone was restless that night, both patients and staff. Wendy Campbell, the head nurse on D ward, checked once or twice to make sure it wasn't a full moon. Normally she'd scoff at such an unscientific notion...but at Creslough Asylum, she'd learned not to laugh.

First floor, A ward and cafeteria, second floor, B ward and therapy rooms; instead of low security, B and C were moderate. Third floor, C ward and the zapper, the basement, D ward—high security—and solitary. There were fewer patients down here, but they were the troublesome ones, like Hugo Planck who screamed about fire and wet himself when he got excited, or Sybil Almand who had to be tube-fed when she went catatonic. None of them were *violent*, really...but accidents happened, like the time a nurse somehow got locked in with the Medium all night. The Medium, semifamous Kelly Ashford, had once had a radio show about psychics but now only giggled and rocked and constantly spoke to invisible people. When morning came, the nurse was a heap of nerves, and Wendy had sometimes heard it told that the Medium had told her she'd die in Creslough.

Said nurse quit that very day, but had a massive stroke when she came back to pick up her last paycheck.

Wendy always shook her head, hearing this bit of the story. You'd think the dumbass would have had it mailed, but people were people.

Like she did every night at eleven, Wendy went on her rounds. Her raspberry scrubs were ironed, their creases sharp enough to cut. Her stethoscope—you always had to have one on her shifts, because the tools made the nurse—was polished, glinting in the low light as she creaked down the faded-yellow linoleum. The pink walls, supposedly soothing, were cracked and pitted, and Nurse Wendy could point to a few of the dents or chips and tell stories of how they happened. Right there next to Hugo's cell was a divot where a twisting, struggling anorexic had somehow managed to run into a gurney so hard it dented the crumbling concrete. It also ruptured the anorexic's spleen, and the young man had been taken to the hospital, where he promptly threw himself through a seventh-story window.

Wendy, her cap of dark curls cut close to her very round head, lumbered up to each door and slid the observation patch aside. She peered into each room, blinking like a disturbed turtle. Most of them were nicely jacketed for the night, because dinnertime had been a disaster. Or a series of separate disasters, since her patients didn't eat in the cafeteria. Hugo had thrown his tray, the Medium began screaming about Judgment Day and not even the regular dose of sedatives could calm her, Henry the Happy Wanker had to have his safety mitts taped on, Pearl the Paranoid had begun throwing herself at the wall, and every single inhabitant of D ward caught the bug and began to be troublesome. Even Marcus the philosopher, who argued with invisible professors about someone named Nee-Chee but was otherwise mild as a kitten, had threatened the swing nurse Annie Diamotti with his spoon, saying he'd cut her heart out. He also leapt at her, but Annie was quick on her feet and dodged, screaming for an orderly.

Creslough used to be a state-of-the-art facility, retrofitted in the forties with every amenity, but the slashes in federal funding rolled downhill, and by the time they reached county level they were gouges. The other floors were bursting at the seams, but down here you couldn't put more than one patient to a room, that's what *solitary* meant. They subdivided in the late eighties, before the tune became "redefine and get their asses off the beds and out onto the streets," but you couldn't magically make more space in the half basement, now, could you?

Pearl the Paranoid snored softly, her face turned toward the observation slit. White hair in a halo, tonight she looked oddly young. With that much sedative in her, she probably *felt* young, too.

Not like stolid Nurse Wendy, whose bulk swayed from side to side as she went from one door to the next. The patients belowstairs called her *Ratchet* when they thought she couldn't hear, and that almost managed to hurt even her leathery feelings. She knew that movie, and the actors used swears and it wasn't anything like a *real* ward, which she would tell them if she had time. But she did not, because *she* was busy. She was the keeper of the crazies, and their nurse.

Tiptap. Tiptap. Tiptap.

Wendy stopped, turning ponderously. Despite her size, she was capable of silence and quick lunges when the occasion called for it. The tiptapping came again, at the end of the hall, light and fast.

Shoes. Footfalls. Someone was walking around in *heels*. The definite, mincing little sounds echoed, bouncing down the corridor. Nurses wore *practical* shoes, and even the admins on the fourth floor had learned flats were best. Nurse Wendy had her ways of discouraging bad behavior, and heels were slutshoes.

They were *disrespectful*, and Wendy didn't care for them. A galvanic jerk went through her once, twice, a fluttering sensation in her belly, as if mental illness were catching and her professional inoculation had just reached its limits.

Another sound intruded. A soft chiming, and then a woman's voice, low and throaty, echoed as well.

"Why are you following me?"

The words drew a golden thread through the entire ward. Nurse Wendy inhaled sharply, and had just enough time to wonder who was in her ward, before every patient, even those sedated for the night, awakened.

Most of them began to scream.

So did Nurse Wendy, as one of the guardians of Creslough found her body an acceptable sleeve and lunged to inhabit its warm mortal caverns.

TO RIDE FOR BREAK
29

Gallow skidded to a stop; Crenn almost ran into him and halted just in time with a soft-whispered obscenity before stepping mincingly aside. Both of them were taking deep heaving breaths, and sweat prickled under Gallow's arms and at the hollow of his lower back.

Even a Half couldn't run forever. Dawn was still hours away, and he wasn't going to make it. The poison-weakness had receded, but he was still shaky.

Braghn Moran's cape fluttered as he glanced back, and that was something to worry about too. Why the fuck was Summer's favorite dancing attendance? The Sluagh was nothing to play around with, a fullblood could fall to them just as easily as a mortal, or anything in between. Stepping between the ravening undead and their prey was a fool's game, and many were the songs of betrayals by those who offered help against the Hunt...and those stupid enough to believe protestations of fidelity or aid.

So Jeremiah had worked his way across the city to here, the roof of the Savoigh Limited, cracked with breakage and fluttering with yellow caution tape just like a sidhe girl's graceful sleeves. "Right there." He pointed, in case the Summer knight could possibly miss the scorchmark starred with opalescent weeping slime. Whoever came up here to cordon it off had to have wondered.

It made him think of Clyde the foreman, and Panko. They'd been in the bar that night when Robin first appeared, desperate to break her trail. Gallow had killed a plagued Unseelie, and that moment had led him here.

Be honest, Jer. It was over the second you saw her. Just like with Daisy. He'd soaked Robin up like thirsty earth under a summer rain. Would probably never see her again.

His ribs heaved, and he managed a few more words. "Puck Goodfellow's deathblight, Moran. You can say you've seen it."

"Indeed." The Summer knight drifted across the roof, picking his steps with care as if he expected a trap or ambush. Robin walked that way, too, and Crenn, as if they expected the ground to give way at any moment. Did it come from being of Summer, or from being a sidhe?

Or, more simply, did it come from just being alive? Every world was treacherous, sideways or not.

Braghn Moran studied the mark. "And you have no trophies, to bring proof of your great deed? The Fatherless carried a bauble or two."

"Ask Unwinter." Jeremiah turned away. His breath was coming back. "I have other concerns."

"Indeed you do." Moran bent to examine the blight more closely. He sniffed, once or twice, tasted the air. When he straightened, his expression had changed somewhat, and Crenn stepped sideways and back at once, giving Jeremiah freedom of movement and putting himself right in the blind spot.

Gallow wanted to twitch, restrained himself with sheer will. Cold silver hunting-cries echoed a few streets behind him—the dead were drifting in his wake. Getting closer every time he stopped to catch his breath and gather his wits.

What little of them remained.

If he'd still been playing at being mortal, he might have been on the crew coming out to repair the damage to the roof. He'd look at the blight and take care to bring salt or silver to cleanse it, and be careful not to step in it, or even too close.

"You are slowing, Half." Braghn Moran's white teeth showed, a snarling marring his sidhe beauty for a moment, and the dark metal in his hair *click-clacked*, a streamlet of dissatisfied sound. "You will not last another hour, let alone until dawn."

"My problem, not yours." The marks on Gallow's arms tingled. "Summer might even keep you as a favorite if you bring my head back to her instead of Puck's."

"She did not send me to do so, though. If I cannot find the Goodfellow's head, I may continue to search wherever I please for it."

Slippery little fuck, aren't you. The marks prickled painfully now, aware of danger growing closer. Was Crenn drawing a knife? The bastard was acting like he actually cared what happened to Jer.

And to Robin.

That's going to be really awkward, if you survive this.

It was almost a relief to have a problem big enough to eclipse every other potential problem in his fucked-up life.

"And right now, it pleases me to aid you." Moran reached, carefully, into his cloak. He produced a long, slender silver whistle, white bone underneath the metal glimmering with its own moonlight. He pursed his lips, and blew.

A long, trilling, thrilling tone echoed across the rooftop. The Veil quivered uneasily, clotting-thick, and Gallow found himself wondering what might happen if Puck Goodfellow's ghost was one that decided to rise.

Could a fullblood rise with the Sluagh? Nobody knew. In any case, he kept a careful distance from the blight, and heard, as if from far away down a train tunnel, a strange reverberating neigh.

Braghn Moran lowered the whistle. "Come, my two Half. We ride for break of day, and many shall be the songs sung of our deeds this night."

"Let's hope we're alive to hear them," Crenn muttered, and Jeremiah's mouth twitched.

Robin had called an elfhorse, once, and paid for it dearly. Braghn Moran was fullblood highborn, so the fleetfoot steeds would come just for the joy of answering the call and running under a night sky.

It had been a long time since Gallow had been a-horse.

The Veil shimmered, coruscating twinkles birthing pixies and their tiny globes of light, burning fiercely blue. The color reminded him of Robin's eyes, and Gallow spared a glance at Crenn.

Alastair's hair was still shaken down over his face, and the twin gleams of his dark eyes were fever-bright. "Don't bother looking at me like that," the hunter of Marrowdowne snapped. "I'm here to help you for her sake, Jeremiah. That's all."

"Suitors aplenty for one little bird," Braghn Moran laughed as the Veil shimmered again, and the *clopping* of hooves drew closer.

They melded out of a rip in the night, white horses broad in the chest and long-legged, their eyes full of stardust and their long manes seafoam-cream. Three of them, crowding warm and vital through the Veil's sudden fraying, and Jeremiah blinked, seeing also chrome and high handlebars, sleek tubes and spinning wheels.

Of course. In the mortal world, they could glamour themselves as they liked, and horses and motorcycles shared the same longing to run.

Braghn Moran whistled again, and saddles bloomed on the wide white backs. One of the elfhorses pranced and sidled a bit, uneasy at the confinement, and settled as the Summer knight spoke a word in the Old Language, soft and crisp as a new-picked apple. The pixies darted about, almost drunk on the glamour exhaling from Moran's cloak and hair; the knight made a sudden movement and the cloak vanished with the Veil, melting. His mailed foot caught a stirrup and he was up in a moment, then indicated the other two steeds with a brief, elegant motion. "Come, come, we must away." The faint moonlight of the steeds poured strangely over his hair.

Crenn's eyes plainly said, *Do you trust him?*

Jeremiah didn't bother replying that he had no choice in the matter. He caught at a set of bell-jangling reins, and his own hobleaf boot caught a stirrup. The old grace hadn't left him; he still mounted tolerably well. Crenn groaned, a short sharp exhalation, once he was settled in the seat.

"I hate this," he muttered.

"Pretend it's a motorcycle." A fey delight filled Jeremiah to the brim, spilling out his mouth in a laugh that rivaled any fullblood's for chill amusement. *Riding. Great way to shake a few ideas loose.* "Lead on, Braghn Moran, and let us ride for dawn's breaking."

The Summer knight touched his heels to his elfhorse's sides, and the steed leapt forward, winking out on one side of the street-abyss and appearing on the other. Moran whistled, a high piercing note, and the other two mounts shot after him.

The Ride began.

MORTAL PAIN
30

Of course Ilara couldn't tell her precisely *where* the damn thing was. *When you get close enough, you will know.* And of course Ilara couldn't come in.

The sign on the building, *Creslough Asylum, est. 1822*, gave Robin a clue, and her first step inside gave her the answer.

The place was a madhouse. Robin Ragged, bracing herself, decided the front door was preferable to getting lost in a tangle of passages.

Bright spatters of imagination and terror splashed the walls, broken bits of the Old Language condensing well after they had been uttered by a mortal by chance or babble-truth. Long illness, or or some brands of insanity, could grant a mortal glimpses of the sideways realms. There were ballads of the mad being held in great honor by the sidhe, including prophets or poets, and also ballads of mortals driven into that nightmare country by a sidhe bored or vengeful.

It was difficult to say which were more numerous.

Splinters of the sideways realms glittered briefly and were gone, and unease pressed against Robin's diaphragm. To brush against those splinters was to invite a chance breath of madness against one's own brain and heart. Yes, mortal blood was an insurance against the contagion, but a tenuous one at best. There was no way the Feathersalt would have risked herself in *here*.

The Veil twisted and ran in great streaks, the eddies cold, then warm against Robin's skin even through the velvet. She might as well not be wearing it, since its value as camouflage was gone, but with her head shorn and her neck missing its familiar gold locket she already felt…

Well, a little *naked*. The sidhe didn't believe in anything as mortal as modesty, but a girl growing up in a trailer might feel a twinge or two. The cold wasn't physical, and neither was the cloying warmth, and the thought of Unwinter with his hands on a piece of truemetal Robin had worn at her throat for many a long year was not a comforting one.

He could find her anywhere, following the tugging of the locket, even as its metal seared his Unwinter flesh.

Tiny bits of blue light flickered in the deeper eddies. Pixies, no doubt, and Robin closed her eyes, listening. The thrum of blood in her ears, the soughing of her breath—four in, four out, did she dare to sing even if faced by something dreadful? Her voice seemed fine, a little huskier than usual. The shusweed should have worn completely off by now, and maybe she hadn't broken anything in her throat, screaming as she fell into the sea.

She penetrated the maze of corridors on the first floor, her shoes clicking time on worn blue linoleum. The front halls were brightly lit; an intake desk with a middle-aged woman in blue scrubs slumped in her chair, resting her chin on her hand as she struggled to stay awake. The dots of blue light around Robin strengthened, and the pixies began to chime, a muffled sleepy song. She halted, watching curiously from one hallway as the nurse behind the bulletproof glass at the intake desk closed her heavy eyelids and drooped further.

Well, that's useful. The intake space was carpeted with short faded nylon, which swallowed her footsteps as she edged quickly across the fluorescent-lit cavern. The elevators were ancient but not nearly as old as the walls, and her sensitive nose untangled several threads. Disinfectant, the unsmell of mortal pain, the chemical reek of medicine, a whiff of ozone. Her left hand twitched as if she would reach for Pepperbuckle's ruff, then fell back to her side as she paused to examine the elevators. They had two doors, an outer shell and an inner grill, and she shuddered at the thought of being caged.

Where should I go? The pixies chattered, their tones soothing but no longer slumbrous. The Sundering was long ago, and this place had definitely been built afterward, maybe catching like a nail on the echo of a long-buried artifact. Maybe this place had been a countryside retreat before it turned into a suburban semiprison.

Down, then. An antique sign pointed her toward stairs, and she knelt to whisper at the heavy industrial lock. A few syllables of the Old Language, their consonants echoing strangely and rippling in her mouth, and she pulled the handle. The door opened smoothly; pixies darted around her in a swarming cloud. They didn't rush at her eyes or bare their tiny wicked teeth. Instead, they ringed her and made little gestures, tiny hands spread and patting at the very edge of her chantment-glow. When she stepped through a thick eddy of the Veil, they grew stronger, and their excited gabbling almost made sense.

They've never done this before. Robin tried not to shiver, pulling the velvet closer as she tapped down the stairs.

A painted sign proclaimed the next level down as WARD D, and she hesitated on the landing. There was one more level, true basement instead of half cellar, but the tugging of instinct made her bend and whisper the lock on *this* door open. Pinpricks ran down her back, and she tensed as she stepped through, finding herself at the end of a long, cold, dark hall, locked doors marching down on either side and only faint gleams from emergency lighting along the ceiling. Each door had a slit in it, some locked with small bars, others open.

The reek of pain and astringent medication was thicker here. The Veil folded like a closed fan, and she had to almost push her way through, her pulse rising. The pixies crowded, one daring to flutter down and touch her shoulder, then another. Little movements told her they were also touching her hair, but again, their tiny hands were soft, and they caressed soothingly instead of biting or jabbing with tiny needle-blades.

Another shadowy instinct drew her on, her heels making faint noises. The entire building was asleep, like an enchanted castle in a ballad. Like Fair Elsein, who sang an entire keep into slumber so she could escape with Barl the Huntsman, or Rothindyl the Pale slipping stealthily through Unwinter's own halls searching for his lover and shield-bearer, Peris.

Peris had been returned to the mortal world, and died on a moor pining, some said. One song held that Unwinter had hunted fair Peris, and that even now the shield-bearer was part of the Sluagh, cursing a faithless sidhe lover as many a mortal had done before.

The pixies circled her, almost like a cloud of fireflies around Summer. They loved to flit about the Queen in a golden screen, especially in the orchard during a long, soft evening in her half of the year, the Gates open and her whims ascendant. Robin brushed them away and they followed the sweep of her hand, one darting down to land on her knuckles for a moment. It blew her a pert little kiss and tumbled off, giggling, only to be cuffed and buffeted by some of the others, whose faces were now pictures of dismay.

"Why are you following me?" Robin asked, very softly. Perhaps in their scattered cacophony she could find another clue?

A deathly hush fell, even the faint buzzing of the lights ceasing. Robin stiffened, a horrifying din broke out, and the entire building heaved and settled once over its foundations.

Something was awake.

DAMN'D SPOT
31

They crossed Summer's border at dusk, winging swift and ungainly-graceful through soft air. Sharp, hooked beaks clacked, black feathers flutter-melted in the freshening breeze. Croaking their throatcut cries, they arrowed over the Fernbrakes and coasted up the long stretch of Silverdell, then flapped furiously to rise on the thermals above a ring of manses and sidhe keeps, the homes of fullblood highborns. Some structures crumbled artfully, others stood white-and-green and proud, swords in the gathering gloom. Still others flickered, pale for a few moments and regaining themselves with an effort, candleflames in a draft.

In the distance Summerhome rose, its towers pitiless-sharp now and serried in ranks like a drow's ever-growing dental frills. The cloud of beaks and wings arrowed toward it, and its shadow bled onto the green hills and the shell-white Road ribboning through Summer's domain.

The flying shadow divided around Summerhome like a river around a rock, curl-foaming on each side. The inksplash resolved into a circling coil, and the beaks opened and closed, clacking and screaming, the feathers dropping faster now. As they floated downward, they *changed*. Elongating, becoming liquid, and flashing once, each shed feather turned crimson and splatted against greenstone-and-porcelain sheathing. The bloodrain stank, a cold wet caustic smell, and would scar and pit any surface except crystalline-threaded thanstone. The harsh, hoarse yells reached a crescendo, and the curse-birds began to fall, plummeting and turning to thick crimson fluid in thin feathered sacks, bursting on impact.

Drenched and dripping, Summer's green banners flopped listlessly.

One of the black bird-things did not melt as it plummeted. It flapped once, breaking the speed of its fall, and stretched its three-fingered lower feet. Its wings glinted, each black feather dipped in gold for a brief moment, and it settled above the massive front door, tapping once, twice, thrice with its beak on the carved stone frieze. A chip of greenstone flaked away from the figure of a stag garlanded with evergrape leaves, spattering on the quartz-veined steps below. Their edges were no longer sharp, those steps, and the bloodrain upon them smoked with tiny chortling hisses.

The herald-bird laughed, a dismal, ratcheting sound. *"Challenge!"* it cried. Once, twice, thrice.

No answer came from Summerhome, but the herald laughed again, its eyes lighting with brief bloody sparks. *"The Field of Gold, at sundown. Bring your banners, bring your knights, and let us have an end."*

It mantled, shaking away spatters of congealing crimson, and took flight again. Each wingbeat was a thunderclap, and it streaked for the edge of Summer's country with the wind behind it, caw-laughing as it went.

Inside the Home, empty passages twisted hither and yon. Some brughnies crept about the kitchens, tending low smoky fires. A few dryads attended the heart of Seelie, but the full-bloods had retired to their own homes, and the heart of Summer's kingdom beat sluggish-erratic.

Broghan the Black stirred slightly. His naked back, striped with long thin scrapes, flickered with muscle and mellifluous scales, each of them lined with silver iridescence. He lay tangled in the deep-green satin well of Summer's most inward bower, perhaps asleep, perhaps feigning slumber. His dark hair spread across a spring-leaf pillow, and the lift of his ribs as he breathed was scarcely visible.

A great oval mirror rose water-clear, held in a frame of oak roots coaxed from the walls and bearing tiny scalloped leaves and jewel-polished acorns now shriveled and withered. It held a shimmering reflection of the entire room. A white sword in the center, the glass eye's pupil, was Summer's loose dusky robe, open down her front. Her knee peeped out, a calf, a tiny foot.

Two pallid birds were her hands, rubbing at each other as she tilted her golden head, the echoes of the challenge falling into the wells of her black eyes. Her hair fell in a mass, ratting into elflocks at the bottom. The hard boil on her wrist had spread down to her palm, and tiny pinpricks on her opposite fingertips showed the spreading as well. Livid branches traced nerve-channels up her left arm to the hollow of her elbow, no longer pearly and perfect. Without the draining glamour, her reflection showed fine lines at eye-corner and lip-edge. Sometimes she had played at a dame's austere beauty, but always with the laughing promise of a youthful nymph beneath.

Even the most cherished blood of all, that of small help-less mortals, had not halted the decline. Shapes and glamours trembled at the edge of her control, and she could not *feel* a full third of her domain. Marrowdowne was sliding deeper into the

Dreaming Sea, salt rising through its green channels and the creatures entombed in its murky depths stirring restlessly. Harrow's Dean, Flyhill, and the Sparn were all prickling-numb, nerves gone to sleep. The dagger of Cor's Heart was insensate. The free sidhe had already begun to creep from the borders of the Low Counties into *her* demesne, hoping for a little bit of insurance against the plague's ravages.

Unwinter had issued a challenge.

She lifted the tiny brocaded bag from the innermost pocket of her robe and drew out a single crystalline tube. It was well made, almost fine enough to seem dwarf-wrought; she held it up, peering at the coruscating liquid inside. Robin Ragged had thought to use this to bargain with Summer for a worthless mortal child, but Gallow had set her at naught. If only Gallow had ceased there, and not turned against his queen—but that was of little account. Soon Summer would be whole again, and lovely, and there were three more ampoules of cure for the plague a mortal scientist had unleashed for love of Summer herself.

The heart of all Seelie frowned at the small ampoule, and a tiny crunching sound was a dart of her displeasure clean-shearing the top away. Her nails, crimson-curved talons now, clicked faintly against the glass. The liquid fizzed, and she lifted the ampoule to her pale lips. One or two of her fine teeth had discolored slightly—not enough to notice, surely, unless you remembered how snowy they had been before.

She tossed the liquid far back into her throat and stood for a moment, her entire body stiffening. Her robe crackled like sap in a hot fire, and the sound brought Broghan Trollsbane out of his real or feigned slumber. He sat bolt upright, dark eyes wide, and saw the Queen of Seelie double over, retching.

A rope of black filth dangled from her mouth, and her black

eyes bugged. She heaved, again and again, and when she was finished, her screams rent the sky above Summerhome, darkening now as they had not done in many a year. Lightning stabbed, diamond-bright, and those who had slunk to their mansions or copses lifted their heads, shuddering.

When the call came to ride against Unwinter, few of them would dare her displeasure now.

That was of little comfort to Summer, who now knew she had been cheated. The vials Jeremiah Gallow had brought her did not hold the cure.

No, Ragged Robin had paid the dwarves dearly to fill the glass with holy water filched from the cathedral of Saint Martin the Redeemer.

The same church the Ragged's mortal mother lay buried near, sleeping quietly under green turf.

MUTE BY DEFAULT
32

The Ragged plunged clatterfoot down the hall, something behind her snorting heavily, its foul breath brushing her nape. It wore rags of raspberry cloth, and its horned turtle-head had been barely glimpsed before Robin fled its stamping approach. It wasn't a true minotaur, of course, the survivors of those horned creatures were of Unseelie and rarely left their blackgrass pastures near the Great Howe. It had only one stubby horn, and that was on its chin, but its eerie darting speed reminded her of an illustration of the great bull-creatures from a vast leather-bound tome in Summer's library, its painted lines moving with almost-animal grace.

This thing bellowed in a deep agonized voice, its new-grown hooves stamping heavily, and the pixies darted before Robin, beckoning. Whether they knew what she was after or simply meant to help her escape she didn't know, because the same tug of instinct that had brought her down into this nasty hole was shrieking at her to *run*, for the love of Stone and Throne, and not look back.

It gibbered and slavered behind her, and the pixies lighted on Robin's hair and arms, plucking at black velvet as if to help her along. She resisted the urge to put her head down—that was a good way to get trapped in a hall-end box *or* run straight into a wall and daze herself. The pixies pointed left and she took that turning, and there was a door at the end of the new hall. Screams echoed from either side, and one of the doors burst open, a small, frail woman with a shock of white hair stagger-ing out. Long sleeves flapped at the end of her skinny arms, and for a moment Robin thought she had grown tentacles before she recognized a straitjacket.

There was no time to wonder how the old woman had burst free; Robin almost knocked her over in her headlong rush. The woman's face, distorted with a never-ending scream—did she even need to *breathe?*—flashed past and was gone, and Robin skidded, the light frantic tattoo of her footstops almost lost in the din.

"*NOT MAD!*" the old woman yelled, and a bright violet flash filled the hall. Robin fumbled at the door, scraping her fingers on thick, cracked paint as she tried to push the lever down.

"*KEPT ME HERE, NOT MAD NOT MAD!*" the woman yelled again, and the beast chasing Robin roared. There was a *thump* and a wet sticky snapping sound, and the pixies darted for the door-lock, chiming in the Old Language. The lock yielded happily, Robin yanked on the door—which *still* refused to budge before she figured out she had to *push* instead and tumbled into a dim, malodorous stairwell, slamming the door and fumbling at the lock from this side. She found the syllables she wanted, spat them, and a golden spark crackled from her lips.

That's never happened before either. She didn't have time to worry about it, though.

These stairs only went down, into the basement below.

Robin let out a harsh half sob. A titanic impact on the other side of the door broke the safety glass in its narrow vertical window, and the thing's bleeding snout jammed against the chickenwire that held the shards in. Robin flinched aside, groping for the banister. It was sticky, almost damp, and the stitch in her side was a vicious claw.

Nowhere to go but down. The thing at the door scrabbled for purchase, its snorting and heaving eclipsing any other noise. Pixies, their indigo light-globes brightening to summersky blue, whirled around her sunwise-deosil, and she could see the end of the linoleum, the stairs turning to ancient, crumbling wood. Sweat poked and prickled under her arms, along her ribs.

Robin pitched herself forward, hoping none of the stairs would break and force her to leap into the darkness, trusting the chantment on her heels.

I shall give thee hooves that will not falter, Morische the Cobbler had said, and he'd wrought well. Still, they couldn't grant her flight.

The stairs turned and she turned with them, the pixies giving her enough light to avoid stumbling, hopping nimbly over the holes of missing steps. The almost-minotaur hit the door again, and dust pattered down, fine as sand.

Let's hope it holds. She followed the pixies' urging, their tiny faces pictures of astonished excitement. They settled in her hair again, along her sleeves, darted before her, swirling above her head in a complicated almost-pattern.

She found the bottom with a jolt, a cavern opening around her, and stumbled on sterile earth that had not seen sunlight in many a year before her shoes sent tingles up her calves, righting and steadying her. Pixies arrowed forward, pointing, and it was *cold*. Her breath didn't plume in the freeze; it was a different branch of chill than Unwinter's. Robin shivered, heard splintering overhead.

The pixies halted over a piece of dirt, no different than the rest. Robin glanced around, the darkness pressing close. The mortals didn't store anything down here, they'd simply built upward. Pixies darted down, shifting tiny handfuls of dirt, Robin fell to her knees and began to claw at the dry-crumbling powder. Small stones rattled aside, she spoke a word in the Old Language and flinched as another golden spark popped from her lips. It didn't *hurt*, but it was downright disconcerting.

Maybe, instead of breaking her voice, she'd just frayed whatever rein she had on it? She was able to speak without letting it loose, but how long would that last? Ending up mute by default, afraid to say anything because the massive destructive music might burst free—

Worry about that later. Right now, dig. The dirt all but jumped away from her hands, chantment behaving with unaccustomed force, and her fingertips struck something strange.

A wooden box, its top so rotten it crumbled to dust as she scrabbled around it. Inside, fraying gossamer silksheen wrapped around a thin curved shape, sidhe fabric of an unfamiliar pattern.

The shape all but leapt toward her hands. Had it been rising from wherever Puck Goodfellow buried it? It *had* to have been deeper than this, and the accretion of time and earth should have just shoved it down further with every passing mortal year. And yet, the mad mortals overhead might have worked their own chantment, and a piece of a great wyrm would be drawn to the hot scent of prey.

Or—and this caused another shudder—maybe it rose through the dirt because the daughter of the one who had buried it was near?

The cloth crumbled too, turning to cobwebs so old they lacked stickiness. Robin stared at a plain wooden hilt wrapped with age-darkened, oiled thongs. The sheath was of stamped leather too fine-grained to be animal *or* human hide.

Sidhe-skin clothed this blade. She turned it in her hands, carefully, in case it wanted to slip loose. A small tug on the hilt, and an inch of crystalline glitter stung her dark-adapted eyes. Pixies cowered, chiming in alarm, and she hurriedly shoved the blade back into its home.

Great. Now she just had to find a way *out* with her prize. The thumping from overhead had ominously ceased.

"Out," she whispered. "A way out."

Pixies scattered, then clustered her again, drawing her on. The only other sidhe she'd seen them display this amount of care for...

...Had been Puck Goodfellow.

Well, that answered that. Maybe, with the Fatherless dead or Twisted past recovery, they were paying attention to his bloodline now. Robin shuddered at the thought, following their soft urgings.

Ah. The ground sloped up, and she glanced overhead. Almost tripped again, her toe striking something light but unexpected, and she sidled like a horse, staring at the black mass in front of her.

Coal. This was a coal cellar. There's a chute.

The pixies pointed, jingling, and there was a final massive noise overhead, accompanied by splintering and cracking.

Robin thrust the knife into one of her velvet robe's larger pockets, and scrambled to climb the forgotten hill of black rock with fire in its heart.

TOO LONG ANYWAY
33

They sang about how elfhorses were an easy ride, so smooth you barely realized how fast you were going.

They *lied*. Crenn held on, hunching over a sleek white neck and feeling every step with a jolt in his teeth, hips, shoulders. His savagely clamped hands were knotted in reins hung with silver bells that almost managed to cover the sound of hunting-cries behind and on either side. The Sluagh were curving around their prey; if they managed to make both ends meet they could strangle any hope of escape. The entire city lay blanketed in a choking fog thick as Marrowdowne's worst stagnation, without the breath of salt from the Dreaming Sea or the fecund reek of rotting vegetation to flavor it. Instead, this mist smelled of flat copper with an undertone of bowel-reek, and a brassy sicksweet note that was easy enough to place, once you'd smelled it before.

Death.

The elfhorses galloped, fractious when they scented the fog. Braghn Moran kept them from melting back through the Veil, the fullblood able to override their urge to protect themselves by vanishing. It was a handy trick, but even a highborn

Summer knight couldn't force them to go faster. Hooves hit pavement in a chiming tattoo, and their white shapes flickered. A few of the mortal onlookers would see white horses; the rest would find it easier to see chrome-and-cream motorcycles, low-slung and belching silver flame from their shining exhausts. Crenn glimpsed flickers of pale faces pressed against the inside of car windows, the elfhorse heaving into a leap and its hooves stamping on thin metal, hissing neighs of displeasure as mortal iron made silver shoes smoke and steam. They crossed a main artery, a sound of crumpling and tearing as a mortal accident unfolded, and plunged into a warehouse district, Braghn Moran evidently thinking to lunge for the edge of town. In the wilderness, there might be fewer pockets of concentrated deathly hatred to bloom into pale vapor and scream those chilling high notes.

Gallow yelled something, the wind whipping syllables out of his mouth. Crenn leaned in the saddle, his knees clamped home, and his right-hand blade flickered, passing through a streak of mist as it stretched long, rancid fingers after Gallow's horse. Braghn Moran shouted another few syllables in the Old Language, and Crenn's skin was alive with adrenaline and the sharp insect prickles of terror.

Jeremiah screamed again, waving his left arm madly, and for a moment Crenn thought another band of mist had snagged him. The hoofbeats rose to a cacophony, and Braghn Moran aimed the horses at a stone wall and bent over his mount's neck, urging them on. Gallow's arm thrashed even more desperately, but his horse followed, and their leaps were marvels of delicate, fluid authority.

Crenn's own elfhorse, however, squealed with terror and balked, and the world turned over. He tumbled free, barely able to instinctively curl his left arm over his head, and he hit the wall with a sickening crunch.

A brief burst of starry darkness swallowed him whole. *How bad? How bad did I hit? Oh God how bad did I hit—*

Then the pain came.

He'd felt something like this once before, when a mortal bullet nestled next to his spine and burning pitch ate his clothes and devoured his skin. His teeth clenched, splintering-hard. *Don't cry out. Don't say a word.*

Tiny little trickle-footsteps, soft silvery sneakings, and the cries gathered around him. He'd helped its prey, and gotten in its way, and the Sluagh was about to feast on him. Gallow would be long gone by the time they finished, and Crenn would be only a rag of sidhe bones and torn flesh, frozen to whatever patch of earth had seen his agonizing demise.

The next time the Sluagh rose, his maddened, hungry ghost would join it.

Don't scream. Don't let them win.

He couldn't have anyway, because all the breath had left him. Alastair's body flopped, uselessly, against the wall. Somehow he was sitting, and he had not lost his right-hand blade.

They clustered around him, shawls and scarves of steamsmoke outlining shattered skulls, wasted arms, twisted legs, muscle-meat torn and bones gone spongy with rot. Ruined faces described only by the mist licking their features leered, their hungry mouths clacking and clicking with tiny sharp sounds.

The vengeful dead drew closer, and Crenn inhaled. Broken ribs stabbed his sides, and though he had set himself not to make a sound, his traitorous breath escaped in a low moan.

"*Robiiiiin,*" he exhaled, the pain a giant red beast with its teeth in his flesh, and forced his broken arm to lift the sword.

NO COCKCROW
34

She spilled out into a chill, damp spring night, and the first few gulps of outside air were sweet as wine. Robin scrambled upright and staggered, pixies swirling madly as the burst-open cellar door quivered—she'd had enough breath to use the Old Language, a word so powerful it had bitten her tongue and filled her mouth with blood she was forced to swallow. If the minotaur-thing followed her out here, she was a *little* more sanguine about her chances.

Robin glanced about, her eyes stinging from the faint light after the cellar's close blackness. Running blindly might catch her in another trap. The night was alive with noise—crackings and rendings behind her, along with a cheated basso howl. Bushes and trees dotted about the madhouse thrashed wildly, though there was no hint of wind, and vast shadows suddenly halted, their malformed heads turning with slow, imperial grace.

Other guardians. Bigger than the minotaur-thing, and probably much nastier as well.

A high, sharp whistle came from the other side of the shuddering building, trilling into a high cold laugh. The Feathersalt was either having a lot of fun, or she was trying to keep the shadows more interested in *her* than Robin. Perhaps both.

Robin turned in a complete circle widdershins, glancing nervously at the black hole of the cellar. The thing thrashing around inside either hadn't found the coal pile, or it couldn't leave the building's confines.

She finished her turn, struggling to breathe deeply. The pixies streamed before her, a foxfire arrow pointing south. She was cold under the black velvet, a chill having nothing to do with the dew falling.

Dawn was approaching. The distant seashell-noise of city traffic had quickened perceptibly, a tide turned and the sun preparing to break over a smog-choked horizon. Robin followed the pixies, stepping quickly but not running, saving her breath for when she would need it. Once she was far enough from the madhouse's clutching grasp, she could whistle for Pepperbuckle, and if they were both quick and lucky, they could leave Ilara to make her own way back to Unwinter.

It was not honourable, but she was under no illusion that the highborn would simply escort Robin back through the Veil. It was stupid to expect anything but betrayal from one who had been one of Summer's highest handmaids for so long. Robin's mortal half had fulfilled a purpose, but—

The pixies reached a dark shadow of bushes and a few spindly trees, and Robin let out a soft sigh of gratitude as she gained the shelter as well. The urge to hide was well-nigh irresistible, to just fold down and cover her ears and wait for dawn. How long until she simply decided to find a burrow in any space of the real or more-than-real that would hold her, and bolt the door? There were limits to what anyone could bear, even a Half.

Tiny hands on her, soothing and stroking, pixies nesting in her cropped hair, settling on her shoulders. Her heart finally began to pound a little less, coppery exertion and sour blood in her her mouth. She longed to spit, denied the urge, struggling with her breathing.

Four in, four out. If you cannot breathe, you cannot sing.

She could have let the song loose on the minotaur-thing, perhaps. Her throat no longer felt raw from shusweed or from screaming as she fell. It bothered her, to be afraid of her only weapon.

Well, it's not the only one now, is it? She slipped her hand into the pocket, felt the cold, smooth hilt with a fingertip. There was another hilt to consider, hanging on the belt at her hips under the coat. Puck Goodfellow's short curved blade, its tip welling with greenish ichor, could serve her well, too.

The pixies scattered as she unbuttoned the velvet, her slim fingers flying, and dropped her left hand to the belt low on her hips, the chantment in its knots humming comfortingly.

A rustle filled the tiny clump of greenery. On the other side of the asylum, a long trilling howl rose into the dregs of night.

Pepperbuckle. Robin's head jerked up, and that saved her as the blow landed on the back of her head, glancing away instead of crushing her skull. It was swift, at least, and she crumpled into a bush. Pixies hissed, rousing with an angry buzz; and Ilara Feathersalt spoke a scythe-sharp word freezing them in place. The fullborn bent, her own quick graceful fingers patting at pocket and fold, and she yanked free the knife she'd sent a Half to fetch from its hiding place.

"Many thanks," the Feathersalt whispered, and Robin, her wits mazed but not completely gone, rolled aside in the bush, slashing upward with Puck's dagger.

It bit, not deeply, and dragged, whether through flesh or cloth Robin couldn't tell. There was a gush of foulness, a hissing, and the Feathersalt might have repaid the blow with interest had not a giant golden blur crashed into the trees.

Tongue lolling, ruff standing straight up, Pepperbuckle bared his teeth at the nastysmell danger, and Ilara faded through the Veil, only her hissed curse remaining. It flapped its black wings, but the hound leapt, catching it before it could achieve flight, and tore the life and hatred from it with a snap.

With that done, he nosed at Robin Ragged, but she had lost consciousness. The creaking of the huge bruise-shadows he'd been allowing to chase him drew nearer, and Pepperbuckle whined.

His head rose proudly, though, and his lip lifted to show pearly teeth. A sword of gold lifted in the east; wind rose, scattering last year's leaves and shaking greenbud branches. There was no cockcrow, but none was needed.

Dawn had risen.

PART THREE

UNWINTER'S DAWN
35

From the black, wyrm-pocked mountains to the shores of the Dreaming Sea, the deep thorn-tangles of the Dak'r Forest to the Ash Plains, silence reigned. Pale flakes swirled from a crystalline vault hung with dry fierce stars of no mortal constellation; splashes of crimson bloomed everywhere as if the land itself was bleeding. It was only the scarlet flax, bursting into luxuriant blossom in every corner of Unwinter's realm for the first time in many a long sidhe memory. Perhaps it was a mockery of Summer's verdant lands, or perhaps it was a mark of the lord of Unseelie's mood.

Black pennons moved, crackling in defiance of the still air. The Keep throbbed, a ferment and tumult mostly sensed by the chest, not heard through the ear. High in the knife-sharp mountains, the rumblings were muted but intense, as great wyrms shifted in their caves and small ones in their burrows. Cave trolls and other large lumpen Unseelie remained watchful in the deep shadows. Dwarven caves were shut, their doors barred, and the muffled din of hammer and hot metal reached such a pitch it added to the barely heard breathlessness outside. Drow towns seethed, and barrow-wights lay behind their own barred doors, their waxen-pale strangler's hands crossed upon their narrow chests and a strange vibration echoing against their walls. On the Ash Plains the lean hunting hounds did not course, and neither the fleetfoot stag nor the swift anthrim with their pronged horns, nor did the deathshead hares flicker through the long blasted grass. The Dak'r was full of slithering unseen motion, sensed but again, not precisely *heard*.

The vile, the unlovely, the nightmarish, the desperate, the criminal, the outcast—all these, and more, were welcome in Unwinter, as long as they obeyed the Unseelie lord's will. The cold half of the mortal year was theirs, and though mortals had grown disbelieving, they were still as... nourishing... as ever.

Just as delicious.

A low crimson glow began along the mountains. It pierced the sleeping dimness, and the Keep shuddered once more, from lowest donjon to its tallest needle-spire. The opalescent moat thrashed, as if the Watcher in the water were about to rise. The drawbridge lowered, the portcullis rising with a harsh music of chains and metal grinding, and the deepest thrill yet ran through every branch, hidden or visible, of Unwinter's domain.

Shadows edged with scarlet moved in the doorway's throat. The persistent underground rumbling stilled, breathless silence taking its place.

A high drilling noise pierced the star-crowded sky. It was the screaming of freezing air compressed under a nightmare mount's clawed hooves.

He melded out of the bloody light, the black metal of his helmet chased with silver that took a ruddy gleam from the glow. It was not his usual high-crowned helm but a wonder of dwarven metalwork, a stag's high branching horns dripping with rusty fluid.

Lion of Danu, was one of his titles. *The Huntsman* was another. He had served First Summer as horse-and-hound master, when it pleased Danu's chosen to go riding in the youth of the world. He had not worn the horns since the Sundering.

The rest of his armor was silver-chased as well, a cardinal cloak descending from spiked shoulders, his gauntlets on the reins unrelieved black. His charger was caparisoned in crimson too, its mane and tail waterfalls of black silk.

The drilling noise was swallowed in another, a vast susurration. Unwinter did not wind his Horn or glance back. He did not lift an armored hand to summon his knights. He did not *command* them to follow.

And yet.

The whisper became a rustle, the rustle deepened to a throbbing, the throbbing swelled into a roar. The highborn fullbloods of Unwinter, pale and wasted, sallied forth clasped in their own black armor, riding by two and three on the nightmare mounts enticed from the Dreaming Sea's foaming edge. The mountains shook and crawled as wyrm and dwarf, troll and half troll, and every other denizen of those warrens burst free. The Dak'r seethed, the poisonous dryads and deepwater naiads with sharp teeth and no love for Summer's sun bidding farewell to their homes. Drow and trow, wights of wood, barrow, and blasted heath broad-shouldered, dripping kelpies and snakelike hounds, every manner of greenjack or creeping-jenny came out. The drow towns emptied of all save the very young or the very fragile, and those cried from their windows at the shame of being unable to follow. Some did anyway, creeping in direct defiance of parental authority or their own infirmity. Twisted and whole, Outcaste and clan-member, they blinked against the rufous glow in the ash-choked sky and flowed in a vast wedge, their leader straight and horned at their head.

Unwinter, the Lion of Danu, Lord of the Hunt and the Hallow, rode to war.

SUMMER'S DUSK
36

A pearly shimmer crested white mountains, indigo clouds under-lit with fierce gold. Green rolling hills shivered under a pall of cold dew, and Summerhome lifted its newly sharpened towers, still blotched and pitted with stinking, caustic rust. Summer's sun was rarely late to rise, no matter how long the queen of Seelie stayed abed, but this morning the thick dark clouds ringing her borders cast a sickly shroud as the rich golden orb struggled to mount the horizon.

The highest window of Summerhome was reached by a winding stair, its steps so long unused they had filled with dust and appeared more a ramp. The fine granules rose in a stinging cloud as she climbed, pausing every so often as if winded.

Here, there were no prying eyes, so Summer the beloved, the beautiful, the light of Seelie and the grace of Danu, did not waste strength on a glamour. She was still slender, but it was the rickety thinness of age instead of the smoothness of youth. Her black eyes, starred with specks of diamond light, stayed half-lidded, and sores clustered her cherry-red lips. The holy water had spilled down her front, spreading a rash of crimson scales, and perhaps it had roughened her throat, for the muttering that drove the dust in a whirl around her was hoarse and cracked, not her own lovely ringing voice.

Surely this limping was merely affectation. Surely Summer, the eternal, the wise, the fount of all things Seelie, simply wished to appear a crone? To test the loyalty of her besieged subjects, for some reason none could fathom, or simply for amusement? Stranger charades had been played at her Court, and ended with blood or betrayal, a clapping of snow-white hands and the greatest gift of all, Summer's beneficent smile.

She climbed, and climbed. The tower vibrated slightly, perhaps because its height made the wind a stroking hand upon its string. Half-heard cries, ragged whispers, soft slithering sounds echoed from the stone walls.

The Speaking Tower, it was called, for here Summer could listen to the voices of her subjects, their wishes and fears seeping from rough mauve rock. The outside was white-and-greenstone, but the inside of the Speaking was a pink throat. How long had it been since she ventured past the small red-tiled chamber at its base, where an inch of shimmering fluid in a shallow uvula bowl collected the sounds for her?

Summer finally reached the end of the stairs and leaned against the wall, one thin hand pressed to her side. A modest sable gown clasped her, no heavy mantle or long oversleeves of cobweb sighs softening her outline. Few sidhe would recognize the style—a simple kirtle, rather high-necked and low-waisted—as the robe of a fullblood highborn handmaid of First Summer's, blue as a dawn that refused to rise above the white mountains.

The dust of her passage, scraped from the stairs by a chantment-wind, spilled out the small window in a coruscating stream. It took a long while, and Summer's breathing grew labored between the syllables. Still, she was fullblood, first among the Seelie, even while weakened a force to be feared. And propitiated.

Dust rose in a sparkling funnel over the Speaking Tower. Summer finally stepped away from the wall and swayed, a trifle unsteadily, to the window. The wind brushed at her skirt and her long tangled hair, polishing her skin. The reddened scales and rash drank at the particles eagerly, and they were sanded away.

Summer peered from the casement, as she had during the Harrowing. When her borders were permeable during that most awful time, Unwinter's raids had pierced them, but the Home had never fallen. He was forced to make his own poor copy of the glorious hills, the woods full of birdsong, the white towers and the merriment that filled every corner of her land. His orchard was a thorn-tangle, and he was not even wise enough to feed his realm as she did. Had she not *earned* her little pleasures, ruling such a fickle, deadly, changeful, creeping, powerful folk?

The dust whispered, whispered. Summer raised her right hand to her mouth, set her once-beautiful teeth against the inside of her wrist, and *bit*.

What oozed forth was not a scarlet mortal ribbon, or the thick blue ichor of a drow. It was not the green thin sap of a dryad, or the blue splash of mer-singer or naiad. Not the brackish ooze of barrow-wight, or the thick golden swelling of a wounded gebrial, or the butterfly-birthing white spray of a heath-troll's bleeding.

No, this was a resin such as the trees in her orchard might ooze. It should have been golden-dark, like buckwheat-blossom honey, but instead it was threaded with tiny branching rivers of leprous-green foulness.

Even a will to match Unwinter's could not keep the plague at bay.

She suckled at her wound, her eyes rolling back under fluttering golden lashes. The dustcloud over the Speaking Tower tightened, a tornado of sandpaper force.

Summer ripped her mouth from the wound, and cried aloud.

The sound belled out through the small arrowslit window with its simple stonework, and every particle of dust flashed bright white. On distant hills and in the moors, deep in the forests and in the wide glades, in the green stench-sinks of Marrowdowne and the clean rushing waters of Hob's End, white jolts of lightning stabbed.

The funnel over the Tower flapped and wheeled now, a storm of white birds with wicked crimson beaks. Their cloudshape collapsed, spreading over Summerhome with a rush of wings, and the birds arrowed forth to visit every corner of Summer's realm, to remind her subjects that *she* was their Queen, their light, their love, and their font.

And that their services were required.

For Summer, for the first time since the Blood Morn that had put an end to the Harrowing, was riding to war.

VANISHING GIRL
37

Emergency vehicles swarmed, their lights flashing fit to give you seizures. Walkie-talkies blatted, and for Chuck Tennington, it was just another day doing search-and-rescue for overtime pay. He'd been thinking more about the alimony he was going to owe than sleeping anyway, and Shep, knowing as much, had called him in to join the sweep for survivors. They were saying gas explosion, but there were no flames, and goddamn if it mattered to Chuck anyway, because Debbie wouldn't even let him see little Mona, Debbie wouldn't even talk to her husband of fifteen years on the phone.

He pushed his baseball cap up a little further and stepped along as part of the human chain searching the grounds. Creslough didn't really house any violent offenders, but if it was a slow news day there would be news copters out here as soon as it was light enough. So far they'd recovered four bodies from the rubble, and a whole bunch of terrified, screaming nutters. They'd even found half a nurse's charred corpse in the hole blasted in the basement; the lifting smoke was from a smoldering pile of ancient coal probably left over from the Roaring

Twenties, for Chrissake. The regular firefighters were dousing it, but the coal didn't want to go out.

A knot of bushes loomed in front of him, and he continued mouthing the standard words. "Anyone here? DFD Station Fifty-Three, emergency response." He almost went around the damn greenery instead of poking into it, just out of sheer exhaustion. Pulling double shifts was brutal enough, but he was suspecting he'd have to pay Debbie's damn shark of a lawyer, too. City and county budget cuts were also making it pretty goddamn likely that even firefighters with seniority and some muscle left would be out of luck real soon too.

Well, it was just a cherry on top of a shit pie, as his granddad always used to say.

The hell of it was, Chuck told himself as he stepped into the dew-heavy mess, he couldn't even be sure any money would go to either Mona *or* Debbie instead of the lawyer. He wasn't even sure what the fucking problem was, just that Debbie had told him out of the blue after an early Tuesday dinner *I want a divorce, Chuck,* and that was that. No explanation, nothing, just told him to pack something and get out.

He almost stepped on the girl.

She lay on her side, a punkrocker shock of coppergold hair slicked down with dampness. Some sort of long black trenchcoat puddled around her, and she was so pale and still that for a moment Chuck thought he'd have to radio in *We've got a ten-eighty-seven here, paramedic in south quadrant,* letting the brave guys with the stethoscopes and the slightly less brave ones with straitjackets come out and find out if she was breathing or not. Then he bent, the trained impulse to help overriding any such craven thoughts.

Just as his knee hit the dirt, he heard a low thrumming growl, and looked up to see a golden retriever the size of a pony staring at him, its eyes flashing bright blue.

The girl—she couldn't be more than twenty, he'd card her for liquor—stirred, pushing at the air with one slim pale hand. Branches moved, showering her with heavy dewdrops, and she rolled over onto her back. Her eyes opened, dark blue as a summer sky at dusk, and the dog growled again, an *I mean business* sound that pushed Chuck's center of gravity back. *Squatter? Homeless? No, she looks too clean. The dog too. But—*

She stared at him for an endless moment, then inhaled as if to scream.

"It's all right." He pitched it as soft as he could. "I'm a fireman, it's all right. Search-and-rescue, I'm here to help you."

The dog twitched, Chuck almost fell on his ass, but the girl simply said, "No." One soft, clear, lovely word.

It reminded him of Debbie's voice, actually, and if that dog came for him things were going to get ugly. He wasn't wearing the protective gear that might keep him from being mauled. Just jeans, T-shirt, flannel shirt, and corduroy work jacket under his brightly colored vest, and he'd stupidly put his face right down at attack-me level.

The dog subsided. More branches shook, as if the wind had risen. It probably had, at dawn there was pretty much always a breeze redolent of exhaust and despair.

She stared at him, then put out her hand again, waving as if she had trouble seeing. He reached out, palms down, keeping a nervous eye on the dog, which sank back on its haunches and regarded him intently in return.

Her warm fingers—maybe she was feverish?—clasped his wrist, touching skin since he'd folded his sleeves back and glove down so he could check his watch regularly. He pulled her up, settling her on her feet, and the dog made no move.

He should have checked her for damage first, and when he thought about it later, that was only one of the things that bothered him. The branches rattled, rattled, and the yells of other searchers rose. He was breaking the chain.

"It'll be all right," he told her numbly.

So pretty, her high cheekbones and wide eyes, a faint tremulous smile touching her pale lips. That hair would be gorgeous if she grew it out, and her trenchcoat was actually *velvet*. He caught a breath of a wonderful perfume—greenness and spiced fruit, a golden thread underneath tying everything together, and it made him think of Debbie laughing after Homecoming that once when he fumbled with the condom and her throaty whisper *It don't matter none, Chuck, I love you.*

He cleared his throat again. "There's emergency shelter, and something to eat. Doctors to look you over. You from the building?" He didn't call it *the asylum* or *the crankhouse* or *Crazyville*, you didn't want to remind them they might have a reason to go wandering away at high speed.

She shook her head, and the gold hoops in her ears—yet another indication she wasn't an indigent—swung lightly. "No." Even softer, almost a whisper. She could be on TV with that voice. Or radio, if anyone but right-wing gun-stroking cranks listened to radio anymore. "I am well enough. Many thanks, mortal."

Mortal? Afterward he wasn't sure what she'd said, and figured he must have heard something else in place of *Mister.*

She let go of his wrist, and a faint smear of gold remained on his skin. He opened his mouth to say something, but a big-ass bug darted at his face out of nowhere, and his involuntary flinch sent him stumbling back against a thin sapling that shook another cargo of moisture-drops pitter-pattering down. It buzzed angrily as he batted at it, his hand swiping nothing but empty air, and he almost yelled but that would give it a way into his *mouth*, good God he hated the creepy-crawlies.

He blinked, rubbing his eyes, and breathed a surprised obscenity.

She was gone. Just a faint blurred outline of her body in the leaf mould, it could have been anything. A tinkling sound, like sleighbells in those Christmas movies, echoed all around him, and he plunged out of the small bit of woods, looking around wildly.

Empty grass stretched on every side of the small overgrown hollow. Whatever way she was running, someone would see her. Still, it bothered him, and he reached for his radio.

He stopped, some clear instinct keeping his finger off the button. A vanishing girl and a dog? Escapees from Creslough, or...or what? What would he say? *I let one get away?* The warning in his guts churned, like that warehouse fire when something had warned him to pull his team out just before the whole structure suddenly collapsed.

When that feeling spoke up, you damn well listened. If you wanted to survive, that is. Georgie Rankin, when he had one too many, would sometimes say he'd seen *faces* in the flames on that one. Mouths open like they were laughing.

You saw a whole lot of shit that could make you wonder, working for the department. Chuck shook his head and hurried to catch up with the other searchers, looking nervously over his shoulder every few steps. He could chalk the whole thing up to imagination, especially the warmth spreading up his wrist. By the time he reached the search line again, his mortal brain had decided such questions were better buried.

Buried *deep*.

Later that afternoon, back at the station, there was a Post-it stuck to his locker. Debbie had called, and when he dialed the phone in Shep's office his heart galloped and his palms were moist.

She picked up. She didn't sound angry. She wanted to talk, she said. Maybe things had been bad, but...well, Mona missed him, and Debbie guessed she did too. She'd thought he was fooling around, with all those late nights, but every single one of them was accounted for on his work schedule, and she supposed she could—

"Baby," Chuck cupped his hand tenderly around the mouthpiece, "you know there ain't never been anyone else, and there never will be." Maybe it was the rawness in his throat or the exhaustion, but Debbie started sniffling, and by the time they hung up they had a tentative meeting planned for the next day. To talk things over. Without the lawyer.

He stood in the darkened office, listening to the din outside as his fellow firefighters changed, passed gossip and gas, cracked jokes, or cursed. He glanced at his watch—noting the time when something amazing happened was trained into every one of Shep's firefighters—and discovered, to his annoyance, that it had stopped just after dawn.

FROM MYSELF
38

Maybe they could have kept running, had Braghn Moran not pointed them directly at the graveyard attached to Saint Martin the Redeemer's glowering granite bulk. The knight may have been unfamiliar with the territory, since his horse leapt first—and dropped, screaming, melting in midair as the blessing of consecrated earth sent it back through the Veil.

Gallow's own mount might have balked, but they were going too quickly. He'd been waving desperately, trying to warn Braghn Moran—then the living, heaving weight under him vanished and he tumbled through free air, lightfoot chantment blooming along his legs and instinct pitching him sideways to avoid a half-felt, unseen obstacle. He hit gravel and rolled, sending up a spray of sharp pebbles and dirt, came to a jolting stop staring up at a high, thin headstone with a carved cross at its crown.

The Sluagh-cries rose around them, the ends of a U closing to make a ring. No escape now, and thick mist boiled against the graveyard gate.

A shadow reared over him. The lance sprang into being, jolting against his palm, the point glowing dull red and the butt socketed firmly against the gravestone behind him. It would cut down his range of motion, but the haft could shorten if necessary.

The fullblood hissed, slapping at the haft just below the blade to push it aside, and Jeremiah almost, *almost* replied with a short sharp movement that would bury iron in the sidhe's guts. Moran's hands were empty, though, and his weight was too far back for him to attempt a lunge of any sort. In fact, the highborn shifted from foot to foot, a flicker of distaste crossing his sharp handsome features, his hair swinging.

Of course. Consecrated ground would be uncomfortable at best for one of Summer's fullbloods. And that heaviness in Moran's hair was some kind of blackened metal, beads strung along the strands clacking with mellow sounds too heavy to be anything but gold.

Jeremiah shook the ringing out of his head. "Crenn?" he croaked.

"I do not know." The hopping from foot to foot became more pronounced. "I did not see the spire, Gallow. I beg your pardon."

"Freely granted." His mouth was dry. It was a cold day in Hell, when a knight of Moran's station begged the pardon of a Half. "They'll rise here soon. You'd best be gone."

"I promised you my aid." His hopping should have made him look ridiculous. Instead, it was a cat's flicking of water from disdainful paws. "I am not faithless, Armormaster."

You might be the only fullblood I'd believe that of, right now. Gallow opened his mouth to tell him it was pointless, that the Sluagh ringed this place and though they could not rise from the graves inside the consecration, it would not bar them from stepping over the border and finding him, once enough of them had gathered. Cold sweat oiled his forehead, his ribs heaved, but whatever he would have said next was lost when Moran stiffened, half turning.

Jeremy heard it too. A low hopeless whisper, with the sonorous edge of a battle-cry.

"*Robin*," it said, a hoarse broken voice, and Jeremiah's skin contracted in atavistic response.

It was Crenn, and he sounded like he was in bad shape.

Jeremiah lunged upright, and Braghn Moran caught his elbow. "Leave him. We may yet escape, if I may find a corner where their Pale God has weakened—"

Yeah. Go ahead, Jer, leave him. It was probably good advice. Braghn Moran *could* help him survive past dawn. It was just barely possible, and if Crenn's horse had melted before it leapt onto church grounds the next step was for the Sluagh to cluster him, sensing death creeping onto a being that had aided their prey.

Alastair Crenn was already dead.

The old familiar loathing swelled under Jeremiah's skin, turning the hard prickling gooseflesh into more oily sweat. He pulled his arm free. "You are a just knight, and a fell one." A standard way of making his gratefulness known, while avoiding the insult of *thanking* a fullblood.

Braghn Moran looked ready to speak again, but Jeremiah pitched forward, bolting over gravel that shushed and scattered as lightfoot chantment brushed it. An ancient, lichen-stained wall with newer cement spreading in leprous patches here and there, it wasn't a serious obstacle when you gathered enough speed.

Leave Crenn, for God's sake. He'd leave you!

Except he hadn't. And he said Robin's name when death loomed. Why would a Half assassin fight in the Ragged's honor?

Well, really, what man *wouldn't*?

He leapt, grabbed the top, muscled himself up like a swimmer at the pool's edge, and balanced for a single moment atop the suddenly thread-thin safety. Glancing down and to the right—Crenn had been flung against the wall, it looked like, and Jeremiah almost winced at the thought. He'd heal, but it would still be painful.

If the Sluagh didn't get him first.

Already the mist pressed in a ragged semicircle around him, thickening as they sensed Jeremiah's presence as well. Scarves of vapor described shattered faces, mutilated limbs, the hitching ungainly movements of the furious, unforgiven—and unforgiving—dead. Crenn's bloody fist held one of his slightly curved blades, its graceful shine trembling.

Leave him. Escape. Do what he thinks you did that night in the Hooverville. You're a faithless fucking sidhe, Jeremiah Gallow, so just do what you're best at, and forget him. You're good at that.

He certainly was. Daisy's face had become a cloudy apparition, replaced by Robin's. The thought that maybe Daisy would rise with the Sluagh if he hadn't laid her to rest in hallowed ground was a torment at best. Crenn *and* Robin both had cause to complain of him. He wasn't kind, or particularly faithful, or even brave. He just did what he had to, moaning to himself about how *hard* it was.

Mist-shrouded faces turned, and a peculiar deep sniffing echoed against the wall. One of the shapes darted forward, trailing a long shawl of greasy mist, and Crenn slashed, a slow futile movement, with his ineffectual blade.

A soft rasping behind him was Braghn Moran, approaching to drag him away or simply to see the former Armormaster meet his end.

Jeremiah Gallow leaned forward, just as he used to on construction sites, testing the idea of leaping out into thin air. Tasting it, using it like a whip on his own bitter-scarred soul.

He shuffled sideways as Braghn Moran arrived on the wall, the fullblood stamping his armored feet as if they pained him. Then Gallow's feet left the precarious safety, he was airborne, and he almost laughed at his own surprise.

Even a Half could get tired of loathing himself, and decide to do something else.

Something better.

He landed, the lance springing into bright being, moonfire snapping off its tasseled end and the point lengthening into a sickle-shape. His front foot slid sideways, the fulcrum of his hip sweeping the blade through the contorted mist-clothed creature, whose empty eyesockets and nose-holes were tiny compared to its giant rotting mouth, crooked-sharp teeth gleaming with their own mad corpseglow.

"Back," Jeremiah Gallow heard himself say. "*Back*, foulness. You shall not have him." *You might have me instead, but I'm tired of running.*

Especially from myself.

It screamed as the blade tore, sparkling, through its midsection, and something yanked hard on the lance, trying to jerk it free of his grasp. Any other weapon would have gone clattering aside, but a dwarven-inked lance could not be wrenched away from its owner.

Even if said owner *wanted* to be rid of it.

The tattoos turned to fire, as if the ink itself was tree-roots pulled from groaning earth. Gallow set his heels, leaning back, and said the only thing he could.

"Thou shalt not," he repeated. "I am Jeremiah Gallow, I am Half, *I do not serve, and thou shalt not take from me.*"

A wet ripping noise, a clanging, pavement cracking in an arc before him and more smokesteam boiling up, thick tentacles reaching for him...

...And cringing away, the ruined semisolid shapes of the dead bowing as one like wheat before a hot wind. The clanging became a sound of horns. Not the high silver hunting-cries, but instruments of ruddy brass trumpeting as the mortal sun's scalp crested the horizon.

Dawn had risen.

MOST DO NOT
39

Slipping free of the net of mortals around the cracked-open asylum was easier than she expected. The empty lots outside the asylum walls were full of mortal garbage—syringes, plastic bags, greasy food wrappers, and other urban effluvia—but they were also free earth, and Robin leaned against Pepperbuckle under an anemic maple lifting its green buds in defiance of wasteland. Her fingertips found the scab on the back of her head; but for chance, Ilara would have dashed her brains out.

The plague made fullbloods strong before it killed them, and Robin thought it very likely the Feathersalt was infected. Leaving Court had not saved her, after all. She was also poisoned by Puck's curved blade. There were enough stories about the wracking Goodfellow's poison would cause its victims to assure Robin the Feathersalt's end was not in doubt, and the only thing to worry about was whether or not she'd manage to strike at Summer before plague or poison felled her.

Still…Summer was old, and powerful, and crafty. She might find a way to take the knife from Ilara, and Unwinter would have to step lively to evade the consequences of those snow-white hands holding a weapon that could kill the Queen...or Unwinter himself, come to think of it.

Robin sighed, wincing as her fingers explored the scab. It would fade by nightfall, and the tension in her neck would too. Sooner, if she found some milk. It would have been nice, really, to let the whole matter reach its conclusion without her presence. Even Jeremiah Gallow's fate was beyond Robin's power to affect.

The pixies echoed her sigh, their orbiting now slow and sedate. Strengthening morning sunlight bleached their blue orbs, but they showed no desire to slip back through the Veil or sparkle in a different color. Several settled on her head, a few on her shoulders, and when she lifted her cupped hands to look at her palms, they perched on her fingertips, bending to look as well. Maybe she would even grow used to the feeling of little bare feet and tiny warm hands tapping at her. The ones on her head took turns descending to her nape, smoothing the crusted blood with soft tiny touches.

"Why are you doing this?" she whispered. For a moment she was unsure if she was asking them, or her very own self.

There was no answer from either quarter. For some reason it pleased them to escort her. Sooner or later they might decide to leave her be, or betray her presence to someone else, but she didn't have the heart to drive them off with iron. There was no point. Let them do what they liked.

"You could at least be useful." She listened to their babble in return, the Old Language salted with slang, mortal syllables, and their own strange twittering words, which changed daily, if not hourly.

Pepperbuckle yawned. It wasn't a show of weariness, he was waiting for Robin to set a direction. His left ear was pricked in her direction, and she again considered vanishing, leaving all the betrayals and fear behind.

Except she'd always be looking over her shoulder, wouldn't she? There was no way to know she was safe until she buried *Glaoseacht* into Summer's flesh and hacked the Jewel free of its home on the Queen's forehead. She could hand Danu's Jewel to Unwinter—always assuming it didn't strike her down for her impudence—along with the knife itself, and walk away.

What's to say he won't use it on you, once you've served your purpose? There was no such thing as *freedom* for a Half.

She smoothed the fur on Pepperbuckle's glossy redgold neck. There was something else, too. She'd already killed once in Sean's name, beating Puck past Twisting into a crippled hulk.

The other half of her vengeance would come when she killed Summer, too, or at the very least witnessed the Queen of Seelie's death with her own eyes. It wouldn't bring him back—all she had of him was the changeling-hound, a monstrous sin she would be murdered for and alongside, without mercy, if Summer guessed how Robin had acquired him.

"I would have lost him sooner or later," she said, testing her voice. Smooth and low, some lingering huskiness remaining. The music under her thoughts was full of minor chords, not dissonant but somber. "Children grow up."

I should know. Daisy did.

So did I.

Those awful words, *sooner or later*. Would she lose Pepperbuckle, too?

That was the trouble. Caring for anything caused it to wither. Perhaps Puck's daughter had her own poisonous cloud. Gallow was dead by now, Sean too, Mama and Daisy, everything gone. Stupid Robin allowed a dog into her heart, too. She should drive him off just to save him from her.

"Would you leave me, if I told you to?" She took her hand away from his sleek lovely fur, took two almost-drunken steps to the edge of the maple's clutching roots. If the mortals did not cut it down, it might grow into a tree fine enough for a dryad to coalesce into.

You know it won't last that long, though. That's what they do, mortal and sidhe alike. They destroy.

Robin sighed. Pepperbuckle looked at her, and his expression was both questioning and long-suffering. His sides heaved with deep doggy breaths, and his pink tongue lolled a little. *Don't ask silly questions,* that expression said. If he was weary, he didn't show it.

Her head gave one last throb of pain and settled into merely aching, which was a blessing indeed.

She needed milk. There was no need to try to track Ilara, she would be returning to Summerhome with the knife. Perhaps there would be a third Summer rising from betrayal and murder, for however long the plague allowed Ilara Feathersalt to keep her prize.

Robin headed away from the tree, her heels not sinking in spring-soft, muddy earth. Another thought halted her, and she swung around, regarding the tree. Pepperbuckle followed, halting at her side and staring at the ruddy light breaking over distant concrete spires and towers with interest, as if dawn fascinated him.

Did her voice still work? She had to know, and she could destroy something as pointlessly as any mortal. As pointlessly and easily as Summer herself.

What was it the Second Lay of Tregannon the Faithless said? *Beware, beware, you become what you hate, And every combat turns the victor into a vanquished mirror.*

Mirror. Robin shuddered, her mouth opened, pixies scattered, and the song burst free.

A wall of golden light whipcracked, throwing up chunks of sod and scorchmelted rock. The song throbbed, cutting earth and stone with equal ferocity, and it almost pushed Robin back. Her heels dug in, her eyes widened, and she cut the song off before it could reach its full volume. Her throat didn't hurt, and her weapon was stronger than ever.

Blinking against the smoke—the mortals might notice, the access road for the madhouse was not far away—she almost turned to leave again, but stopped, staring. For a moment, she almost forgot to breathe, and when she did it was a soft shuddering gasp.

The song had divided around the maple. For the first time, the music had obeyed her instead of sweeping away everything in its path as an indiscriminate wedge of destruction throwing dappled golden light everywhere. Not only that, but the buds weighing winter-naked branches unfurled, the tree standing a little straighter, looking much more solid. As if a dryad might open her eyes in the bark at any moment, stretching and yawning prettily as she stepped forth, moss-and-brown clothing her skin and her hair a long fall of exuberant green.

Pepperbuckle, unimpressed, leaned to the side so he could lift his back leg, scratching, and finished the movement with a luxurious stretch.

The pixies clustered to examine the tree and the smoking furrows laser-cut around it. When they lost interest, they returned to Robin, caressing her wet cheeks and crooning.

The Ragged, wakened from a daze, turned and beckoned her dog.

So things *could* change, after all.

But, she told herself as she walked quickly away, breathing in for four counts and out for four, most did not.

MAD PURPOSE
40

They called themselves the Wild Boys, and the Sevens were their little secret. Once, the town had sat in the middle of wheat-growing land, and in late summer some hollows or forgotten corners still held tasseled golden heads among weeds and the edges of forgotten irrigation ditches.

Even the best of towns can metastasize into a city, sometimes almost overnight.

During the big boom in the late seventies and early eighties, factory workers needed somewhere to live, so all the farmland was unceremoniously turned into cheap housing. When the inevitable crash came, a protracted strangling death visited the trailer parks and already-crumbling apartment complexes. The Sevens held one of each, squeezed together just on the edge of downtown, hidden by the freeway's concrete tangle.

If you knew how to do it, you could slip through the fence near the West 80 interchange and follow thin dusty paths through blackberries grown high enough to meet over your head. If you were lucky, or had a guide, or memorized the route—though Brat swore the paths *changed* sometimes—you would eventually come out in a belt of worn-out bushes with dispirited yellow tingeing their leaves, their branches full of shredded plastic bags the wind fingered with a whisper and their roots forcing through a jumble of assorted rubbish. You could spend your time heaving rocks through the few surviving unbroken windows. If you knew about the path under the blackberry tangle in the empty lot off Third and Falada, you could even get there from the strip of good panhandle territory, one of those urban slices full of unwashed vitality and cardboard flats on the sidewalk holding a dreadlocked kid strumming a guitar or tiny quirky stores selling "handmade" jewelry to boutique shoppers kidding themselves about social justice.

Inside the Sevens, though, it was much quieter. Nothing but the wind and the drone of the freeway. There were squatters, sure, and one or two burned-out hulks where a spark or a stray cigarette had spread, growing like Godzilla and starving to death soon after. A few of the mobiles were shredded from the inside like tin cans, and the Boys stayed well away from those.

Meth labs were dangerous, even after they'd burned.

When Tomtom hit the streets at age thirteen, unable to deal with his foster father daily beating the crap out of him, he'd started panhandling on Llorona Avenue and wandering in the Sevens. Others followed, one by one. Juice was fourteen, Brat twelve, Popper relatively old at sixteen but as immature as any. Pinkie, Rom, Glue Clue, and a snotnosed kid who wanted to be called Tiger but was instead addressed as Kitten all made the regulars at one time or another, and there were a few affiliates—one or two slummers who were nevertheless accepted faces and some kids brought in because they had forties or weed to share, but not invited to stay.

Other kids showed up sometimes, hoping to be christened with a name and allowed to roam through the overgrown trash, sidle along the cracked pavement, fire a rock or two at the lifeless streetlamps, maybe even climb up to the third floor of one of the abandoned apartment blocks, where the Wild Boys had their squat. A few stayed. Most didn't. Sometimes you only saw a kid once, and stories grew up thick and rank as the blackberry brambles—*the bushes ate him*, or *some gang kid had a knife*, or *the cops, man, the fucking cops*. Once or twice an "adult"—one of the older homeless—made it past the tangle-paths, but the Wild Boys somehow seemed to know, and gathered around the intruders, white cells clustering a foreign particle. Sometimes a rock was thrown, sometimes a knife was flashed, and the foreigner was escorted back to the blackberries and driven away.

A hazy late afternoon found all the old-timers in the squat, a sea of huddled bodies in manky sleeping bags and crusted blankets scrounged from who-knew-where. The boarded windows admitted small shafts of reddish sunshine. Tomtom woke and ambled, yawning, for the stairs; as he reached the door to the roof he scratched under his narrow ribs and yawned again.

Pissing off the roof was a privilege only accorded to the Wild Boys themselves. Guests had to go downstairs.

Lord of his tiny wasteland realm, Tomtom shook his matted hair back and stretched. He was about to do his morning yell off the roof, an ululating Tarzan call reaching every corner of his domain, but paused, dark eyes narrowed and his sharp nose twitching slightly.

Something was different.

Thick haze over the city made the sun a reddened sky-blister sliding wearily to the western horizon. Tomtom stared, his mouth ajar a little, and rubbed his eyes, luxuriating in clearing away the crust. When he opened his eyelids again, the sun was still the same, and he stared across the shell-pattern of mobile-home roofs below, each crack and hole and spindly tree familiar.

He finally figured it out as the door behind him opened again. Brat shuffled out, and so did Kitten, his asthmatic wheeze not helped by the fact that the stupid kid was already sucking on a menthol.

They reached the edge of the roof, Brat on his right and Kitten on his left, and Kit didn't waste time with talking, just whipped it out and let loose.

Brat stood for a few seconds, then slowly unzipped. "The shadows are wrong," she said finally, flatly, as if she expected to be contradicted.

Relieved that he wasn't the only one to see it, Tomtom nodded. "Yeah."

"What?" Kitten blinked through the smoke. Menthols were *nasty*, but sometimes you could boil them and drink the liquid, and that gave you nice fucking hallucinations. Poor man's acid, Glue Clue called it.

"Don't you feel it?" Brat's blue eyes were wide and distrustful. She had a homemade Styrofoam pee cup, and she wasn't about to let any of the guys piss off the roof when *she* couldn't. They laughed at her until Tomtom said *Kind of cool, right?* Then Rom had piped up about how he read in a book somewhere that in some tribes the women peed standing up, and Popper said something about Kegels and keeled over hee-hawing until Tomtom gave him a smack on the head and told him to show some fucking respect. "Something's gonna happen."

Tomtom sniffed the breeze. It smelled just like the Sevens usually did—garbage, exhaust, rotting insulation, and the raw green juicy reek of spring forcing its way up through cracks and vents. There was another burning tinge, one something in him recognized. A dormant longing almost, almost waking.

"Shit's gonna happen," he agreed. "Maybe someone's gonna attack."

It wasn't out of the question, another gang could decide the Sevens was perfect and try to move in. It had happened before, the Bricks had tried twice and the Dragons once—Tomtom still had a scar from one of the knife-carrying bastards. They all three absorbed this. Brat's urine splashed in a low arc, and when she was done she shook the cup with a flick of her fingers and zipped up.

Tomtom's pulse sped up, a rapid tattoo. It showed in his scrawny, dirt-ringed neck. "Kitten, go down and wake everyone up. Get Glue to take those kids from last night out, and send Popper up here, I'm gonna have him watch. We're on war, bro."

Normally Kit would make some sort of stupid remark, but he was pale as he squinted down at their menaced territory. "Okay." Then he was gone, his footsteps pounding. That left Tomtom alone with Brat.

Which was kind of what he wanted. "What do you think?"

"I don't think it's another gang." She scratched under her red bandanna, then used her teeth to clean her fingers, a sign of deep worry and concentration. "It feels *big*."

"Yeah. Run for the storehouse, take Rom with you. Did Juice come back?"

"Yeah, at dawn. He brought Hot Pockets."

So there would be breakfast after all. The prospect made him feel a little better.

Brat punched him lightly on the arm—her very own mark of affection just for him—and left.

Tomtom, his brow furrowed, stared at their tiny world. Something was moving in the bushes, and there were odd... flashes, maybe? Hard to tell from up here, but *something* was happening down there. For a minute he considered calling Brat back, but she was fast and smart, and she'd know what to bring from the storehouse. Which was just an old broken-down shed attached to an even more broken-down mobile, nasty-sharp thistles crowding it on all sides.

It was the inside that counted, though. You wanted to think the entire world worked like that, but the truth was, you could only make a little piece of it into the place where your outside didn't matter. Once you had that place, you had to do whatever it took to keep it.

If war was coming, the Wild Boys would be prepared.

THRICE FALSE
41

The mortal sun, robbed of its destructive power by a deathly smoke-haze, peered down upon the Field. So did Summer's brazen sky-coin, similarly cloaked; the choking screen was Unwinter's doing. This was the only possible place, a level ground shared by the free sidhe, the Seelie, and the Unseelie, rubbing through the mortal world, the sharp edge of a knife under thick silk. Creasing, rubbing, wearing through, little bubbles of wild chantment spinning at the Veil's ripples and eddies. Pixies sputtered briefly into being, shivered as they scented what was to come, and winked out. A few of the braver ones flittered in the depths of brambles, chiming excitedly. There was a hushed, feverish sound to their tinkling speeches, and once, as a skinny mortal girl with a red rag tied about her head scurried past a particularly ugly knot of thorn-laden suckers, they darted out to look after she'd passed. A perfume of *almost* hung on her, but instead of following curiously they scutter-flew back into the thorns, nervous at leaving their precarious shelter.

A hot wind arrived from nowhere, mouthing the fresh new green on bough, branch, and weed. Thick, pungent, unhealthy growth slipped through each plant. Thistles stretched before their time, their puffs turned a purplish maroon instead of blue-violet; blackberries leafed extravagantly, their thorns stretching to hand-long needles. Sickly saplings bulked out like gluttonous middle-aged mortals, dandelions stretched sunflower-large blossoms all at once, their leaves turning to leathery, blackening arms covering flashes of maggot-white taproot. Mobile homes groaned, sudden growth pressing against wall and foundation, door and overgrown window, vines sliding stealthily even across the poisonous blight of mortal chemicals in large burned patches. The cinderblock mass of the single apartment building trembled almost imperceptibly, and another pair of mortal children on the roof stared at each other. *Did you feel that?*

Faint cries floated on the hot breeze. Clashing and jingling, and a haggard chorus of sprightly tunes played just a *little* wrongly, just a slight touch out of tune. The mortal sun sank, quickly, two fingerwidths above the horizon.

With lengthening shadows, the cold came. Frost touched, at first lightly but then with more authority, blighting the unnatural vegetation. The cold rose from the ground itself, pavement exhaling a treacherous, shallow moan as it contracted. Blackberry suckers withered, their sap drunk dry, leaves on the fattened saplings shriveling. Along with the merry singing something else came—a killing silence, broken only by a vast soft sense of movement in the ink-black shadows. The flickers of almost-seen motion became more definite. Three mortal children broke from the concrete block and ran for the edge of the Sevens, pale and huge-eyed.

"*Idiots!*" someone screamed. "*Come back!*"

The blackberry tangle swallowed them. Thrashing vines woke to sudden frenzied life. After a short while there was a choked cry, lost in another sound—the music, breaking like a white ocean wave weighed down by filthy foam.

The Seelie…appeared.

The eastern end of the Sevens was suddenly alive with curdled golden light. First came the highborn fullbloods on white elfhorses, caparisoned in silver, gold, cobalt, viridian— a panoply of color and grace, high plumes floating from dwarven-wrought armor older than the cities of mortals. Behind them, a crowd—woodwights and dryads, satyrs piping and for once not chasing the treegirls or water maidens, selkies stamping and tossing their long seal-dark hair, shimmering in scale-armor, and behind them all, giants from the high moors stepping carefully, massive stone clubs on their shoulders. The dwarves came in phalanxes, drawn from their barred homes by some threat or blandishment.

At their head *she* rode, a burning-thin, pallid Broghan the Black at her side. Summer's golden hair was once again smooth, piled high atop her head in a cage of bone and piercing ebon pins, her moss-green dress sewn with the scales of selkie armor and reinforced by poisonous *lara* thorns pricking outward, the Jewel on her forehead crackling spark after spark as her palfrey walked. The elfhorse rolled its eyes, foam touching its graceful mouth as if it bore something too terrifying to flee upon its cringing back.

Her Armormaster all but swayed in his saddle, and his eyes were dull. Summer straightened, tall and sleek, and he sagged. The glass badge flashed on his chest, but none of the other fullblood knights had leapt at the chance to challenge him and take it.

The Seelie did not hang back, but neither did they hurry to follow. Fortunately Summer's pace was slow, a sedate, stately walk.

A fresh surge of chill poured over the Sevens, and for a moment it seemed the entire space had become a wheatfield again. Gold sparked on every surface, the shadows filling with coruscating silver, and in the west, a low crimson glow matched the last bloody gleams of the dying mortal sun.

Stonetrolls and barrow-wights birthed from the shadows, cawing in amazed amusement as the mortal sun did not harm them. A rumble underfoot was the passage of wyrms, and the sky darkened with the shadow of vast wingbeats. The darker treefolk—elms, hollies, thorn and sloe, black willow and towering cedar, the tangled arms of *upas* and the slim tall yews, all had given up their wights. Kelpies stamped, flickering between horse and human, their long matted hair streaming with water salt or fresh.

In their midst, the pale faces of Unwinter's highborn fullbloods floated over blackened armor chased with the red of lava. Many of the dwarven Black tribes marched, carefully keeping the bulk of the army between them and the phalanxes of the Outcaste, the unclean of their kind. Drow and trow marched, some playing skirling pipes and others clapping time, a different pulsation than Summer's limping music. The barrow-wights lifted their new-moon blades or clashed their flint daggers together, and a vast heterogenous mass of halfblood, outcast, Twisted, or simply unsightly marched as well, their faces of every hue and their limbs—hoof, claw, tentacle, knotted fingers, or any other shape—moving freely, with swaggering grace.

Before the tilted concrete block of the apartment building was a wide space that had once been parking. Now, crazy-cracked both by mortal seasons and the tugging of the Veil, it yawned emptily until Unwinter kneed his mount forward. The scream of frozen air under its delicate clawed steps added another thread to the clashing, discordant music.

Summer rode forward as well, Broghan's elfhorse following a few paces behind. The Armormaster clutched at his pommel, but his chin lifted haughtily and his dark gaze was as proud as ever. The ragged rashbloom at his pale throat, a mark of dainty teeth, glared in the gloom.

They regarded each other, Summer and Unwinter. His visor was open, but a shadow obscured his thin face except for two burning coals.

Silence fell like a hawk stooping to prey. Each sidhe stilled, and even the pixies hiding in deep thornbrakes did not chatter.

Finally, Summer moved as if she would speak, her carmine lips opening. But Unwinter did not let her.

"*Traitor,*" he said, a terrible weight of condemnation in the word. "*You loosed a plague upon every one of Danu's Folk.*"

She laughed, a small movement of her head as if she wished to toss her hair. The sound was cold as any evening on the Ash Plains while the wind whips and even the well-furred moonlight hares do not venture forth.

"Aye," she said. "A mortal made it for me, to purge the corruption from the sidhe."

A rustle ran through the ranks of Seelie, stilling as her gloved hands tensed on the reins, her elfmount stamping one hoof.

"*Your crimes are many,*" Unwinter continued, as if she had not spoken. "*I name thee thrice false, Eaakaanthe.*" The syllables dropped through the Old Language, Summer's secret truename spoken before all assembled, and the sound caused no few of the sidhe to clap their hands over their ears or flinch. Unwinter's fullblood knights lowered their visors, the small click of each securing ending the rumbling echoes. "*False lover.*" He paused. "*False queen.*" Another breathless pause, and Broghan the Black stirred as if he would intrude upon the conversation.

"*False Summer,*" Unwinter said, his tone cold with unutterable loathing.

She was very pale, very still. Her age showed in that stillness—nothing young can become so immovable.

"You were a false knight, Haarhnhe of Unwinter," she whispered, her carmine lips wet with a quick kittenish flicker of her pink, delectable tongue. *She* did not pronounce his truename, and perhaps a few among her army might have been forgiven for thinking there was, after all, something Summer did not know.

"*I went past the Veil for you, and brought you white berries. What use did you put them to, Eaakaanthe?*" Her name was now a low hollow moan, its edges cold as Unseelie blackmetal blades.

Another rustle went through the Seelie ranks. Brogan the Black slumped afresh. Did he seem even thinner now?

The shrouded sun slipped further toward the rim of the earth.

Who knows what Unwinter would have said next, had he not been interrupted?

The Veil brushed back, and between the two, a single slim hooded shape appeared. Her cloak, of mist and cobweb lace applied in thick layers, was of the finest the weavers of Hob's End could make. When she pushed the hood back, a pale platinum head rose from it, and Ilara Feathersalt smiled at Summer.

It was not a pleasant smile.

"I know what she did," she cried, and the sun sank completely.

Summer's expression changed slightly. Dawning comprehension made the Jewel flash again at her forehead, and Broghan the Black slid from atop his mount, crumpling in midair. Cracks raced through his falling frame, black dust puffing through, and the wind whisked at the drained husk of a Seelie knight, dead before he hit the mortal earth.

In the distance, a thin silver hunting-cry rang. It was not one of Unwinter's, and it sent a fresh chill ripping through the Sevens.

The Sluagh had arrived.

TWIN MOVEMENTS
42

At the very edge of the Sevens, between a small lot full of nodding heads of rotten grain and a listing, blasted shack, a golden smear slipped free of the Veil as well. The hound staggered a step or two, shaking its dangerous, graceful head, and on its back a shadow in a black velvet coat clung. *Find her, boy*, Robin had whispered in Pepperbuckle's ear, and the hound had complied.

As soon as she slid from his back, shaking her head to free it of a ringing din she didn't quite realize was all around her, the pixies appeared too, clustering her with bright-blue glow. They darted at her, landing on shoulders, hair, hands, any part of her they could reach except her face. More spiraled around her, so agitated they shrieked loudly enough for mortal ears.

"*Stop!*" she yelled, and they halted, wings humming so they could hover, staring at her with their little faces set in identical expressions of dismay.

The ringing didn't go away, but her ears adjusted, and she glanced about to orient herself.

Ahead of her, a listing trailer with half its roof gone leered, all its windows broken and frost-rimed. For a moment a rushing filled her head and she almost staggered, thinking she was back in the tower with the heavy footsteps and the chorus of groaning, grinding voices, each one attached to a terrifying, lurching corpse.

Look who's come home!

Pepperbuckle sneezed. The pixies were crawling over him, too, and he didn't look as if he minded. They picked through his fur, taking turns scratching behind his ears and at the base of his tail, and when he shook he did so gently, not to dislodge them.

It was, she finally decided, not a trailer she had ever lived in. She closed her eyes, listening intently, and under the pixie-babble there was another sound.

Crashing. Metal clashing. Screams of bloodlust or death. Thin silver hunting-cries, thrilling up into the ultrasonic and sending ice-cube claws down the muscle in her arms and legs.

The Sluagh was here. For a moment she contemplated grabbing Pepperbuckle's ruff and fleeing. Somewhere, anywhere, was better than this place.

Gallow.

She could not help but hope that he'd managed the impossible, and lived through a night's chase, through dawn and another dusk. If he had, he might need her help, and if not, well, there was the song, and whatever vengeance she could wreak after she was finished with Summer.

If such a thing were possible. Her ears caught the ringing of Seelie metal, the battle-cries of barrow-wights, and the rock-scrubbing groan of giants. The Veil trembled, so thin she could walk through it just like a fullblood, her surroundings pulsing with stray chantment and spike-sharp bloodlust.

She had heard songs of the great battles of the Sundering, and for a moment she thought she'd stepped into one of them, an echo trapped in the Veil's many folds.

There were no trailer parks in Seelie, though. Well, there was Marsdell and Crennaught, where the maimed and Twisted who did not care to hie to Unwinter eked out precarious existences. Or Marrowdowne, where Alastair Crenn retreated to. The swamp was a refuge of sorts, one that left green in your hair and moss on your teeth. None of them were this unglamorous, though.

Well. Ilara Feathersalt was here, and the Veil reverberated with chaos. Had she struck Summer down already?

A small form shot out of the trailer's broken back door, angling across Robin's field of vision toward another broken-down tin shack. A flash of camouflage pants and a filthy-stiff jacket, a bright crimson splotch and matted, elflock-tangled hair of indeterminate color. Pepperbuckle bolted, shaking pixies free, and only Robin's sharp "*No!*" stopped him midsnap.

It was a dirty mortal girl, her red kerchief knocked astray and the sharpness of sidhe on her pale face. Something in the slant of the cheekbones, the wide eyes, and the shape of her mouth, shouted it. Pepperbuckle held her by the scruff, eyeing Robin as if to ask for directions. *See, I caught this!* Every line of him, from tail to nose, expressed pride, and his tail was wagging hard enough to detach and fly free, boomerang-style.

The girl stared at Robin, pixie-light casting knife-sharp shadows on her small kittenish face, and the past folded over into the present again. Was that what Robin had looked like, rising from skinnydipping in the pond to see Puck Goodfellow watching, frankly but somehow not lewdly, his high-pointed ears and strange clothing telling her in a flash that the world was much deeper and wider than adults ever suspected?

A fully mortal child would have burst into tears. This little part-sidhe, though, stared at Robin defiantly, dark eyes full of fire and her filth looking like a conscious choice. The pride was an aching in Robin's chest, because she remembered it herself, the determination to go hungry rather than beg for a scrap.

The same ruthless, rotten, begging pride in Jeremiah Gallow's gaze when he looked at her, as if he saw Daisy's ghost in the flesh and wanted to get closer even if it was an evanescent phantom.

A silver-frozen horn-call came again, and the girl flinched. Even then she didn't look precisely afraid. Well, she looked too terrified to feel it, and Robin understood.

Oh, God. An agonizing choice. Run to help or avenge Gallow, who probably needed every bit of aid he could scrape together if he was still breathing, or stop to reassure the girl, push her through a fold in the Veil so her sidhe side would awaken—though really, if it hadn't by now, with all this chantment floating around, maybe even a dip in one of Summer's streams wouldn't do it.

She settled for striding to Pepperbuckle, grabbing the girl by the back of her jacket, and hauling her free. "You can't eat that." She had to raise her voice to carry over the din. She let go of the girl, who whirled and stared at her, defiantly, the same sullen hunger turning her mouth down.

The same thin shoulders, but her hair was dark under the dirt and grease turning it into a headful of elflocks.

Robin caught the girl's chin and exhaled in her face, the sparks falling from her lips splashing. It was an instinctive movement, and some hidden fire in the thin child's chest woke, reflected far back in her eyes.

Another sidhe. Another little girl caught between the worlds.

She let go, and the child stumble-staggered away. Another dim form shot from the trailer's back door, but it headed straight for the mass of blackberries, and Robin almost winced at the reception it would garner. Anyone with any sense wouldn't run right into living brambles.

They were always hungry.

"Do you want to come with me?" The words left her unwillingly. Another responsibility, another potential failure, another small life turned to dust or shards because Robin Ragged could not stop caring. Could not stop trying, over and over, to save what little she could, to preserve something small and fragile that would otherwise be caught in the cyclone.

The girl pulled at her jacket, settling it, shaking Robin's fingers free. Another silver horn-call rose, and they both shuddered, a twin movement. Even Pepperbuckle whined, his ears folding back and his tail halting.

Robin snapped a glance over her shoulder.

Thick, greasy white mist was rising from the writhing blackberries. Their tendrils whipped, shaken into a fury, and when Robin turned back the girl was gone. Pepperbuckle was taut as a guitar string, obviously wanting to chase her down, but Robin shook her head and pitched forward, running before she realized it.

If there were Summer knights fighting and Ilara had come here, no doubt Summer herself was here too, glorying in the bloodbath.

All other considerations aside, Robin Ragged had business with the Queen of Seelie. Now was the best time to conclude it.

As she ran, Puck Goodfellow's reluctant daughter plunged her hand below her black velvet coat, yanking free her sire's short, curved dagger.

THE DUSKEN RIDE
43

The worst wasn't the shapes suggested under the rotting cheese-cloth vapor-veils. It wasn't the leering sideways glances, or the way the corpsehorse underneath him swayed as if bits of muscle were peeling off as it galloped. It wasn't even the spooky skittering speed of the damn things, stuttering in and out of the visible with stomach-churning wrongness, so different from a fullblood's appearing.

It was Jeremiah's eyes, milky pale now, no iris or pupil. Just… white, without even the tinge of yellow that was a mortal sclera. Without even the faint adumbration that tinted a sidhe's.

Alastair Crenn held miserably to the smoky mane of a corpsehorse, one that kept pace with Gallow's own as the world spun and shivered around them, streaks of black oil on a greased, spinning plate. He'd been ready to die, honestly. Shattered against a graveyard wall and lifting his useless sword.

Then, Gallow dropping out of the sky like the avenging asshole he thought he was, and he told the Sluagh to back the fuck off.

Then…things got hazy. Trying to remember only brought up a white-hot image, a streaming of eggwhite goop like the foaming borders of a Marrowdowne skirler's nest, streaking for

Gallow, webbing him from top to bottom. A contemptuous sidhe laugh, enough to make a fullblood proud, and Braghn Moran landing beside Crenn, his six-fingered hand closing on Alastair's bleeding shoulder and a flood of healing-chantment scorch-wracking him with different agony.

I do not serve, Jeremiah said, the words like brass gongs. The Sluagh had swallowed him . . . but they had not *eaten.*

Now Alastair Crenn rode through a nightmare next to Gallow, and the only thing more uncomfortable than the corpsehorse trembling underneath his thighs was the thought that maybe, just *maybe,* he wasn't dead, and Jeremiah had done the impossible.

It would be, he told himself, just like the bastard.

The automaton wearing Gallow's face lifted the awful silver curving thing to his mouth, and the flaring of ribs under Gallow's red armor—he wasn't clothed in white steamsmoke, like the rest of them—was an awful reminder that he might still be living in there.

The Horn sounded, and Crenn bent over the corpsehorse's stinking neck, silver nails sinking through his eardrums. The sound was curiously distant, buffered perhaps by his place in the cavalcade, but it didn't help. Everything in him twisted sideways at that horrific, inhuman call, and each time a little of the mortal in him died. Or maybe was torn away, added to the smoking, appalling mass behind him.

On Gallow's other side Braghn Moran rode, pale and fey, clutching the reins of his own shattered mount just as Crenn did. It was slight comfort to know that a highborn fullblood was just as deathly afraid as a Half, for once.

They burst through a final suffocating black curtain made of screams of agony and despairing unbelief, the echoes of countless murders and betrayals, howls of inhuman rage and wails of all-too-mortal despair. Corpse-hooves thudded down against cracked concrete covered in juicy blackrotting weeds, and Crenn leaned over the side of his mount and heaved dryly. There was nothing left in his stomach, but his body still tried to rid itself of any superfluous weight. He couldn't see if Moran was feeling the same way, but that was just as well—highbloods tended to hate those who had witnessed them in any less-than-graceful state.

When he straightened, clinging to the saddle with more luck than skill, it was just in time to brace himself for the great clash. The Sluagh threaded through Unwinter's assembled force, not even deigning to glance at the Unseelie who screamed and flinched aside from their thick white grease-ropes. Unwinter's knights had already met Summer's with a jolt, elfhorses and nightmare mounts both crying aloud, and the Sluagh curved forward on either flank, ready to swallow every sidhe who had ridden to war with the Seelie.

The giants were the first to crack, howling as they fled, stamping and smashing woodwights and dryad archers alike with their heedless flight. The Red Clans melted away, dwarves deciding their alliance with Summer had not included holding fast against the ravening undead; great cracks widened in the floor of the battle as they retreated, earth swallowing them. Naiad, dryad, and selkie continued to fight, surging forward to protect the Queen, who sat upon her white palfrey and stared at the melee with a blank, avid expression.

That's not right. Crenn squinted. *What the hell?*

Summer looked old.

Summer had *changed*.

Unwinter, atop his charger, had not; he lifted his gauntleted hands and crimson lightning crackled from thickening clouds.

A slim cloaked figure stood before Summer, the two of them locked in a bubble of silence while the highborn fullblood on every side battled, clash of sickle and new-moon blades, their

263

mounts screaming and rearing to fight with hoof and tooth. Trolls on either side of the conflict fled in every direction, knocking over friend and foe alike, and the dryads had almost reached Summer.

Crenn's heart almost stopped. He was tumbling from the corpsehorse's back before he realized the cloaked female before Summer was too tall to be Robin, and had a shock of pale hair besides, not ruddy gold. Only a single glint of gold caught a dart of dying sunlight in her platinum mane.

The cloaked sidhe girl lunged, and in her hand was an icy star-glimmer. Summer's palfrey reared, sharp hooves thrashing, and fell. Summer rose from the tangle of white limbs and jets of crimson and silver, and the Seelie queen opened her red, crack-cornered mouth. Leprous green spots crawled up her cheeks, but the Jewel on her forehead flashed, and as the glittering dagger plunged into her stick-withered, upraised arm, Summer's curse blasted the cloaked, pale-haired sidhe, who hopped aside.

But not nimbly enough. She crumpled, and Summer shook her arm, flinging the glittering blade free.

"*ILARA!*" Braghn Moran's anguished cry split the battle-din. Crenn landed, breath driven out of him in an inelegant huff, and a streak of redgold bolted by, nose to the ground.

Crenn ran. His own cry, with all the force of anguish behind it, pierced the noise as well, but he didn't hear it. He was blind and deaf, save for one thing—a second sidhe-slim, sidhe-graceful female form, this one clothed in black velvet, moving with quick dodges, almost dancing through the fray, bearing down on Summer as well.

"ROBIN!" he howled, jerking his twinblades from their back-sheaths. A knot of drow and selkies jolted across his path, the melee shrinking, and he flung himself into battle.

A WELL-MADE CUR
44

Someone was calling her name, but the Ragged didn't care. Besides, much care and dodging was needed to skirt the sidhe locked in death-dealing dance all around her. Seelie roused by desperation, Unwinter's forces roused by bloodlust and the scent of certain victory, neither of them mattered.

All that mattered was the wriggling paleness on ichor-soaked concrete, its once-golden hair fast knotting and turning to dishwater. The Jewel flashed over and over, a distress signal, and Robin bore down on the queen of all Seelie step by step.

Pepperbuckle darted aside, his basso growl lost in the confusion. Summer contorted, gained her feet in a lunge, almost tripped as her feet caught in her long mantle. It was absurd, a skinny slattern-hag wearing the rich robe of royalty, and Robin's mouth opened.

A long furrow tore across the pavement, almost brushing Summer's hem. The Queen whirled, darting to the other side, but the song curled on itself, a snake of deadly golden light, and flashed before her in a wall. The Jewel dimmed, its light no longer piercing-bright but mere glitters, rapidly clouding. More crimson lightning crackle-flashed among the Seelie lines, and the selkies shrieked, throwing down their arms. Defeat spread in concentric rings, naiads and dryads fleeing, pixies appearing, swarming Robin's shoulders and head, lifting over her in a spiral, semaphore-blinking almost-patterns as if she were Summer now, watching some groveling thing in her orchard as fireflies veered overhead, drunk on her glow.

Summer fell backward, her heel catching on her mantle again, and the crack of her body hitting the pavement was lost in the bloodcurdling yells of the Unseelie, realizing they had broken Summer's lines. Robin kept walking, her pace unhurried now, there was no need to dodge. Fat ropes of oily white mist threaded through the combat, and Robin finally halted, staring down as Summer writhed supine, plagued madness shining in her black, black eyes. No sparks remained in Summer's gaze; her face was simply bearing twin holes into nothingness.

"*You!*" Summer moaned. "*You* did this!"

Robin shook her head. Four in, four out, the song boiled under her conscious thoughts, ready. If she unleashed it on this plague-stricken skeleton, she might even break Danu's Jewel.

It had to be said, though. "You made the plague, Summer." The sparks flew from her lips, momentarily stinging, pixies darting to catch them, their glow-globes flashing bright blue in the gathering dusk. "Now you may die of it."

"*No!*" Summer screamed as she contorted. Black boils rose on her pasty skin now, great streaks of green threading down her breast, her legs turned to thrashing sticks flaying the mantle from the inside. "*I will kill you first, you treacherous Half slut!*"

You already have. But I came back.

The Jewel...cracked. It was only a hairline fissure at the top of its roundness, but the sound drilled through Robin's head and halted the screaming chaos around her.

Except for that voice, still calling Robin's name. Pepper-buckle loped to Robin's side, his nose flaring as he caught scent of Summer. His lip lifted and he growled, a steady dangerous thrum.

"You...You made..." Summer's black eyes widened, and Robin nodded. No use in denying it, and Pepperbuckle was a well-made cur, indeed.

I should strike her down. I should. She should let the song loose, and cleanse the world of this sweet-rotting filth. For Daisy, for Sean, for all those Summer had killed, for the half-dozen mortal children who had died on her flint knife only a day ago.

Was it only a day? It felt like a lifetime.

Her decision surprised her. Robin's lips parted.

"You're not worth killing." A wondering tone, as if she had just realized it. Robin's hand dropped to Pepperbuckle's fur. He stopped growling, but his comforting warmth never faltered.

TREACHEROUS TOO
45

A cracking, a groan, and Braghn Moran's bright blade severed the life from the flapping curse. He dropped the hilt, metal chiming musical on frost-cracked concrete, and fell to his knees, gathering up the thin, shivering pale-haired sidhe woman. "Ilara," he said, softly. "Hush. Hush, my love. All will be well."

The Feathersalt arched, wracked by poison and plague, the single golden bead in her hair tugging as it sensed the nearness of its kindred. "I...the Ragged...she poisoned..." She choked, and Bragh Moran cradled her closer.

"Do not speak. I never swore my troth to another, though I was hard pressed to." The words tumbled out of him, each one a promise. The glamour-ash fell from his hair, and bright golden dwarf-wrought starflowers bloomed among the dark strands. "We shall ride to the Dreaming Sea, my love, and—"

Her right hand, curled into a fist, glittered as she drove *Glaoseacht* into her knight's belly. He stiffened in shock, and black-laced blood dripped from the corners of Ilara's mouth.

"You...see," she choked. "I...can be...treacherous too... my *love*."

Braghn Moran's hand curled around hers. Tightened, with bruising force, as the final spasms wracked Ilara's body. A jet of noisome wet tar burbled up her throat, out her mouth, and cracks spread through her now green-tinted skin. Dust raced, she convulsed again, and her flesh liquified, turning to sludge and rotting her cobweb-cloak and the dress underneath. Her free hand turned to dry sand, uncurling to drop a small, lost glimmer—a dwarven-wrought promise ring, landing in the flood of muck she had become. Such things were favors often given, knight to lady, lady to knight, and kept to the end of the affair.

Or beyond.

Braghn Moran, erstwhile favorite of Summer, found himself clasping the knife buried in his gut. He jerked it free, his arms empty at last, and flung back his head. His keening cry ribboned through a great silence falling over the battlefield, a private agony in the midst of catastrophe. The golden flowers in his hair blurred and ran together, shriveling, each a star of molten pain.

He rose, his armor shedding plague-rot and shining like a hurtful star, and left his blade next to the bubbling caustic mass that had been his lady. *Glaoseacht* dripped in his left fist, and as he cast about the battlefield, his gaze lighted on a redgold head atop black velvet.

Braghn Moran took a step, staggering as the pain struck him, and regained his balance. His dark eyes lit with ferocious pale sparks, the very color of Ilara's hair, and he took another.

A SINGLE CRACK
46

Jeremiah Gallow, film-eyed and spine-straight, clamped his knees tighter on the corpse-charger's sides. He lifted a gloved hand, his armor running with that peculiar swirling foxfire glow of dead bodies exhaling in a swamp, much as the marks on his chest and arms were writhing underneath. A cold clarity settled on his shoulders, and the Sluagh...stilled.

Every mist-described head turned unerringly in his direction, every shrouded ungainly beast-mount halted, a statue of terror in the middle of cringing, shivering Summer sidhe or grinning, victory-certain Unseelie.

Summer was routed. Jeremiah, the ice-burning dream of revenge swirling around him, found he could think again. Running with the Sluagh was just as exhausting as running *from* them.

Slowly, so slowly, he became aware of something *else*. A red flame, still and quiet, not far from him. No, not red. Gold. Or both, a sword of burning purity trembling at the edge of an abyss. The Sluagh hissed as one, jealous of its new master.

Had it always been so simple? You just made up your mind, and *did*. No second-guessing, no self-loathing, all that vanished in the ice. He had simply decided that running was no use, he'd been doing it all his life, and if it was going to work it would have by now.

It was, perhaps, the only way to master the unforgiven—and unforgiving—dead. No wonder Unwinter couldn't have told him. It was one of the stupid-simple things you had to learn on your own, usually when you'd tried every other avenue and come up blank.

He wanted to say her name, but if he did, they might descend upon her. So, instead, he filled his lungs, fighting the constriction of his ribs as the chill mailed fist of their expectation tightened around him.

You will not have Crenn, you will not have me, and you will not have Robin Ragged.

"You have hunted your fill," he heard a distant, dreamy voice say. The edges of each syllable cut screaming mortal air, reverberated through the Veil, and he realized the words were his own.

I sound like him. Like Unwinter.

The Sluagh struggled against the pressure of his will, and it was hard to contain them. The final test, not just to master the Hunt and lead it but to send it away when he decided enough had been done. Gallow could let them run until they spent their fury, however long that took, traversing moonless nights with the cavalcade, more surely their slave with each death meted out.

Well, what's to stop me?

Daisy's pensive, worn, mortal face. *You ain't as bad as you think you are, Jer.* Except he was, and hating himself for it would serve nothing. There wasn't room in this fight for that luxury.

Robin's voice, a golden wall descending from nowhere, sweeping aside the Unseelie. His own words to Summer. *A Half girl truer than cold iron itself, who makes you look the faithless hag you are.*

Last of all, Alastair Crenn, slumped wheezing against a graveyard wall, prepared to die alone. Would Jeremiah be half as brave in his position?

Half of this, half of that. Time to see what I can make whole.

"You have hunted your fill," he repeated, now conscious of making his tongue move, his lips, his lungs forcing air through his throat to give the words to resisting air.

The Sluagh roiled, restlessly, one or two slinking closer to his corpse-charger, stretching out their mutilated smoke-clad hands. Their aching roared through him, the sullen pointless rage at the indignity of everything, of life itself, and wasn't that the heart of the joke?

He could control them, because he had felt that rage. Was made of it, down to his very core.

His breath crested at the top of the inhale, every mist-shrouded spirit straining against his control, and he spoke the final word.

"*Begone!*" Jeremiah Gallow, once-Armormaster, now Lord of the Hunt, cried.

NOT YOURS TO METE
47

A great silence hung over the smoking, misty battlefield. Crenn kept going in the direction he'd seen Robin take, nervously edging past motionless Sluagh and motionless sidhe, both side's troops caught suspended as if in crystal. Stabbing drow and leering trow, fleeing dryad and falling troll, their blades flashed in the stillness.

Everything had turned to very clear water, hard to force his way through, but something had ignited in him. It was very much like the kindling of his sidhe side, the first few breaths of a different air intoxicating and punishing at once.

There were other flickers of movement. A green flash, as Summer's Jewel threaded with more hair-fine cracks. A slinking shadow, dark-haired, with a strange reddish light filling the grooves in his armor, a hurtful glitter in his right fist and his hair full of fire.

It was Braghn Moran, his face a mask of effort, none of the smiling sidhe beauty left. He was aiming for the same thing Crenn was—a black velvet cape-coat, a ragged mass of slightly curling redgold atop it starred with flash-frozen mist-moisture, a faint hint of her cheekbone sweet enough to make a man's heart cry for mercy. She was turning her back on the shrieking scarecrow that had been Summer, and pixies hung around her, their blue globes clean and distinct. Pepperbuckle, caught in the act of glancing up at his mistress adoringly, looked sleepy, his blue eyes half-lidded.

Braghn Moran lifted the glittering knife, and Crenn strained afresh against invisible bonds. *No. NO!*

The stasis broke. Time snapped like the gut-strings of a lyre-bird hung to dry and fingered by a harsh hand, and—

Crunch. He hit Braghn Moran hard, and the glitterblade went flying. The knight hissed, staggering, and Crenn's dual blades flashed, the left one laterally in the songstrike, meant to fold your opponent over like a just-finished minstrel bowing to his patron. His right blade halted, Crenn straining his entire body to the side, his much-abused mortal boots finally disintegrating under the strain and icy pavement burning his feet. That blade descended with as much muscle as he could put behind it at this angle, and he was vaguely aware of Pepperbuckle's coughing growl and Robin's short, surprised gasp.

The stroke was clean, and Braghn Moran's flaming, severed head landed with a heavy thud. Rot flashed through his slumping body, a high jet of unstained blue ichor curving in a strangely perfect arc before splatting.

Robin, paper white, whirled and dove for the painful-bright glitterblade. She almost reached it, but a great cold shadow fell over her, and Unwinter's boot descended just before her seeking fingers.

"*Robin!*" Crenn yelled again, and the thought that he was about to throw himself at Unwinter passed through him in a brief flash before burning into ash.

The lord of the Unseelie bent. One gauntleted fist scraped

slightly as his fingers closed around the hilt, and the other reached down... and offered itself, spreading, to Robin Ragged.

"*My lady,*" he said, with cold solemnity, and Robin flinched. Crenn's feet, flayed by the frozen-sandpaper concrete, left bloody marks; he almost fell.

The Sluagh made a vast noise, a hot wind tonguing a wet cornfield. Rustling and rubbing, the sigh rose, and Crenn realized two things—Unwinter was drawing the Ragged to her feet, and the Sluagh were fading.

And another thing made three. Bloody prints steamed on the concrete, and he winced as lightfoot chantment bloomed instinctively underfoot. It wouldn't kill him, but the healing would be goddamn uncomfortable.

Unwinter paused, glancing over Robin's head at Alastair Crenn. The bloody sparks in the dark covering his face glinted, swelling with cruel amusement, and the darkness slid aside to reveal the haggard, weary visage of a sidhe lord. Fine black cracks spread up his left cheek, hard black pinprick-bumps at their intersections.

Plague.

Robin let out a sobbing noise. Pepperbuckle cowered behind her, and Crenn almost tripped over the hound as he reached them, his arm circling Robin's waist, dragging her back.

Unwinter smiled, more grim amusement stretching his thin mouth. "*Be still, Hunter of Marrowdowne. I mean the Ragged no harm.*"

"My Lord—" Robin's voice broke on something like a sob. The pixies buzzed angrily, one or two of the bravest darting for Crenn. She struggled in his grasp, but only briefly. "Unwinter..."

"*Peace, little bird. This death is not yours to mete.*"

Clanking, creaking, clattering, the sound of dropped weapons.

Many of Summer's sidhe took this opportunity to flee; Unwinter's scurried in pursuit, silently or with bloodcurdling yells. The fullblood highborn of Summer, their fine golden armor spattered with all manner of ichor, blood, and foulness, mingled with the armed Unwinter knights who had ridden with their lord since the Sundering, his faithful few.

They made no move to aid their mistress, those day-armored lords. Those who had not heard Ilara Feathersalt had been told in murmurs of that lady's testimony, how Eaakaanthe of Summer had sent her lover through the Veil for white shadowberries, and how those berries, crushed, went into unsuspecting First Summer's cup, filled by her favorite handmaiden.

Summer's twist-writhing faded as his shadow fell over her. She was as withered as any Twisted jennygreen now, and the Jewel cracked further as she shook her raddled head, great strings of cloudy hair spread over mortal concrete. She drew in tortuous, echoing breaths.

Robin Ragged twisted in Crenn's arms. She looked up, and the flash of surprise crossing her face tore at him.

Who did she think was rescuing her? Gallow? Probably.

Light bootsteps, a distinctive gait. Jeremiah Gallow appeared, walking slowly, as if his joints pained him. His dark hair held a pale streak over his left ear now, where the first Sluagh to reach him had hit. A silver medallion glinted against his red leather armor, and he halted, gazing at Robin. His irises had lightened, no longer green but almost colorless, his pupils dark wells in the middle.

Even if he'd survived, the Hunt had marked him. That strange, light gaze rested on Crenn briefly, and comprehension filled Gallow's features for a moment.

Silent, Unwinter gazed down at his love, who had been so blithe and merry when the world was new and mortals only a bad future-dreaming. He sank down, one knee touching the concrete, and the Unseelie knights knelt with him. After a moment, the Summer knights did as well, paling as they realized what they were witnessing.

"*Eaakaanthe*," he breathed, and for a moment an appleblossom breeze touched the battlefield, whisking past the dead or dying, ruffling a flash of mortal red tucked in a tiny declivity shielded by frost-blackened bushes. "*I loved you too well.*"

She reached up to him, and a faint ghost of her beauty returned, transparent. "My…love…" she whispered. "Mercy…mercy…" A kittenish expression on that ravaged, bruise-cracked face, and those who knew Summer's fickleness held their breath, wondering if it would stay Haarhnhe of Unwinter's hand.

He smiled, wearily. It was a gentle expression, for all his gaze boiled with scarlet. A single thread of crimson touched his plague-blackened cheek, welling from his eye.

She beckoned. "A…final…embrace?" A hungry glitter in her black, black eyes, and the Jewel made a high groaning noise, a pine in strong wind just before it shatters.

"*We already had one, Eaakaanthe.*"

And Unwinter's arm flashed as he drove *Glaoseacht*, the Fang of old, into Summer's chest. The Jewel shrilled, bursting free and rolling across the cold concrete, and Unwinter tipped his head back, his throat working.

Summer's black eyes closed. Dry dust crawled through her hair, cupped her scalp, raced up from her tender, bony feet, and the Fang, driven into the ground underneath, flashed once more.

Alastair Crenn forced his arms to loosen, and he let Robin Ragged go.

SUICIDE BY HALF
48

Jeremiah's bones ached. Every other part of him did, too. He glanced at Robin again, Crenn glowering behind her like a watchful guardian angel, and the sweet pain the sight of her sent through him did more than anything else to restore him.

Who knows what he would have said, then, if Summer's decay had not become irrevocable?

Robin's hands, both clasped over her mouth, flew free as the ground quaked. A deep grinding noise began, and every Summer sidhe still on the battlefield felt it, a wrenching, welling pain. Pixies streamed away from Robin; Unwinter rose and rose, his full height even blacker and more massive. The grinding subsided, but all of Summer's subjects knew what was happening.

Summer itself, the land that sustained them, was fading.

Robin bolted, her heels clattering on the concrete, after the pixies. Unwinter turned, unerringly, toward Jeremiah Gallow.

"*Gallow*," he said, two inexorable syllables. "*You challenged me once.*"

The lance tingled, its familiar weight in his palms. It burned—the Sluagh had changed him, and the iron scorched until his mortal half could reassert itself. The struggle was brief but left him sweating, and Unwinter nodded. His helm's visor dropped, and the clawing of Summer's vitality leaching receded. Were they all free sidhe now, except Unwinter's?

He could *see* it, Summerhome crumbling, the proud towers shaking. The Dreaming Sea rising in towering, glassy waves, tearing at the white-sugar shore. Marrowdowne shrinking, Hob's End fading and Cor's Heart drying into dust, the fraying working inward, color seeping loose, the apple trees of Summer's orchard turning translucent and another image rising behind them, dark thorn-tangles and the corpseglow lamps of drow burrows and trow towns peeking through the umbrous dusk. The white mountains grew taller, sharper, dells and copses spreading and twining with vines and vile, pale flowers.

"I stand ready," Gallow said formally. One last thing to do. "Provided you swear to Robin's health, Unwinter."

Unwinter's head dipped in a single nod. "I swear to you on my truename, Jeremiah Gallow, that the Ragged shall enjoy the protection of me and of mine. *Forever.*"

That's a whole lot less comforting than it should be. No time to pin him down, though. Unwinter reached for his side, and his greatsword rose, frost dripping from razor edges, the ruby in its hilt lighting with its own bloodclot glow. The lance finished its burning, yanking Jeremiah aside, and the battle unfolded before him, already narrowing to one conclusion.

Why? I'm Half, and barely standing, why does he—

Unwinter blurred forward and Jeremiah danced aside, the lance's head turning crimson and wicked-serrated. A clash and a slither, Unwinter stepping back almost mincingly to gain enough room for another strike. The lance could easily flick in, open him up under the ribs—why, in God's name, was the bastard playing?

Unwinter came at him again, with a darting rush far too quick for his blade to hope to arrive in time, a visible mistake. Jeremiah *twisted*, the lance slapping the greatsword aside...

...And again, he fought the urge to cut the other sidhe down. *He's not fighting. What is this?*

"*GALLOW!*" Unwinter roared, lifting the chiming greatsword with both hands. "*KILL ME!*"

Well, if Jeremiah could want a fair price for his exit, the lord of Unwinter would want no less. With both Summer and Unwinter dead, would the Sundering heal—or would all of them bleed out through the wound?

Behind him, a shadow darted—it was Alastair Crenn, wrenching the glittering knife free of Summer's scorched outline. How many eternities had she ruled, and now nothing was left but a stain on the pavement? Alastair hopped up lithely into a crouch, grimacing as if his torn feet pained him, and gathered himself.

He was prepared to fall on Unwinter himself. For Jeremiah? Or for the Ragged?

Probably for her, Jeremiah admitted, and faded backward, shuffling. The assembled sidhe stared, sensing something amiss, Summer knights grimacing as a high ringing sound pulled an emerald thread through the smoke-wracked battlefield.

He's trying to commit suicide by Half, Jeremiah realized, and might have laughed—except Unwinter halted, sword still upraised.

And then, the unthinkable.

Unwinter...fell. His armor crackled, glamour folding aside, and the leprous-green sheen clustering all up and down his left side, eating through black dwarven-wrought metal.

From *inside*.

A flash of russet, of cream, and of blue—Robin Ragged

skidded to a stop next to Unwinter's supine form, neatly dodging an uncoordinated blow as the lord of Unseelie convulsed.

He was plagued, too.

Robin had shed the black coat, carrying it in a wad. She dug frantically at her belt, and jerked free something strange—a small curved case, oddly familiar. Gallow straightened, the lance losing none of its solidity as every Unwinter knight started to his feet.

Pipes. Gallow's jaw threatened to drop. *She has Puck's pipes. How...*

She wrenched the biggest reed free, leaning back to dodge another of Unwinter's queerly uncoordinated thrashings.

No wonder he wanted a clean death, compared to this.

A small glass tube turned in Robin's quick, nimble fingers. Crenn glanced at Jeremiah, who shook his head slightly, and they both turned a fraction, facing Unwinter's knights, who each laid hand to blade-hilt in an oddly synchronized movement as well.

Robin cursed, a single sharp word that splintered glass, and she breathed another syllable or two in the Old Language. Realmaking sparked, and Jeremiah glanced at her again, hoping she knew what she was doing.

The glass tube had become an old-fashioned syringe, glittering in her hands. She raised her fist, and the needle stretched, long and wicked enough to pierce armor.

I have the cure, Unwinter!

"Get back," he warned the Unwinter fullbloods, and hoped they weren't going to fight him. They might kill, where Unwinter had refused to. "She's curing him, get *back*!"

And Robin's fist flashed down, stabbing.

DAISY, COME BACK
49

The world stopped. Her hands tingled with Realmaking, and the needle slowed, then quickened as it forced a way through the armor and into flesh beneath.

Unwinter screamed, the massive noise passing by her ear like a freight train's roar, wind stinging her eyes and yanking her hair. She hung on, grimly, and slapped her free hand over the plunger. *Hope I remembered how a syringe is made clearly enough*, she thought, and *pushed*, muscle standing out in her arms and shoulders as the thick sludge-material stirred inside the glass tube.

And, *I hope Puck didn't hide the real cure elsewhere.*

Last of all, *I hope Jeremiah and Crenn are all right.*

So much hope. Unwinter's fist arrived out of nowhere, and she couldn't dodge this one in time. Stars flashed, she *flew*, but she had pushed the plunger down all the way, she was *sure* of it, hadn't she?

Hadn't she?

She hit something hard with a crunch, it gave more resiliently than she expected, and she tumbled to the ground in a heap, Alastair Crenn's limbs tangling with hers. Somehow he had his shoulder in the way, so her head bounced on *him* instead of on concrete. Stunned and breathless, she went limp, Unwinter's howl blasting a crimson streak straight up into the clouded sky.

The world turned sideways, and Robin Ragged surfaced a few moments later, her head ringing, her cheek bruised, and a long scrape up her arm from the concrete. Crenn lay crumpled underneath her, and Pepperbuckle's claws scrabbled as he reached her, his long pink tongue frantically licking the side of her face, his wet cold nose and hot breath confusing her.

Crenn's dark eyes opened. This close, she could see the fine grain of his skin, the line between his pupil and iris, the exact sheen of his hair. The moss had crumbled away; the curls were black and springy, and looked very soft.

They stared at each other, their noses a bare inch apart, and deep in his gaze, something familiar stirred.

He had no right to look so lost. No right at all to look so hopeful, so despairing. He had gagged her with shusweed and brought her to Summer. Summer had taken his scars away.

Yet he'd saved her life twice now.

Robin. A deep, imperative voice. *You're not done yet.*

She rolled aside, wishing she hadn't seen his vulnerability *or* his slight flinch as she pushed herself away. He probably thought she loathed him.

Well, she did, didn't she? Or she could have, just like she could have left Sean to his fate or Gallow to his, if only she didn't care. If only their pain or sweetness did not strike an answer in her, if only she could have refused to see.

Well, it didn't matter. She grabbed a handful of Pepperbuckle's fur, he made no noise as she hauled herself upright.

"Don't," Jeremiah Gallow said behind her. "Don't make me kill you."

She whirled, and saw Unwinter's convulsions had quieted. Hopefully the cure was working.

Jeremiah Gallow, the new white streak in his hair glaring in the dimness of what was only a mortal night now, stood with his glowing lance slanting slightly up, held across his body like a bar. It was a pikeman's defense, and the mass of Unwinter's fullbloods, their pale faces alight with bloodlust, pressed toward him.

Her face hurt. Her heels clattered as she lunged for the wad of black velvet. Pixies crawled over it, piping at her in the stillness, and it seemed to take forever to reach the material, yank it up—

A single green gleam fell into her palm, shrunk to the size of a marble, singing in distress. She closed her fingers gingerly over it and ran for Gallow, and her expression must have been wild, for the assembled fullbloods fell back.

They remembered her voice, and were wary of it, at least.

Behind her, Unwinter groaned. The sound wasn't cold enough to hurt, but it was unmistakably *his* voice. He would probably live. And if he did, he was Unwinter, and there had to be something else.

There had to be a Summer.

Do it, Robin. Do it now.

"Jer!" she yelled, and her voice wasn't her own for a moment. It was lighter, and laughing, a timbre and cadence she knew as well as she knew her own. "*Turn around!*"

It was Daisy's voice, and she hated herself for using it even as Jeremiah turned, the lance slipping between his fingers and winking out—

And Robin Ragged rammed Danu's Jewel against his armored chest as his arms closed around her. Realmaking sparked and oscillated around her fingers again, and Jeremiah was squeezing her hard enough to rob her of breath.

Did he think she was Daisy, come back to him? Her heart and her face both ached.

The Jewel stabbed through armor, through fine linen, and met flesh. Realmaking pierced, shone, spun, and Jeremiah Gallow stiffened. He screamed, a long trailing cry of anguish, and if he had not been slightly changed by the Sluagh he might well have died of shock in that instant alone.

She caught him as he sagged. But he was so much heavier than she, especially in armor, and they both went down in a tangle, Robin's knee barking the cold paving painfully. She bent over him, and a tremor passed through every Summer sidhe.

Forgive me, Robin Ragged wanted to say. *I can't let all of Summer die, and you and me and Pepperbuckle with it.*

But she didn't have the breath.

DID DANU...
50

🌹⚔️

*P*ain. *The agony poured through Jeremiah Gallow, in chan-*
nels still smoking-raw from the passage of the unforgiven dead.
Summer trembled, and Danu's Jewel screamed. Her folk were of
the moonlight and the cold spring dawn, of glamour and cruelty,
of dancing and making merry, of elfhorse and elflock.

In some place beyond the Veil, did the goddess herself lift her
head, sensing their cries? Did she peer into her fountain, and did
her ageless brow wrinkle slightly as she saw a battlefield, blood
spilled not in her honor but for vile selfishness? Did she regret, even
for a moment, her creation, or the birthing of her second children,
who even now swarmed the kingdom she had given them, poison-
ing it with filth and rubble?

None were blameless, not even a goddess.

Did Danu peer a little more closely, stirring just slightly in
one direction? Did one gentle fingertip come down, touching the
trembling surface of her fountain, rippling outward as one thing
changed and another did not? Who could tell?

A great hush swept through the Veil, those small ripples touch-
ing each other, and did the fingertip dip again, ever so gently, just
the faintest breath of a nudge?

Sooner or later, all children grow. Control is not possible.

But encouragement and aid, well... those are always possible.

Did Danu Herself smile as she regarded them, these children fighting over dropped toys, now clinging to each other and weeping? Tears of relief, or tears of pain, a green gleam on the chest of a knight...

Did Danu pause? Did she breathe across the surface of the fountain, as her garden shimmered half-wild in the folds of the Veil, a tamed wilderness echoed in light and shadow all through the real and more-than-real?

Or is she merely a fiction, and the slices of real and more-than-real, stacked in a glorious fan, nothing more than the sum of choice, of consequence?

What is known is merely this: Danu's Jewel...

...had found a new bearer.

Summer was alive.

LAST OWED
51

When he regained consciousness, he was surprised it didn't hurt.

The first thing he saw was a white streak floating in dimness. The sidhe bending over him was attenuated from some illness, his cheeks thin and his long nose wrinkled slightly. For all that, he looked very familiar.

Alastair Crenn stared with blurring eyes, testing his fingers and toes. They appeared to be all there. A thin, iron-strong arm slid under his shoulders, and he was lifted. The horn at his mouth held *lithori*, an expensive squeezing of evergrape and chantment, a fiery clarity sliding down his throat and detonating in his stomach.

The streak in his hair was even more pronounced now, and Jeremiah Gallow's bleached irises glowed slightly. He laid Crenn back against soft, snow-white pillows, and through a casement came a fragrant breeze redolent of blossom and cut grass.

Lithori was a restorative. After a little while, Crenn found his left hand patting at his belt, and Gallow smiled.

"Relax." Even his voice was slightly changed. Deeper, more

resonant. "We took your swords off so you could rest. You have new boots, too."

Crenn's lips wanted to shape the word *where*, but that was stupid. He settled for the only other question.

"Robin?" he croaked. His throat was dry. Gallow propped him up, steadied his hand around the horn of *lithori* before answering.

"I asked her to stay." The former Armormaster settled into a chair at the bedside. The room was close and cosy, an applewood fire burning fragrant and bright, but not overheating. The cool breeze from the window came again, touching Crenn's hands and face.

Persistent unease sharpened into a realization.

Gallow didn't *smell* right. The smoke-tang of iron clinging to mortal blood didn't exude from him nearly as strongly.

"I said *Summer needs a lady*." Gallow's broad shoulders hunched, and he picked up something dark and curved from the chair's arm. "She said I'd no doubt find many applicants for the position."

The wince made sense. Crenn's hands steadied. The evergrape was working wonders. Plus, if he was any judge, he was in Summer. But that didn't smell right, either.

"Ouch," Crenn said finally, and could almost feel the ruefulness spread over his own expression. Nice to know he wasn't the only one rejected. "So...um..."

A slight easing crossed Gallow's face. "I think she's north, at the edge of Marrowdowne." Gallow frowned, turning the curved shape over in his hands. "But things are...difficult. The merger is underway."

Crenn decided he could sit up without the pillows. He did so, cautiously testing every limb. The *lithori* burned, and the sharp rich colors around him told him he wasn't anywhere near the mortal realm.

But if it wasn't Summer, then *where*?

"Take it very slowly, Jer." He had to clear his throat twice. "But not too slowly, because after I can stand, and thank you for the boots, I'm going after Robin."

"I thought as much." Jeremiah nodded. "Crenn..." He dropped the curved thing in his lap and unbuttoned his fine linen shirt, Hob's End weaving by the look of it. A green glow spread up his chest. "Robin. I think she...I don't know. She cured Unwinter, too. He's in his Keep, but I sometimes see him in the halls, here. And he sees me. The Sluagh began it, tipping me away from Half." The tattoos moved sluggishly, cradling the Jewel. Its light ribboned through them, a thin thread at the center of every inked line. Somehow, Danu's mark of favor wasn't repelled by the iron in the tats, or by mortal blood. "The Sundering is healing. Summer and Unwinter are merging. It's starting at the Keep and the Home, and spreading out."

Crenn's throat was dry. He set the rhyton carefully on the small inlaid table crouching near the bedside as well. How long had Jeremiah been sitting there, waiting for him to wake up? "And when it's done?"

Jeremiah shrugged. "Then he can have the Jewel and welcome. If I can find a way to get rid of it without dying."

"That, um, could be a problem."

Gallow smiled. It was a flicker of his old self, and it faded almost as soon as Crenn witnessed it. "Which is why I want you to promise me something."

"Do I have to?" Crenn winced, swinging his legs out of the bed. The new boots were there, as promised—brown hobleafs, light and supple, matching Crenn's leathers perfectly. It occurred to him that sarcasm might not be the best avenue. If Jer was growing—or being *pulled*—away from his mortal side, it could be distinctly unhealthy.

"Don't worry, you'll like it." Gallow stood, crossed to the window casement. His back was rigid, and for a moment Crenn's eyelids twitched. It was like seeing a photo develop on a plate in a bath of shimmering chemicals, a ghost-image.

Spiked armor, broad shoulders, and a shock of white thistle-down hair. A soft chill spread through the room, the crispness of an autumn night.

He busied himself with bending to twitch his chantment-cleaned socks and enclose his feet in the hobleafs. Their chantments woke, humming slightly, and he almost didn't hear what Gallow would ask of him, for the new King said it as if he had a rock in his throat, as if it pained him.

Crenn straightened. He stared at Jeremiah's back. He said nothing.

"Please, Al." The fading shadow of his old friend—his *oldest* friend, his only friend, even though Crenn hated him—spoke through an almost-sidhe's throat. "I would rather it be...a friend."

Goddamn it. You selfish bastard.

The very same selfish bastard had leapt in front of the ravening undead for him. Maybe Gallow hated him, too.

Maybe mortal hate was close to love. Who knew?

The curved thing in the chair was a shard of mortal glass, its crusted edge wrapped with a few thin gold-red hairs. It shimmered, just as the glitter-knife of Unwinter's had, and Crenn's gorge rose.

A glass knife for Unwinter, and one for Summer. Was Jer hoping he'd take it?

"Yes," he said finally. Harshly, through the obstruction in his throat. "I swear it to you, I will."

Jeremiah nodded, a brisk movement. "I shall hold you to your promise, Alastair Crenn. Should you have need of me, just say my name."

Which one? Crenn was going to ask, before it occurred to him that he was probably the only person who would know it. But maybe Robin did too.

The knowledge throbbed in the Old Language, under his skin and bone and breath. Knowing Summer's truename was dangerous.

Crenn did not make a similar promise, though he wanted to. Instead, he stood and moved for the wooden door, deliberately stepping mortal-heavy, making noise. So Jer, or whatever was left of him, would know where Alastair Crenn's loyalties lay.

He stopped, his hand on the doorknob. "Jer?"

"Al." It was a cool tone, almost but not quite a fullblood's mockery.

"I know you didn't…you weren't with her that night. The schoolteacher." *I can't even remember her name now.* Silence. Crenn paid out the last of what he owed to the mortal Jeremiah, save the one promise he suspected he'd have to fulfill sooner or later. And wouldn't Ragged Robin hate him then, too? A man couldn't win. "I always knew."

The bitterness filled his mouth. Was it a lie?

That was the trouble with Half. You could never be sure.

Crenn closed the door softly, leaving the new Summer to his own thoughts, and hurried away. He had left the glass shard in the chair by the bedside.

He had to find a door.

EVER AND ALWAYS
52

The Keep shimmered, its wet black stone gleaming under a different light though a pall of smoke hung above one of its towers. The library was gutted, but the astrolabes still spun, slowing and tarnishing by imperceptible degrees. The roads in Unwinter's realm were still milky quartz, but brighter now, and on the Ash Plains the scarlet flax now held a blush of green on the undersides of its pale leaves. That Dak'r was just as tangled, the mountains just as sharp...but the light of every fire and forge was richer now, with a tinge of gold to its ruddiness. The constant rain of pale cinders had turned to soft spatters of feathery snow.

Robin's eyes were grainy. The cream slid down her throat in long swallows, and Unwinter watched the movement. When she finished, wiping at her mouth with her fingers, the soothing spread all through her.

Everywhere but her heart.

Pepperbuckle sat next to her chair. Harne of Unwinter rested his long pale hands on the other side of the small table, and if Robin stretched her leg out, she could tap his knee with her toe.

Not that she would dare, but still.

She licked her lips. Unwinter watched, the pinpricks of crimson in his pupils flashing once, dimming slightly.

They regarded each other. The fire crackled, and a cold wind touched the shutters—but it was not as frigid as it had been. Unwinter's thistledown hair had darkened, almost gray instead of parchment-pale.

Finally, Robin scraped up the last of her courage. "I didn't kill Summer."

The Lord of Unwinter shrugged. "*I did not expect you to.*" The words were chill, but not hurtful. His tone had lost none of its edge, or its power.

It had merely...changed.

"Still, I promised," Robin persisted.

"*You promised only to free the Jewel.*" Unwinter indicated the window with a brief, expressive motion. "*I see him in my halls, Ragged. As he no doubt glimpses me in his. The Sundering is done.*"

Robin's gaze dropped to the table. She studied the flagon of cream.

"*Do you wish for more?*"

She shook her head, her earrings swinging slightly. Her hair was growing out quickly, remembering its former length. Her bare shoulders didn't steam in the chill. The black velvet coat-cloak probably still lay where it had landed during the battle. "No, my lord Unwinter."

Unwinter's pale, graceful fingers flicked. A golden gleam spun, depending from a fine chain—her locket.

Daisy had worn its twin. She was probably buried with it.

Robin's eyes prickled. She denied the tears, breathing steadily. Four in, four out.

Unwinter raised his other hand. Chantment flashed, and metal made a thin singing noise of stress and freezing. A bloody gleam filled the shadows with slumbrous crimson for a brief moment, and Unwinter offered the locket across the table.

Now, a red gem was set in the locket's lid. *"Should you have need of any aid,"* he said, almost kindly, *"simply touch, and I will answer."*

It wouldn't be politic to refuse, no matter how useful she'd been. So she took it, her fingers brushing Unwinter's chilly flesh for a bare moment. His eyelids dropped halfway, and for a moment, his face blurred slightly, a different—and familiar—man's features showing.

That was all.

The chain was cold, but warmed immediately. The clasp recognized her, and when the locket settled just under the notch at the top of her breastbone her chest hurt again, a swift lancing pain she ignored.

She stood, her chair scraping back along the stone floor. Was she simply too weary to feel terrified of Unwinter? Perhaps. "You are gracious, my lord."

"And you are careful. Your sire is dead, Robin Ragged, and the pixies recognize you."

It gave her a chill to think Puck had survived the crowbar and Robin's song. It gave her a double chill to think she hadn't known, and he had been stalking her afresh until Gallow struck him down. Now even Unwinter acknowledged the Fatherless was dead.

It wasn't as comforting as it could have been. Really, nothing ever was.

"Yes." She gazed into those blood-pricked eyes, steadily.

"Do you return to Summer now?"

Robin shook her head. Touched the locket, careful to avoid the gem. "No, my lord. Summer is not for me."

"Gallow would have it otherwise."

"Perhaps he would." Robin put her left foot behind and curtsied, as prettily as she ever had to False Summer. "I bid you farewell, Lord of Unwinter."

"I will see you again, little bird. Soon Summer and Unwinter will be one, and you will come home."

She could have told him there was no home for a Half, but in the end, she simply turned and took the first few unsteady steps into her future. Pepperbuckle lunged to his feet and shook his fine coat, padding after her, his nails clicking on stone. She reached the heavy black wooden door without further incident, but as it opened Unwinter spoke again.

"Robin Ragged, I would ask something of you."

Her throat was dry. "My lord."

"I would have someone remember me." Harshness melted out of his tone. *"When the Sundering is also a memory, and all are merry in green fields or winter's snow."*

"Yes, my lord." She swallowed, hard. *I can do that.* "I will. Ever, and always."

Both of you.

The door closed softly. Some of the halls looked queerly familiar, overlapping in her memory with the familiar corridors of Summerhome. She turned left, then right, feeling her way, and paused.

At the end of a long hallway, a green gleam. The shape was ghostly—broad shoulders, a flash of white in dark hair, a startled motion as if he had turned, expecting her footstep.

Robin, Jeremiah Gallow had said. *Please.*

The Ragged turned, walked quickly in the opposite direction. There was no bone-frilled Steward to guide her, but instinct, and Pepperbuckle, led her to the front gates. The moat was smooth as glass, the Watcher quiescent in its depths. Robin

Ragged walked with her chin up and her shoulders straight, a single shimmering diamond dewdrop on her right cheek.

It was gone before she found a small overgrown door set into a thorny hillside. Traceries of green ran on the undersides of the bramble-vines, strengthening as Unwinter slid closer and closer to Summer. The more-than-real would be whole again. There would be no need for the flint knife or the bloodied doorway; the Tiend would take other forms. Stone and Throne would be one.

She spread her fingers against the door, glancing over her shoulder. The Keep loomed black and sharp, smoke fraying above. Just before she blinked, it turned white, and a soft apple-blossom breeze touched her cheek.

When she opened her eyes again, the flash was gone. The door opened reluctantly, but Robin pushed, and finally she stepped through, vanishing from the more-than-real in a flicker of russet, cream, and gold.

And one crimson spark.

LAST OF THE WILD BOYS
53

The child hunched against a concrete wall, shivering. This wasn't like other fights, kids throwing stones and yelling, not like the nightmare of the trailer or apartment or even the tract house, crouching while adults screamed and things crashed against the wall. It still echoed all around her, everything topsy-turvy, the malice settling in her bones and making her ache, ache, ache. Her broken arm, and the time that man sprained her ankle, and other hurts, all come back to say hello.

Where were the other kids? Where was Tomtom? He was nice, and he took her seriously. His dirty face lived in her heart all the time, a soft sweet stinging, and she had run for the storehouse without stopping, Rom behind her and her head ringing with the importance of the mission.

Then, the redheaded lady, and the things made of mist, and the scratching of the blackberry vines and poor Rom's screams...

Brat cowered in the frost-covered bushes all that night, even after sanity came back and the noises and shaking faded away. Near dawn, cold and bladder-full, she crept out of her little hidey-hole and into a listing, icy trailer to pee. Her cup was back at the squat, and she didn't want to trust any of the trash around here near her privates. Boys had it so *easy*, and she had decided, way back when she was plain old Eleanor Gunderson, that she wanted to be like them, thinking maybe the easy would rub off.

It never did.

Her chest felt funny. The frost wasn't bothering her as much. It was like she had a little heater starting up inside her, and it smelled like the redheaded woman's breath. Brat crept outside again, taking shelter next to the trailer's listing, rotted porch. She could see anything sneaking around from here, and maybe plan out how to get back to the squat.

Morning strengthened, and Brat moved every once in a while, flitting from cover to cover like a tiny soldier, her red bandanna bobbing.

Around noon she found Tomtom's body. He lay on his back, his arms spread wide and his lips turned blue, and something had pecked at his eyes. He stared at the sky with the ragged red holes, and Brat stood, hugging herself. She nudged him once or twice with her foot, ready for him to hop upright and say *Did I scareya, Brat?* and laugh in his whistling way. He was the leader, the bravest and the best, and the craziness had killed him.

That's what it was. Seeing things with wings and hooves and human faces and flittering tiny people and *giants*, actual *giants*, was crazy.

She lost track of time, standing there and swaying, and only roused when she heard something that didn't belong in the Sevens.

Click-click-click. Taptap. Click-click click. Tapping little footsteps, in the quiet.

That was when Brat realized she couldn't hear the traffic,

even though the Sevens were right up against the freeway. Instead, there was only the wind, and that persistent movement at the edge of her vision, like the world wasn't going to stay still. Like it was just waiting for her to blink so it could change into something else, maybe a deep dark forest like she used to have nightmares about, pale hands reaching through spikethorn branches and curving to catch at her...

The clicking drew nearer, nearer, and finally she appeared.

The redheaded woman.

Brat might have turned to run, but her legs had frozen, and the woman wasn't wearing black anymore. Instead, she wore a silken blue dress, its hem fluttering, and beside her a dog as big as a small horse pranced. He wasn't like the mongrels other street kids had or the pampered Shit-Zoos one of her foster families had brushed and babytalked. He was redgold, the color of her hair, and he looked straight at Brat like he knew her, with bright-blue eyes more direct than a dog's should ever be.

The tapping footsteps slowed. The redheaded woman was so beautiful it hurt to look at her. At her throat, a locket gleamed, and set in it was a single bloody gem like an eye.

Someone gave her that, Brat thought. *Someone she maybe doesn't like very much.*

The woman finally stopped, a reasonable distance away. She looked at Tomtom's body, and Brat was suddenly sure she was going to sneer, like the ladies in high heels sometimes did when they passed Tomtom playing his guitar on the street. It was a swift expression, like he was a stain or a bad smell, and each time she saw it Brat's eyes would narrow, and the hate would fill her like big red clouds.

The lady didn't sneer, though. She just studied him, and looked sad.

She was so *beautiful,* from her tumblecurl crop of redgold hair to her creamy shoulders, to the folds of the blue silken dress, all the way down pale dancer-muscled legs to her black high heels. Maybe she'd known Tomtom, to look at him that way. Brat felt herself bulge like a punctured beachball. She hunched her shoulders.

The woman's gaze passed over her, and Brat tried not to straighten self-consciously. Tried not to feel the dirt on her skin—because if boys thought you were pretty they would do things to you, and even if you were ugly they sometimes would, but less often. Besides, Tomtom said the body would clean itself, modern detergents just got in the way and polluted the planet.

The dog sat down, its tongue lolling, and its teeth were huge, too. Curiously, though, it didn't seem like she had to be afraid of it. It was just so *big*.

She and the woman watched each other. Little spatters of light bloomed around the redhead, and if Brat squinted she could see the crazy fluttering in the lights.

It looked like little people with wings. Some wore whispers of frayed, cobwebby clothing, others were smooth and hairless-naked, unembarrassed.

"His name was Tomtom." Brat blushed, hotly, and the words spilled out, taking her by surprise. "The others are dead." She knew it was true as soon as she said it.

She was the last of the Wild Boys, and she wasn't even a *boy*.

The woman thought this over. Then she spoke.

"I'm sorry."

Her voice was golden. Soft, and low, and honey-sweet, it spread soothing all the way down Brat's aching little body. A dusting of golden freckles on the woman's nose glowed. She was too perfect to be real, except...

Brat frowned. The woman *was* real.

Realer than real, even.

Did that mean the craziness was real too?

Amazingly, the woman folded down. She crouched, her blue skirt pooling around her, and studied Brat from below, her wide dark-blue eyes moving in unhurried arcs. The spatters of light brightened, and the heat in Brat's chest intensified. The persistent coughing from cold and cigarettes, the deep gnawing never-fully-satisfied hunger, the pain from one of her baby teeth rotting in her head, had all vanished.

Brat actually felt *good*.

"You saw the battle." The woman tilted her chin. "Right?"

Brat nodded, digging her left toe into the concrete as if she was five and Called to the Carpet. That was what the Shit-Zoo woman had called it. *You're gonna be Called to the Carpet, you little brat.*

"And you see the pixies." The woman indicated the flying blue glimmers. "We're from Summer, little one. The more-than-real."

Hearing her own thoughts given voice was terrifying and comforting at once. Brat's hands loosened at her sides.

The honey-voice continued, soft and sure. "You're...different. You've always seen things other people don't. Known things they don't." It wasn't a question. "I can take you with me, little one, or I can show you how to go somewhere else. Somewhere just as dangerous as *this* place, but...beautiful too."

"Why didn't you stay there?" It sounded angry, but Brat was honestly just curious.

The woman didn't get angry in return, though. "I...I had to leave." The sadness came back, flooding her face, and for a moment she looked tired. But still lovely. "That's all."

Brat looked down at Tomtom's empty shell. The police would come. There would be questions. The older homeless would flood into the Sevens, and Brat couldn't hold them back by herself.

She was, after all, only twelve, and dimly realized she was bargaining for something much bigger than her age would permit her to compass. Others like the woman might come, but they might not be...kind.

Compassion, like hatred, can be sensed. A twelve-year-old's bullshit detector sifted through everything else, and found the secret Robin Ragged kept even from herself.

Brat felt for her red bandanna. It was Tomtom's, actually, and she crouched next to his head, his raw oozing eyesockets staring past her. When she draped the red cloth over his face, she felt better. Lighter.

When she looked up, the woman had stood. Brat searched for something to say, and she finally crept crabwise toward her, almost-cringing. The dog studied Brat intently, his bright warm tongue lolling. Pinker than pink, a color too vibrant for the pale savage nightmare Brat been born into.

The woman offered her soft white hand. The little lights around her began to dart toward Brat too, chiming softly. They were saying something the child *almost* understood, but comprehension slipped away, and she reached up with her own dirty paw.

"I'll go with you," she whispered, and the redheaded woman tugged gently on her hand.

"Stand up, little one. Do you have a name? You can choose one, if you like."

"What's yours?"

"Robin. Robin Ragged."

"I'm Ell," Brat mouthed, as if she could make it true by saying it. "Ell Wild."

"Ell Wild," Robin repeated, and nodded. "I am very pleased to meet you, indeed."

As simply as that, she was no longer Brat, just like when she met Tomtom she was no longer Samantha but Brat, and when she fled the last foster home she was no longer Eleanor but Samantha.

Maybe this name would stick. "Ch-charmed," Ell stuttered, like she'd heard men do in movies.

For some reason, that made Robin smile, a soft pained curve of her lips. "I can teach you that, too." She looked up, glancing at the sun. Another spring storm was moving in, black clouds in the north gathering. The rain would wash the Sevens clean, and maybe it was the only shower Tomtom would have liked. "Come, little one. We've far to go before dark."

"Will it rain on us?" Ell clung to her warm hand, and was ready to trot to keep up with an adult's long paces. But Robin shortened her stride, and on her other side the dog paced, glancing curiously at Ell every few steps. In a friendly way, like he could tell she liked dogs, and was ready to like her in return.

"Sooner or later, it always does," Robin Ragged replied.

ALMOST INDIRECT
54

Later, the Sevens sprawled exhausted and bleached, steaming damply. The sodden red rag over a boy's corpse was the only blot of color in the graying landscape, the clouds turned to an oppressive stormlid. Lightning stabbed and thunder crackled, the battlefield warming and finding it was again, only, mortal ground.

A shadow slipped along the roads, stepping over rotting bones and sponge-soft swellings, avoiding puddles of half-spent curses and the sharp stabbing fishbones of naiads and selkies. The mortals would see only branches and trash, shiny but worthless pebbles and melting gray cobwebs. To them, his almost-indirect route would seem an aimless amble through a junkyard, instead of a careful quartering of the cursed wasteland where False Summer—for so the Seelie sidhe now named her, eager to ingratiate themselves with their new lord, even though he was *Half*—fell. Ballads were being composed, and his own name featured in a few of them.

Alastair Crenn could not care less.

He found what he sought deep in the heart of the tangle, where a mortal corpse lay on its back, its face covered. The shape of the wet cloth describing the features made him shudder slightly, but he bent, keen dark eyes finding tiny traces. She'd stood here for quite some time, then...

He lifted his head, sniffing. With his hair tied back, it was much easier.

A thin thread of spiced fruit on the rainwashed breeze. Thunder muttered again, but the hunter closed his eyes, inhaling.

Only a few hours old. There was Pepperbuckle's trace, too, a long fine curling redgold hair.

Crenn found the trail, and set off at a lope.

PERHAPS, SURETY
55

Perhaps Alastair Crenn did find her. Perhaps she did not welcome his appearance; perhaps he said *I am sorry* and she replied *It is not enough.*

Of a surety, though, is his answer, the only answer possible when retreat is not an option.

Tell me what would be enough, and I will do it. I have no other choice.

Oh, the sidhe whisper; oh, the sidhe gossip. But on this they all agree: Robin Ragged rambles, with a hound and a child.

And wherever she goes, a hunter is not far behind.

GLOSSARY

Barrow-wight: Fullblood Unseelie wights whose homes are long "barrows." Gold loses its luster in their presence.

Brughnies: House-sidhe; they delight in cooking and cleaning. A well-ordered kitchen is their joy.

The Fatherless: Robin Goodfellow, also called Puck, the nominal leader of the free sidhe.

Folk: Sidhe, or clan within the sidhe, or generally a group, race, or species.

Ghilliedhu: "Birch-girl"; dryads of the birch clan, held to be great beauties.

Grentooth: A jack-wight, often amphibious, with mossy teeth and a septic bite.

Kelpie: A river sidhe, capable of appearing as a black horse and luring its victims to drowning.

Kobolding: A crafty race of sidhe, often amassing great wealth, living underground. Related to goblins, distantly related to the dwarven clans.

Quirpiece: A silver coin, used to hold a particular chantment.

GLOSSARY

Realmaker: A sidhe whose chantments do not fade at dawn. Very rare.

Seelie: Sidhe of Summer's Court, or holding fealty to Summer.

Selkie: A sealskin sidhe.

Sidhe: The Fair Folk, the Little People, the Children of Danu.

Sluagh: The ravening horde of the unforgiven dead.

Tainted: Possessing mortal blood.

Twisted: A sidhe altered and mutated, often by proximity to cold iron, unable to use sidhe chantments or glamour.

Unseelie: Sidhe of Unwinter's Court, or holding fealty to Unwinter.

Wight: "Being," or "creature"; used to refer to certain classes of sidhe.

Woodwight: A wight whose home or form is a tree, whose blood is resinous.

ACKNOWLEDGMENTS

Thanks are due to my children, who were, as usual, very patient with their distracted mother living half in another world while finishing a book. They are also due to Devi Pillai, the best editor I could have; Miriam Kriss, who told me I could do it and was, as usual, right; and Mel Sanders, who kept me sane, as she is wont to do.

A very large measure of gratitude must also go to Kelly O'Connor, who did not lose her temper with me even when I was very difficult during production.

The Folk are merry, the Folk are fell, the Folk are bonny, and it's just as well.

As always, the final thank-you goes to you, my dear Readers. Come, make yourselves comfortable, pour yourself whatever drink you desire, and let me tell you another story...

extras

orbit

meet the author

Photo credit: Daron Gildrow

LILITH SAINTCROW was born in New Mexico, bounced around the world as an Air Force brat, and fell in love with writing when she was ten years old. She currently lives in Vancouver, Washington.

introducing

If you enjoyed
WASTELAND KING
look out for
the next novel

by Lilith Saintcrow

It could have been aliens, it could have been a trans-dimensional rift, nobody knows for sure. What's known is that there was an Event, the Rifts opened up, and everyone caught inside died.

Since the Event, though, certain people have gone into the drift... and come back, bearing priceless bits of technology that are almost magical in their advancement. When Ashe—the best Rifter of her generation—dies, the authorities offer her student, Svinga, a choice: go in and bring out the thing that killed her, or rot in jail. But Svin, of course, has other plans...

Maki screamed, letting off a burst of fire at the stand of spindly trees and thick underbrush. Tremaine vanished into its maw, and the Rifter grabbed the back of Barko's jacket, hauling him backward again. The bald scientist went down hard, the sound of his teeth clicking together almost audible over the rifle's barks—projectile instead of plasma, because you couldn't ever tell what plasma would do in a Rift. It wasn't worth it, so the plas-switches on the Currago5K rifles had been disabled. The pin on the Surya Naga submachine the demo man carried had been tripped, too.

"He's gone!" she yelled. "Fucking forget it!"

Hicks, his knees digging into the grass, swore viciously. *"Cease fire! Cease fire, you fuckbuckle motherfucker! Hold your fire!"* Behind him, Brood had prudently hit the ground, and bullets plowed into the shrubs and shaking, spindly trees. They were plo-rounds, and anything flammable should have gone up in seconds. Certainly anything woodlike should have burst into flames.

Instead, the trees writhed and the shrubs ran like ink on an oiled plate, extending long thorn-liquid runners up the hill. Dust puffed up, the serrated grass whipping wildly, and the Rifter uncoiled over Barko in an amazing leap. She hit Maki squarely, and even though she was much smaller, the unexpected impact threw the man sideways. Bullets spattered overhead, and Brood punched Hicks on the closest thing he could reach to get his commander's attention.

That just happened to be Hicks's left buttock. Which cramped, viciously, because Brood had a helluva windup.

"Motherfucker!" Hicks howled, but he knew exactly *why* the sonofabitch had done it.

The thing was heading up the hill, sending out its shrub-tentacles, clawing against grass and earth. The Rifter screamed, a high hawklike cry, lost under the sound of crunching and gunfire. Maki stopped firing, and Brood was on his back, fumbling at his chest while the thing heaved itself another few feet up the slope.

It looked angry, and it was making a *sound*. A low grumbling roar, gathering strength. The trees were less trees now, and more spinelike, leaves suddenly little fleshy pods with tabs crusting their edges. The "leaves" crawled over the spines, and as the thing scrabbled closer, Hicks could swear he saw them scurrying along, nuzzling at the scars bullets had torn. Lapping at them, swarming like white blood cells gathering to form an angry pus-filled pocket.

Hicks lurched to his feet. Maki was no longer screaming. Barko was, a hoarse cry of despair. Eschkov, his backpack left behind, stumbled down the slope towards them, hands outstretched and his spectacles askew. A lonely flash jetted off one lens, and he almost ran into Hicks, his soft skinny hands closing with desperate strength on the officer's pack straps. He bagan pulling, hauling Hicks up the hill.

Brood's hand finally came away from his chest, full of the sour metal apple of a concuss-grenade. "*Clear!*" he screamed, pulling the pin, and tossed it at the thing. He rolled over and scrabbled, getting his legs inelegantly but efficiently under him, and almost ran into Hicks, who stared at the goddamn thing as the grenade bounced once, vanishing into its quivering depths.

"*Get down!*" the Rifter yelled, and kicked Senkin's feet from under him. She threw herself on top of Barko, and Hicks had a brief second to wonder why before the grenade popped and the noise exploded outward.

A gigantic warm hand cupped every inch of his back, legs, head, neck—everything. He *flew*, weightless for a moment, and the impact knocked all the sense out of him for a brief gentle second before the pain began.

Crunch. The world spun away, came back on a greased leaf full of tearing edges. He hung between Senkin and Brood as they slid down the other side of the hill, and the Rifter was bellowing at them to *move you cocksuckers move!* She had some-thing in her hands—one of those queer opalescent rocks, and as she ran she twisted at it, tendons standing out under pale skin. It cracked, a thin thread of darkness appearing at its heart. She had a snotrag, a faded red one, and popped the rock into it as she ran.

Then she whirled, digging her heels in, and skidded to a stop, the twin furrows plowed by her boots glaring against the matted grass. The noise behind them spiraled up into a boulder-rubbing screech.

The thing was fucking *pissed.*

It crested the rise in a humpback wave, shedding those fleshy leaf-bits, whatever wet sound they made lost in the roar-ing. They fell, bloodsick knobs of tissue, and when they hit the grass, small puffs of caustic smoke belched up. The Rifter raised the fist with the red snotrag and began to whirl the trapped rock inside.

The thing heaved itself fully over the rise. Brood was down on one knee, shooting at it, wasting ammo. Hicks tried to shake the noise out of his head, tried to *think.* The roar turned everything inside him to jelly, knocked his head back on the smallish stem his neck had become, and the pain came again, diamondtooth ants biting down his back and legs.

The Rifter's face was alive, bright color high on her cheeks. Her eyes weren't bulging so much as *shining,* and she whirled the makeshift sling just like the illustration of King David Hicks could remember in one of his battered childhood books. His mother would read them to him, if she wasn't too bone-tired after a long day of slinging other people's wet laun-dry, and she would tell him the stories behind the stories—how David even then was a king, and his bloodline would bring the Messiah when it was time for God to call his chosen people home. How King Solomon had built his palace with demons as his slaves, the great ring glinting on his finger, how the wise *rebbes* made massive men of clay and breathed life into them to protect the ghetto.

There were other stories, but all Hicks was seeing was the Goliath coming down the hill, gaining speed, and Brood was screaming as he emptied one clip, then another at it. The bullets tore into it without effect, and the Rifter let out another high, keening screech. A snap of her arm, and the white, faintly glowing rock described a high arc.

For a moment it looked like she'd miscalculated, but the impossible happened. The rock *curved*, and the dark thread along its middle peeled open, a single spark buried in its depths dilating.

The Rifter turned on her heel and launched herself at Senkin, who was holding Hicks up because Brood had gone fucking killcrazy. She hit with a *crunch*, and the Rifter yelled something he couldn't hear. His head rang, and there was a soft, ridiculous *whoosh* before the flung rock exploded.

Fallen sideways, his head bouncing against the serrated grass, Hicks stared.

The flame was blue, and it didn't act like it should. It spread like liquid, but leapt and danced, and a cloying, feverish heat blasted down the hillside as the spine-backed thing writhed, throwing even more of those tiny gobbets everywhere. One landed near Hicks's nose, and he watched it, dreamily, as the round mouth on its end, ringed with concentric rows of inward-slanting, triangular teeth, opened and closed.

Fuck of a sphincter. The thought was very far away. Everything grayed out.

When he came back, touching down in his body like a dropped popper into a magseal catch, he was on his back and Eschkov was finishing a very capable field-splint on his left leg. Senkin had an emergency kit open, and pushed Hicks's sleeve up; he smoothed a red painpatch onto his commander's biceps. The narcotic would begin spreading immediately. Senkin's mouth moved, but the words were only a faint, fuzzy, faraway buzz.

Shock. I'm in shock.

Barko, on his other side, held up a syringe of amber liquid. He tapped it, twice, and cleared any air before bending over Hicks's arm, which had a tourniquet around it he couldn't feel. Barko's lips were moving, but maybe the man wasn't talking. It looked, instead, an awful lot like he was praying.

Hicks's head tipped back. There was Brood, at a weird angle because his field of vision was sliding, standing watch. Maki, his head wrapped in a bandage already bearing a rosette of blood leaking through, was watching the other way.

The Rifter crouched in the middle distance, her peach-fuzz stubble slicked to her scalp with grime and blood. Had she run her hands back over her head, like Barko was always doing? Her hollow cheeks were striped with weird, greasy soot. She wasn't looking at Hicks.

Instead, she was studying Brood's back, and her expression wasn't quite unguarded, but it was ... thoughtful.

She knows he's Copeland's. I wonder if she'll ...

It was dangerous in here. More dangerous than they had ever imagined. The thing had looked like *trees*, for fucksake. Had the Rifter left them there knowing one of the scientists would be unable to resist the temptation? Or had Tremaine just been that stupid?

One more thought came circling back before the warmth of the painpatch crept up his shoulder to his neck and made everything seem just-fucking-fine-and-dandy.

Someone else is going to die. I'm hurt bad.

It might be me.

introducing

If you enjoyed
WASTELAND KING
look out for

WAKE OF VULTURES

The Shadow: Book 1

by Lilia Bowen

Nettie Lonesome lives in a land of hard people and hard ground dusted with sand. She's a half-breed who dresses like a boy, raised by folks who don't call her a slave but use her like one. She knows of nothing else. That is, until the day a stranger attacks her. When nothing, not even a sickle to the eye can stop him, Nettie stabs him through the heart with a chunk of wood, and he turns into black sand.

And just like that, Nettie can see.

But her newfound ability is a blessing and a curse. Even if she doesn't understand what's under her own skin, she can sense what everyone else is hiding—at least physically. The world is full of evil, and now she knows the source of all the sand in the desert. Haunted by the spirits, Nettie has no choice but to set out on a quest that might lead to her true kin…if the monsters along the way don't kill her first.

CHAPTER

1

Nettie Lonesome had two things in the world that were worth a sweet goddamn: her old boots and her one-eyed mule, Blue. Neither item actually belonged to her. But then again, nothing did. Not even the whisper-thin blanket she lay under, pretending to be asleep and wishing the black mare would get out of the water trough before things went south.

The last fourteen years of Nettie's life had passed in a shriveled corner of Durango territory under the leaking roof of this wind-chapped lean-to with Pap and Mam, not quite a slave and nowhere close to something like a daughter. Their faces, white and wobbling as new butter under a smear of prairie dirt, held no kindness. The boots and the mule had belonged to Pap, right up until the day he'd exhausted their use, a sentiment he threatened to apply to her every time she was just a little too slow with the porridge.

"Nettie! Girl, you take care of that wild filly, or I'll put one in her goddamn skull!"

Pap got in a lather when he'd been drinking, which was pretty much always. At least this time his anger was aimed at a critter instead of Nettie. When the witch-hearted black filly had first shown up on the farm, Pap had laid claim and pronounced her a fine chunk of flesh and a sign of the Creator's good graces. If Nettie broke her and sold her for a decent price, she'd be closer to paying back Pap for taking her in as a baby when nobody else had wanted her but the hungry, circling vultures. The value Pap placed on feeding and housing a half-Injun, half-black orphan girl always seemed to go up instead of down, no matter that Nettie did most of the work around the homestead these days. Maybe that was why she'd not been taught her sums: Then she'd know her own damn worth, to the penny.

But the dainty black mare outside wouldn't be roped, much less saddled and gentled, and Nettie had failed to sell her to the cowpokes at the Double TK Ranch next door. Her idol, Monty, was a top hand and always had a kind word. But even he had put a boot on Pap's poorly kept fence, laughed through his mustache, and hollered that a horse that couldn't be caught couldn't be sold. No matter how many times Pap drove the filly away with poorly thrown bottles, stones, and bullets, the critter crept back under cover of night to ruin the water by dancing a jig in the trough, which meant another blistering trip to the creek with a leaky bucket for Nettie.

Splash, splash. Whinny.

Could a horse laugh? Nettie figured this one could.

Pap, however, was a humorless bastard who didn't get a joke that didn't involve bruises.

"Unless you wanna go live in the flats, eatin' bugs, you'd best get on, girl."

Nettie rolled off her worn-out straw tick, hoping there weren't any scorpions or centipedes on the dusty dirt floor. By the moon's scant light she shook out Pap's old boots and shoved her bare feet into into the cracked leather.

Splash, splash.

The shotgun cocked loud enough to be heard across the border, and Nettie dove into Mam's old wool cloak and ran toward the stockyard with her long, thick braids slapping against her back. Mam said nothing, just rocked in her chair by the window, a bottle cradled in her arm like a baby's corpse. Grabbing the rawhide whip from its nail by the warped door, Nettie hurried past Pap on the porch and stumbled across the yard, around two mostly roofless barns, and toward the wet black shape taunting her in the moonlight against a backdrop of stars.

"Get on, mare. Go!"

A monster in a flapping jacket with a waving whip would send any horse with sense wheeling in the opposite direction, but this horse had apparently been dancing in the creek on the day sense was handed out. The mare stood in the water trough and stared at Nettie like she was a damn strange bird, her dark eyes blinking with moonlight and her lips pulled back over long, white teeth.

Nettie slowed. She wasn't one to quirt a horse, but if the mare kept causing a ruckus, Pap would shoot her without a second or even a first thought—and he wasn't so deep in his bottle that he was sure to miss. Getting smacked with rawhide had to be better than getting shot in the head, so Nettie doubled up her shouting and prepared herself for the heartache that would accompany the smack of a whip on unmarred hide. She didn't even own the horse, much less the right to beat it. Nettie had grown up trying to be the opposite of Pap, and hurting something that didn't come with claws and a stinger went against her grain.

"Shoo, fool, or I'll have to whip you," she said, creeping closer. The horse didn't budge, and for the millionth time, Nettie swung the whip around the horse's neck like a rope, all gentle-like. But, as ever, the mare tossed her head at exactly the right moment, and the braided leather snickered against the wooden water trough instead.

"Godamighty, why won't you move on? Ain't nobody wants you, if you won't be rode or bred. Dumb mare."

At that, the horse reared up with a wild scream, spraying water as she pawed the air. Before Nettie could leap back to avoid the splatter, the mare had wheeled and galloped into the night. The starlight showed her streaking across the prairie with a speed Nettie herself would've enjoyed, especially if it meant she could turn her back on Pap's dirt-poor farm and no-good cattle company forever. Doubling over to stare at her scuffed boots while she caught her breath, Nettie felt her hope disappear with hoofbeats in the night.

A low and painfully unfamiliar laugh trembled out of the barn's shadow, and Nettie cocked the whip back so that it was ready to strike.

"Who's that? Jed?"

But it wasn't Jed, the mule-kicked, sometimes stable boy, and she already knew it.

"Looks like that black mare's giving you a spot of trouble, darlin'. If you were smart, you'd set fire to her tail."

A figure peeled away from the barn, jerky-thin and slithery in a too-short coat with buttons that glinted like extra stars. The man's hat was pulled low, his brown hair overshaggy and his lily-white hand on his gun in a manner both unfriendly and relaxed that Nettie found insulting.

"You best run off, mister. Pap don't like strangers on his land, especially when he's only a bottle in. If it's horses you want, we ain't got none worth selling. If you want work and you're dumb and blind, best come back in the morning when he's slept off the mezcal."

"I wouldn't work for that good-for-nothing piss-pot even if I needed work."

The stranger switched sides with his toothpick and looked Nettie up and down like a horse he was thinking about stealing. Her fist tightened on the whip handle, her fingers going cold. She wouldn't defend Pap or his land or his sorry excuses for cattle, but she'd defend the only thing other than Blue that mostly belonged to her. Men had been pawing at her for two years now, and nobody'd yet come close to reaching her soft parts, not even Pap.

"Then you'd best move on, mister."

The feller spit his toothpick out on the ground and took a step forward, all quiet-like because he wore no spurs. And that was Nettie's first clue that he wasn't what he seemed.

"Naw, I'll stay. Pretty little thing like you to keep me company."

That was Nettie's second clue. Nobody called her pretty unless they wanted something. She looked around the yard, but all she saw were sand, chaparral, bone-dry cow patties, and the remains of a fence that Pap hadn't seen fit to fix. Mam was surely asleep, and Pap had gone inside, or maybe around back to piss. It was just the stranger and her. And the whip.

"Bullshit," she spit.

"Put down that whip before you hurt yourself, girl."

"Don't reckon I will."

The stranger stroked his pistol and started to circle her. Nettie shook the whip out behind her as she spun in place to face him and hunched over in a crouch. He stopped circling when the barn yawned behind her, barely a shell of a thing but darker than sin in the corners. And then he took a step forward, his silver pistol out and flashing starlight. Against her will, she took a step back. Inch by inch he drove her into the barn with slow, easy steps. Her feet rattled in the big boots, her fingers numb around the whip she had forgotten how to use.

"What is it you think you're gonna do to me, mister?"

It came out breathless, goddamn her tongue.

His mouth turned up like a cat in the sun. "Something nice. Something somebody probably done to you already. Your master or pappy, maybe."

She pushed air out through her nose like a bull. "Ain't got a pappy. Or a master."

"Then I guess nobody'll mind, will they?"

That was pretty much it for Nettie Lonesome. She spun on her heel and ran into the barn, right where he'd been pushing her to go. But she didn't flop down on the hay or toss down the mangy blanket that had dried into folds in the broke-down, three-wheeled rig. No, she snatched the sickle from the wall and spun to face him under the hole in the roof. Starlight fell down on her ink-black braids and glinted off the parts of the curved blade that weren't rusted up.

"I reckon I'd mind," she said.

Nettie wasn't a little thing, at least not height-wise, and she'd figured that seeing a pissed-off woman with a weapon in each hand would be enough to drive off the curious feller and send him back to the whores at the Leaping Lizard, where he apparently belonged. But the stranger just laughed and cracked his knuckles like he was glad for a fight and would take his pleasure with his fists instead of his twig.

"You wanna play first? Go on, girl. Have your fun. You think you're facin' down a coydog, but you found a timber wolf."

As he stepped into the barn, the stranger went into shadow for just a second, and that was when Nettie struck. Her whip whistled for his feet and managed to catch one ankle, yanking hard enough to pluck him off his feet and onto the back of his fancy jacket. A puff of dust went up as he thumped on the ground, but he just crossed his ankles and stared at her and laughed. Which pissed her off more. Dropping the whip handle, Nettie took the sickle in both hands and went for the stranger's legs, hoping that a good slash would keep him from chasing her but not get her sent to the hangman's noose. But her blade whistled over a patch of nothing. The man was gone, her whip with him.

Nettie stepped into the doorway to watch him run away, her heart thumping underneath the tight muslin binding she always wore over her chest. She squinted into the long, flat night, one hand on the hinge of what used to be a barn door, back before the church was willing to pay cash money for Pap's old lumber. But the stranger wasn't hightailing it across the prairie. Which meant...

"Looking for someone, darlin'?"

She spun, sickle in hand, and sliced into something that felt like a ham with the round part of the blade. Hot blood spattered over her, burning like lye.

"Goddammit, girl! What'd you do that for?"

She ripped the sickle out with a sick splash, but the man wasn't standing in the barn, much less falling to the floor. He was hanging upside-down from a cross-beam, cradling his arm. It made no goddamn sense, and Nettie couldn't stand a thing that made no sense, so she struck again while he was poking around his wound.

This time, she caught him in the neck. This time, he fell.

The stranger landed in the dirt and popped right back up into a crouch. The slice in his neck looked like the first carving in an undercooked roast, but the blood was slurry and smelled like rotten meat. And the stranger was sneering at her.

"Girl, you just made the biggest mistake of your short, useless life."

Then he sprang at her.

There was no way he should've been able to jump at her like that with those wounds, and she brought her hands straight up without thinking. Luckily, her fist still held the sickle, and the stranger took it right in the face, the point of the blade jerking into his eyeball with a moist squish. Nettie turned away and lost most of last night's meager dinner in a noisy splatter against the wall of the barn. When she spun back around, she was surprised to find that the fool hadn't fallen or died or done anything helpful to her cause. Without a word, he calmly pulled the blade out of his eye and wiped a dribble of black glop off his cheek.

His smile was a cold, dark thing that sent Nettie's feet toward Pap and the crooked house and anything but the stranger who wouldn't die, wouldn't scream, and wouldn't leave her alone. She'd never felt safe a day in her life, but now she recognized the chill hand of death, reaching for her. Her feet trembled in the too-big boots as she stumbled backward across the bumpy yard, tripping on stones and bits of trash. Turning her back on the demon man seemed intolerably stupid. She just had to get past the round pen, and then she'd be halfway to the house. Pap wouldn't be worth much by now, but he had a gun by his side. Maybe the stranger would give up if he saw a man instead of just a half-breed girl nobody cared about.

Nettie turned to run and tripped on a fallen chunk of fence, going down hard on hands and skinned knees. When she looked up, she saw butternut-brown pants stippled with blood and no-spur boots tapping.

"Pap!" she shouted. "Pap, help!"

She was gulping in a big breath to holler again when the

stranger's boot caught her right under the ribs and knocked it all back out. The force of the kick flipped her over onto her back, and she scrabbled away from the stranger and toward the ramshackle round pen of old, gray branches and junk roped together, just barely enough fence to trick a colt into staying put. They'd slaughtered a pig in here, once, and now Nettie knew how he felt.

As soon as her back fetched up against the pen, the stranger crouched in front of her, one eye closed and weeping black and the other brim-full with evil over the bloody slice in his neck. He looked like a dead man, a corpse groom, and Nettie was pretty sure she was in the hell Mam kept threatening her with.

"Ain't nobody coming. Ain't nobody cares about a girl like you. Ain't nobody gonna need to, not after what you done to me."

The stranger leaned down and made like he was going to kiss her with his mouth wide open, and Nettie did the only thing that came to mind. She grabbed up a stout twig from the wall of the pen and stabbed him in the chest as hard as she damn could.

She expected the stick to break against his shirt like the time she'd seen a buggy bash apart against the general store during a twister. But the twig sunk right in like a hot knife in butter. The stranger shuddered and fell on her, his mouth working as gloppy red-black liquid bubbled out. She didn't trust blood anymore, not after the first splat had burned her, and she wasn't much for being found under a corpse, so Nettie shoved him off hard and shot to her feet, blowing air as hard as a galloping horse.

The stranger was rolling around on the ground, plucking at his chest. Thick clouds blotted out the meager starlight, and she had nothing like the view she'd have tomorrow under the white-hot, unrelenting sun. But even a girl who'd never killed a man before knew when something was wrong. She kicked him over with the toe of her boot, tit for tat, and he was light as a tumbleweed when he landed on his back.

The twig jutted up out of a black splotch in his shirt, and the slice in his neck had curled over like gone meat. His bad eye was a swamp of black, but then, everything was black at midnight. His mouth was open, the lips drawing back over too-white teeth, several of which looked like they'd come out of a panther. He wasn't breathing, and Pap wasn't coming, and Nettie's finger reached out as if it had a mind of its own and flicked one big, shiny, curved tooth.

The goddamn thing fell back into the dead man's gaping throat. Nettie jumped away, skitty as the black filly, and her boot toe brushed the dead man's shoulder, and his entire body collapsed in on itself like a puffball, thousands of sparkly motes piling up in the place he'd occupied and spilling out through his empty clothes. Utterly bewildered, she knelt and brushed the pile with trembling fingers. It was sand. Nothing but sand. A soft wind came up just then and blew some of the stranger away, revealing one of those big, curved teeth where his head had been. It didn't make a goddamn lick of sense, but it could've gone far worse.

Still wary, she stood and shook out his clothes, noting that everything was in better than fine condition, except for his white shirt, which had a twig-sized hole in the breast, surrounded by a smear of black. She knew enough of laundering and sewing to make it nice enough, and the black blood on his pants looked, to her eye, manly and tough. Even the stranger's boots were of better quality than any that had ever set foot on Pap's land, snakeskin with fancy chasing. With her own, too-big boots, she smeared the sand back into the hard, dry ground as if the stranger had never existed. All that was left was the four big panther teeth, and she put those in her pocket and tried to forget about them.

After checking the yard for anything livelier than a scorpion, she rolled up the clothes around the boots and hid them in the old rig in the barn. Knowing Pap would pester her if she left signs of a scuffle, she wiped the black glop off the sickle and hung it up, along with the whip, out of Pap's drunken reach. She didn't need any more whip scars on her back than she already had.

Out by the round pen, the sand that had once been a devil of a stranger had all blown away. There was no sign of what had almost happened, just a few more deadwood twigs pulled from the lopsided fence. On good days, Nettie spent a fair bit of time doing the dangerous work of breaking colts or doctoring cattle in here for Pap, then picking up the twigs that got knocked off and roping them back in with whatever twine she could scavenge from the town. Wood wasn't cheap, and there wasn't much of it. But Nettie's hands were twitchy still, and so she picked up the black-splattered stick and wove it back into the fence, wishing she lived in a world where her life was worth more than a mule, more than boots, more than a stranger's cold smile in the barn. She'd had her first victory, but no one would ever believe her, and if they did, she wouldn't be cheered. She'd be hanged.

That stranger—he had been all kinds of wrong. And the way that he'd wanted to touch her—that felt wrong, too. Nettie couldn't recall being touched in kindness, not in all her years with Pap and Mam. Maybe that was why she understood horses. Mustangs were wild things captured by thoughtless men, roped and branded and beaten until their heads hung low, until it took spurs and whips to move them in rage and fear. But Nettie could feel the wildness inside their hearts, beating under skin that quivered under the flat of her palm. She didn't break a horse, she gentled it. And until someone touched her with that same kindness, she would continue to shy away, to bare her teeth and lower her head.

Someone, surely, had been kind to her once, long ago. She could feel it in her bones. But Pap said she'd been tossed out like trash, left on the prairie to die. Which she almost had, tonight. Again.

Pap and Mam were asleep on the porch, snoring loud as thunder. When Nettie crept past them and into the house, she had four shiny teeth in one fist, a wad of cash from the stranger's pocket, and more questions than there were stars.

VISIT THE ORBIT BLOG AT

www.orbitbooks.net

FEATURING

BREAKING NEWS
FORTHCOMING RELEASES
LINKS TO AUTHOR SITES
EXCLUSIVE INTERVIEWS
EARLY EXTRACTS

AND COMMENTARY FROM OUR EDITORS

WITH REGULAR UPDATES FROM OUR TEAM,
ORBITBOOKS.NET IS YOUR SOURCE
FOR ALL THINGS ORBITAL.

WHILE YOU'RE THERE, JOIN OUR E-MAIL LIST
TO RECEIVE INFORMATION ON SPECIAL OFFERS,
GIVEAWAYS, AND MORE.

imagine. explore. engage.